THE GRAVEDIGGER'S SON

Patrick Moody

Illustrations by Graham Carter

Sky Pony Press
New York

First Edition

This is a work of fiction. Names, characters, places, and incidents are from the author's imagination, and used fictitiously.

Sky Pony Press books may be purchased in bulk at special discounts for sales promotion, corporate gifts, fund-raising, or educational purposes. Special editions can also be created to specifications. For details, contact the Special Sales Department, Sky Pony Press, 307 West 36th Street, 11th Floor, New York, NY 10018 or info@skyhorsepublishing.com.

Sky Pony® is a registered trademark of Skyhorse Publishing, Inc.®, a Delaware corporation.

www.patrick-moody.com
www.graham-carter.co.uk

Visit our website at www.skyponypress.com
Books, authors, and more at www.skyponypressblog.com

10 9 8 7 6 5 4 3 2 1

Library of Congress Cataloging-in-Publication Data available on file.

Jacket illustration by Graham Carter
Jacket design by Sammy Yuen

Hardcover ISBN: 978-1-5107-1073-3
E-book ISBN: 978-1-5107-1074-0

Printed in the United States of America

For Maggie

So live, that when thy summons comes to join
The innumerable caravan, which moves
To that mysterious realm, where each shall take
His chamber in the silent halls of death,
Thou go not, like the quarry-slave at night,
Scourged to his dungeon, but, sustained and soothed
By an unfaltering trust, approach thy grave,
Like one who wraps the drapery of his couch
About him, and lies down to pleasant dreams.

William Cullen Bryant, "Thanatopsis"

One

Ian Fossor sat close to the fire, mindlessly poking at the embers with a stick. He liked to watch them flicker and spark. Fizzle and pop. It helped him pass the long nights in the graveyard, especially when he grew tired of his lessons.

"Now, now, lad. Look up here."

Ian lifted his eyes to his teacher, which was a difficult task. Bertrum wasn't the easiest thing to look at. There were a couple of reasons for this. One, he had the odd habit of staring. It unnerved Ian, especially because his teacher never blinked. Two, he wasn't exactly . . . *alive*.

"Eighth row, southeast corner of the lot, two stones from the left."

"I know the stone," Ian replied, frustrated.

"Well then, mister *too-big-for-his-britches*, does that stone have a *name*?"

"Of course it does. Mary Cook."

"And what's the date on poor ol' Mary?"

"There *is* none. She made her headstone special, so no one would know how old she was."

"Aye. That she did."

Ian sighed. He looked around the little camp they'd set up, surrounded on all sides by pale granite slabs glinting in the light of the fire.

"Bertrum, we've gone over *every* stone in this part of the Yard. Can't we stop for the night?"

"No. And we'll go over them tomorrow, and the night after that, and the next night, and—"

"That's all we ever do," Ian protested.

Eyes still trained on the fire, he ran his hand over the spine of the book he'd shoved into the pocket of his cloak. *Rare and Curious Plants, Volume IV.* He wished he could take it out and have a read, but Bertrum would say that was disrespectful. Why couldn't Bertrum ask what color frost juniper turned in full bloom, or how many petals grew on star moss when it clung to a fern? Ian usually faltered a bit when asked to recite the names on the tombstones, but he could point out every flower in the cemetery, every type of tree in the thickets, every type of wheat and grass swaying in the meadows.

"Aye," Bertrum snapped. "That's all we ever do. And that's all we're gonna keep *on* doin'."

Bertrum leaned forward to light his pipe in the flames, singeing a bit of flesh off his cheek in the process.

Bertrum was the only caretaker the cemetery had ever

known, and the Gravedigger was supposed to trust him with his life. Bertrum loomed over Ian, a giant of a man, although four hundred years had shrunken him a bit, and he had to limp around with the aid of a crutch.

The old grouch was falling apart. Years of toil had left him in a sorry state of disrepair. Ian often had to help his teacher bandage up limbs that had fallen off during their long midnight walks. It wasn't uncommon for Bertrum to lose a finger or a toe on their treks, sometimes even an arm or a leg when his demonstrations became a bit too animated. The loss of Bertrum's limbs was as common as a stubbed toe or a splinter. He'd already lost an eye, and his nose had vanished long before Ian was born.

He'd once been a village blacksmith and, later on, a soldier. He loved to tell Ian about marching under royal banners, evading death and sharing victories with his men, about how he hunted down his fair share of enemy knights, chasing them through valleys and forests, through long hazy summers and bone-chilling winters. The old grump still got teary-eyed when he talked about those days.

Once Ian turned eleven, and was old enough to begin learning the family trade, his father had seen fit to appoint Bertrum as his tutor. For the past year, the reanimated blacksmith had met Ian every night to teach him the art of Speaking with the Dead.

"A Digger must know all those who slumber in his yard," he'd growl. "For there'll soon be a day when one of 'em comes-a-callin'."

"I know," Ian would huff, night after night.

That particular night was no different. Bertrum's patience with Ian's moodiness had worn thin, and it showed.

"Oh, ye do, do ye? Well, ya little know-it-all, how's about ye recite the Digger's Code?"

"Now?"

Bertrum took a long pull off the pipe, nodding gravely.

Ian crossed his arms, reciting the words that had been drilled into his head since birth. The first rule of the Digger's Code spilled out easily, so much so that Ian didn't have to think about the words: "'The Dead are not the Living. They shall not walk above ground nor breathe the air of mortal man.'"

"Aye," Bertrum grunted.

As far as Ian could tell, old Bertrum was the one exception to that particular rule. For good reason, though. Ian had quickly learned that Bertrum's past wasn't all colorful and heroic. He'd heard the story many times before. He knew it just as well as the Digger's Code:

There was once a great king, and a soldier to guard 'im. An old soldier, weary 'n worn from too many battles, who spent more time layin' about than keepin' an eye on his lordship. One night, there was a storm, and in that storm up crept an assassin, too cunnin' and quick for the old soldier to notice. Slipped into the castle like smoke and shadow. And durin' the night, the king was slain . . . while the soldier who shoulda been watchin' 'im lay fast asleep in his bedclothes, snorin' away like the oaf he were . . .

Bertrum had been awakened by Ian's ancestors and granted his one true desire: a second chance to serve with honor, to protect with life and limb, and keep a never-ending watch for the rest of his days. He had served as the Fossor family's

4

retainer ever since, constantly vigilant, and though his limbs were a bit worse for wear, his mind was razor sharp. His grumpiness, however, only seemed to grow worse with time.

Ian prodded at the flames once more. "They shall not walk above the ground," he muttered under his breath. "Except for you, that is."

The old corpse shot Ian a look with his good eye, grunting like a boar. "I heard that, lad. Very clever. Clever's all well and good, but even the clever can fall. Sometimes harder than simpler folk. And I'll have ye know that yer father's father's father's *father* woke me so I could keep an eye on this place! It'd be in shambles if it weren't for me. *Humph!* Second rule!"

"'A Digger shall not grow attached to the Dead. Show compassion for the pain of the restless souls, but love them not, for that is the path to confusion and danger.'"

"Ye need to *understand* 'em, boy. The Dead long to be heard. They long for company, for a sympathetic ear. But they'll never be yer kin. Third?"

"'The bones of the Dead must return to the earth, where they shall find rest.'"

"Aye. Always. Don't want any *more* corpses walkin' about, muckin' up the place for the rest of ye air breathers. This oldn's more'n enough. Four."

"'The Dead are dead, and nothing can change that. Mortal life is a gift given only once. It cannot be lived eternally.'"

"And don't you forget it, lad. Last one, now."

"'A Digger must not refuse a request from the Dead. He must do everything within his power to set things right, and guide restless souls to the Great Beyond, where they will find peace everlasting.'"

Bertrum leaned back, pipe smoke billowing out of his empty eye socket. "Very good. We'll make a Digger out of ye, yet."

Ian turned back to the flames, not even sure he *wanted* to be one. The more he recited those old words, the more stale and distant they felt.

"Well," Bertrum growled, taking a long, puffy pull of the pipe, "I suppose that's enough readin' and recitin' for one night. Off to bed wi'ye." He motioned toward the manor far off in the distance. "It's a long walk to a warm bed, lad. And *don't* go wanderin' the way yer did the last time. Straight to the manor."

With that, the old blacksmith plopped himself down in front of the fire, one of his ears dangling loosely from the side of his head.

Ian dusted himself off as he walked into the darkness of the graveyard. A cool wind rose up and gusted through the markers. He listened as it whined and howled through the old, crumbling rock. Wind did strange things in a place like that. It made sounds Ian never heard anywhere else. It was like a wailing spirit, lost and tormented, crying out into the night. Sometimes, the sounds grew so strange they brought visions. All too often, Ian found himself barraged by them on the lonely trek home. A shadow here. A figure there. Always black. Always darting out of sight.

When Ian was younger, he would chase the shadows. They would lurch out from behind a tombstone or from the top of one of the old mausoleums, dancing in the corner of his eye. Ian would run and jump and dive and tumble after them. And just when he was sure he'd found them, they'd disappear, waiting to trick him the next night.

Over time, he'd learned to ignore the shades. They only served to frighten little boys, and Ian Fossor was convinced that he was not a frightened little boy. Well, not *usually*.

There *was* one thing that scared him—an old tomb near the center of the Yard—the Fossor Family Crypt. It had been chiseled from dark granite, its walls rough, corners sharp and spiky like an evil castle straight from a fairy tale. Ian got a chill whenever he went near it, even in bright daylight.

Fossor Manor sat at the edge of the cemetery, separated from the graves by a wrought iron fence. Ian thought about the night's lesson as he trudged up the cobblestone path to his door.

Bertrum had been sour during their lesson. More sour than usual. It couldn't have been easy for him, stomping around the graveyard night after night. The old guy was . . . well . . . getting *older*.

Ian knew that his own attitude hadn't been helping matters, either. Just the night before, Bertrum had caught him trying to dissect the bud of an elder rose when he *should* have been sharpening his shovel. His love of plants had spilled into his training hours, and the old grouch had noticed. Ian wondered if Bertrum had finally begun to realize that his charge's heart was no longer in Gravedigging. Perhaps he did. Perhaps he saw it plain as day, but chose not to acknowledge it.

As Ian walked up the front steps, he thought about apologizing. He'd make it up to Bertrum, somehow. Maybe a new crutch would set things right. He'd noticed the ankle on Bertrum's other leg had begun to loosen. Maybe a new cast was in order. He'd gotten quite good at making them in his spare time. That dangling ear needed a few stiches, too.

Ian found his father slumped down in his armchair in front of the fireplace, staring into the flames. He'd Spoken earlier that day. His father always sat so on days when he Spoke. It seemed to be the one practice that calmed his nerves. His black shovel rested on curved iron rods set over the hearth. Ian watched the flames dance across the obsidian. A strong scent of freshly tilled soil permeated the room.

Bertrum warned Ian to give his father some space after a night of talking to the Dead. "Best to just leave him be," he'd say. "Speakin' to 'em ain't as easy as speakin' to you or me. It's different. Takes a lot outta ya. Drains the soul."

Ian would nod, never fully understanding. The knowledge that one day *he'd* have to Speak made him shiver with dread. He hated the thought of it.

Though it wasn't like he would have much choice in the matter. You couldn't just run from something you were born to do. Gravedigging was in his blood. His people were the first to stack the bodies in the royal catacombs. The first to put the ancient Dead to rest in days of old. The Fossors were a line stretching back for thousands of years, unbroken and unchanging.

Ian stared up at the portraits on the walls of the study: old, dusty paintings of Gravediggers past. There were so many of them. The row of frames stretched across the room, a line of ancestors all watching from above.

He started his viewing, as he always did, with the founding member of his Gravedigging clan: Ingmar Fossor. Old Ingmar was bearded and gaunt. His eyes stared icily down from the frame. They always seemed to be judging Ian, faces forever cast in a disappointed frown.

Ian sneered, sticking out his tongue at his great-great-great-great-great-great-great-grandfather, then moved down the line: Ibsen, Ichabod, Ignatious, Ibrahim, Isidore, Ilmer, Imbert, Iago, Irmin, Isaiah, Ishmael, and Ivan surrounded him on all sides. He knew there were others, but for the life of him he couldn't bring their names to mind. And those were only the Diggers, themselves. Never mind their wives and sisters, second sons, and countless daughters. They, too, had portraits hung all over the house, from the kitchen to the dining hall, with more stacked in the basement and attic when the newer generations simply ran out of room.

Ian always wondered why each Fossor man's name started with the same letter. Tradition, he supposed. Tradition seemed to be the only thing that mattered. Tradition had kept his family together for centuries. Why question it? After all, he was the youngest Fossor now. Not much he could do to change things, even if he wanted to.

His father turned in his chair. He yawned, stretching his limbs like an enormous cat. "You're home late," he said, sleepily rubbing the bridge of his nose. Isaac Fossor looked at his son and smiled.

Isaac had always been a bit of an intimidating figure. He stood almost seven feet tall, gaunt and sinewy, shoulders wide and thick from years of digging with that heavy, obsidian shovel. His hair tumbled down to his shoulders, long locks outlining a rough, chiseled face.

Ian stared at his father's hair, unable to take his eyes off of it. Though still a relatively young man, Isaac Fossor's hair was whiter than the purest snow.

Every Gravedigger's was.

From the moment a Digger started to Speak, the color

would fade. The change was slow at first: the brown or black would go gray, a hair here, a hair there. After a Digger had Spoken enough times, the whole head would turn a bright white, aging them far beyond their mortal years.

When a Gravedigger Spoke, he touched the Void, the vast rift between the worlds of the Living and the Dead, where restless souls stayed trapped like fireflies in a jar. To enter the Void was to touch Death itself, but a Digger could make the journey unscathed. Ian didn't suppose there was any training in the world that could truly prepare someone for that.

Ian feared the Void, that stomping ground of the restless Dead, a place of endless dark and cold. It was the gateway to the Great Beyond, the realm of eternal rest. Gravediggers were like shepherds, his father had once told him. It was their duty to usher tormented souls through the darkness, and lead them to the light.

The Great Beyond . . .

Ian had spent many nights awake in his bed trying to picture it: a vast, unending place where time did not exist. He tried to envision what it looked like, but there were no pictures in any of his books, no descriptions or stories. Bertrum kept tight-lipped whenever he'd ask. Even his father rarely spoke of it.

Isaac stood, joints and bones snapping and popping as he stretched his massive body. He removed the enormous black shovel from its place above the fireplace and proceeded to polish the rune-etched handle with a damp rag. Ian watched the care his father put into the shovel's upkeep. Isaac treated the tool with such reverence that Ian sometimes felt overlooked in comparison.

"Is Bertrum still making you recite the Code?"

"Every night." Ian sighed. "Tomorrow, I'm to start my naming lessons. Markers and tombstones."

Isaac gave a tired smile. "And after that, inscription and stone carving, if I'm not mistaken. He did the same with me. It's no fun, I know. But I'm afraid we all have to suffer under Bertrum's rule until we can look after ourselves out there. Try not to let it bother you. You'll thank him, one day."

Ian sometimes forgot that his father had sat in the cemetery with Bertrum when *he* was a child, learning the same lessons, listening to the same lectures. Probably even feeling the same feelings. It was a comforting thought. It made Ian feel less alone.

"Up to bed, now," Isaac said. "Better to face that old taskmaster bright-eyed and rested." He turned back to the fireplace, and lost himself again in thought.

Ian trudged up the stairs to his room, sneering at yet another series of portraits that sneered right back from their cobweb-covered frames, faces cruel and warped in the glow of the oil lamps. Sometimes, he wished he could take them down and hide them in the attic. Or cover them up with sheets. Or convince his father to hang up some actual *artwork*.

But a Gravedigger never complains. A Gravedigger endures.

Ian entered the washroom and shrugged off his cloak, letting it drop onto the ever-growing pile of towels and breeches. He inspected his scalp in the mirror.

Tilting his head to one side, he slowly ran his fingers through his hair, carefully looking over every inch. Still black. Ian breathed a deep sigh of relief.

He tripped over the piles of laundry littering his bedroom floor, distracted by the wind whistling through an open window. The curtains fluttered and flapped like ghosts. Most children would've been a little frightened, but Ian was no stranger to things that go bump in the night. Turns out, ghosts aren't real. The only Dead that walked were the people his father woke, and, truth be told, they were never the sort you needed to be afraid of.

Ian wandered over to the window, gazing out at the lake behind the manor. The peaceful, rippling water gleamed under the light of the moon, stretching out to the forest looming in the distance. Ian looked, as he did every night, out to the small island at the lake's center. On it stood a lone mausoleum, its marble walls bright in the midnight gloom. It always seemed to glow a soothing shade of gray, a beacon amid the surrounding black water, catching his eye like a flash of lightning in an empty meadow.

The mausoleum was special to Ian. It was the resting place of his mother. She'd died when he was very young. A great sickness had taken her, he'd been told, though he never learned more, no matter how much he asked. Ian would often try to remember her face, but all he got were blurry visions. A feature here or there. Nothing concrete. If he were to draw his mother's picture, it would just be a blank circle. What he *did* recall was the sound of her voice, soft and warm like a lullaby, even when she wasn't singing. He could still hear the gentle notes, lilting and calm, more beautiful than any bard's song. Ian clung to that sound. He promised himself that he'd never forget it.

He'd tried many times to get his father to talk about her, but Isaac would retreat into the same state as when he

Spoke—somber and serious. He'd talked of her only once, when Ian was very small. Isaac had said that he loved her more than anyone could love another person, and never a night passed when he did not dream of her.

Ian had always wondered why she'd been buried on the island in the lake. When he was younger, he'd pestered Bertrum endlessly about it. "But *why?*" he'd demanded, stomping his tiny foot into the ground. "Why is she all the way out *there?* And why can't I visit her?"

"Now, now," Bertrum had said. "It's complicated, lad. Ye see, yer father . . . *hmmmph* . . . he can Speak wi' the Dead, right? Well, when yer mum passed on, he made sure that'd never happen with *her*. He put her in a boat and rowed her out to that island, yonder. Built her a coffin 'o solid granite. Built the mausoleum to house it outta the hardest stone he could work with. Locked her up good and tight and far, far away, ya see, so there'd be no chance o' him ever havin' to Speak to her in . . . in that condition. Ye follow me, son?"

"*I* would Speak to her, if I were him."

"Oh, my boy, I don't think there's nothin' more yer father wants in this entire world. But I'm afraid it won't happen. It *can't*. It'd be too much for him. Speakin' to her . . . it may . . . well . . . let's just say it wouldn't be good for *you*, lad. 'Cause if anythin' were ta happen to yer father, I'm afraid it'd just be you and me for a while. . . ."

It was as much of an answer as he was ever going to get, and Ian supposed it would have to do.

Someday he would go out there. Sometime in the distant future, if he ever learned to swim or if he built a boat or a raft. He didn't want to wake her or anything like that. He just wanted to visit. To tell her about his life and catch her up on all she'd missed out on.

After watering the river lilies in the vase that sat on his nightstand, Ian slipped under the covers and prepared to drift off to sleep. It never came easily. While most his age counted sheep, Ian thought about the Dead. He conjured up images of the long-departed, their spindly hands reaching out to him, longing to Speak, their spirits wallowing in the murk and shadow of the Void. There was a coldness around Death that he could never get used to, a feeling of such intense loneliness that it made his heart ache.

Two

"RISE AND SHINE, FOSSORS! THERE'RE VISITORS FOR YE!" Bertrum's voice thundered from the entry hall.

Ian startled awake. He should have been used to this routine by now, yet Bertrum's bellowing scared the living daylights out of him every time. A rooster's crow would have been a gentle song compared to the old corpse's howling.

Yawning, Ian tumbled out of bed, tiredly wiping the crust from the corners of his eyes, tripping over the laundry piles as he hastily threw on a cloak over his bedclothes.

"LET'S GO, YOUNG FOSSOR. YER FATHER'S ALREADY OUT THE DOOR!"

"I'm coming!" Ian yelled, stubbing his toe as he stumbled down the stairs, head still foggy from a night of troubled dreams. He'd had a nightmare about his mother. Again. It had been the fifth one that week.

Every night it was the same: he would row up to the island in a rickety boat, silently gliding across the still, black water as clouds flitted by an orange moon. The mausoleum would glow in the evening light, pulling him forward like a magnet. He would dock, ungracefully wobbling as he stepped out onto dry land, dragging a sledgehammer behind him. Nervous and shaking, he'd venture forward, pulling open the door with all his might before lighting a torch and slowly stepping into the pitch-black.

The room was always freezing. His breath would trail out from between his lips in puffs like he was standing in a snowstorm. With cautious steps, he'd edge closer to the center of the room in which the granite coffin lay. With all of his might, he'd lift the sledgehammer above his head, gritting his teeth as he swung it down, pounding against the stone. Again and again he would strike the coffin, hacking away chunks of rock until it was battered enough to open. Then he'd throw down the hammer and grasp both sides of the lid.

That's when he'd wake up.

For five nights, Ian had gone through that whole grueling process over and over. Each night brought him a little closer to opening the coffin. He wished he could stop. It would be so nice to dream about something else. If only it were that easy.

But even if Ian had bad dreams, he could usually count on Bertrum and his wake-up calls to haul him back to reality.

He found the old corpse milling around the foyer, impatiently tapping his boot against the floor. "Yer a bit late this mornin'," he grunted.

"Please, Bertrum. I just woke up!"

"Aye," Bertrum said, mussing Ian's bed-matted hair. "Best get outside, now. Yer father's gone down the walk to meet with 'em. Go on, out wi' ye!"

With that, the old grouch swung the front door open, grabbed the boy by the scruff of his neck, and effortlessly shoved him into the morning breeze.

As Ian stomped down the gravel walkway, he saw his father ahead, cloak billowing as with long, powerful strides he moved toward the front gate. Isaac Fossor marched with dignity, like a general or a prince. Ian felt like a puppy trailing after him: small and insignificant, a faulty, half-hearted copy. He would have stood straighter, he thought, tried to be a little more like his dad, if it weren't so bloody early.

Ian watched as Isaac stopped at the gate, mouthing a greeting before allowing two figures to pass through the iron bars. A woman and a girl stopped just inside pausing to exchange a word with the Gravedigger before he ushered them back toward the house. The woman stayed close to his side, while the girl spotted Ian and broke into a sprint, her feet slapping against the gravel as she barreled toward him.

The ladies were a familiar sight. The woman was Joanna, the girl, her daughter and apprentice, Fiona. They had a very special relationship with the Fossor family and visited regularly for a very specific purpose. They were Voicecatchers.

Gravediggers needed to know *where* to dig. The ability to Speak to the Dead was pointless if you didn't know *who* to speak to. Voicecatchers, blessed with the ability to tap into the murky mists of the Void, received the Call. Once contacted from beyond the grave, they carried their message to the Digger, whose job was more, well . . . hands on.

Ian always wondered how the Voicecatchers were Called. Fiona had tried describing it, but her explanations were always fuzzy and vague. She said that her mother would wake up in the middle of the night with a shout, like she'd had a bad dream. Her mother had told her that Voicecatchers were always contacted in their sleep, when the channel between the worlds of the Living and the Dead opened a bit wider. The message didn't come in words, exactly. A Voice would Call from the dark, though wordless and faint, followed by pictures, one after another, fitted like a misty puzzle. At least, Fiona had told him that's what it was supposed to feel like. She'd never really know until it happened.

Fiona and Ian had known each other since they were toddlers. They were bound by ancient custom. When their apprenticeships were over, they'd work together, just as their parents did now. Truth be told, Fiona was the only friend Ian had who was actually *alive*.

In many ways, she was his connection to the world beyond the cemetery gates. He felt a lot better when Fiona stopped by for a visit. They'd often spend the afternoons playing hide-and-seek among the tombstones or having picnics beneath the drooping arms of the weeping willows.

Ian loved to spend time with Fiona in his garden, which was hidden away in a far corner of the cemetery. It was his favorite place. He'd spend his free time there toiling in the soil, watching his flowers grow, learning the properties of each plant. He knew which cured fever, which stayed a pounding headache, which soothed burns, and even the combinations that could aid sleep or ease an upset stomach.

He would spend hours showing Fiona the daffodils and roses, the lilies and marigolds, dragons' tails and wizards' bells, the mint and thyme patches, lovingly singing to the petals as he sprinkled them with the contents of his watering can. In those brief moments, the flowers helped Ian forget about Digging.

Though Fiona was a magic user, she lived in the real world. She studied with other children at the Guilds in the Capital, learning arithmetic, embroidery, alchemy, and a slew of other useful subjects. She often brought Ian books from the Guild Library—basic Healing manuals and more advanced anatomy texts. Ian secretly devoured them away from Bertrum's prying eye.

As a Voicecatcher, Fiona wasn't completely bound to the cemetery the way Ian was. Her mother had insisted that Fiona learn as much as possible before she received her first Call.

Fiona had even visited the royal palace and all the lands surrounding it. Ian would listen as she told him stories about her travels, mesmerized at even the most boring and mundane details.

Unfortunately, Ian didn't have that luxury. There were no Guild professors to teach him. Only Bertrum, with his graveside lectures. Only the Code, and the endless list of the Dead. Digging was one of the most ancient arts, its spiritual and physical knowledge passed only from Digger to apprentice. Father to son, or uncle to nephew. House Fossor was one of the few Digging clans in their part of the world, and the Yard, nearly as large as the Capital itself, had many needs. There was always work to be done. Not only was Ian expected to dig graves and perform funerary rites, he was also constantly mending tools and tending the cemetery grounds, working the land, repairing statues and mausoleums: tombs large and small. He'd soon learn to work the forge, where he'd eventually master the art of blacksmithing, and stone carving, as well. The Dead weren't the only things that required attention. A Digger in training had little time to spare.

Ian had spent many a day complaining about his predicament, telling Fiona how stuck he felt, trapped like an animal in a cage. For Fiona, the graveyard was a place of wonder and adventure. For Ian, it was little more than a prison.

Still, she always found a way to lift his spirits. "It's a great honor, being a Digger," she'd say. "It's an important job. The Dead need help, too, same as anybody. You can fix their problems. Lend them an ear. Put their minds at ease. An entire family's troubles, decades or *centuries* of grief, can be fixed just by waking up the right person and getting answers. All that worry, all that woe they carry into the Void, *gone*. All because of *you*! Doesn't that make you happy?"

It did, Ian supposed, but he still insisted she was lucky. *Her* training didn't involve being scolded by a grouchy corpse for hours at a time. Once he became a Digger in his own right, he'd venture out into the world beyond the cemetery gates. Just never in the way he wanted.

"Hi," Fiona cried, almost crashing into him as she skidded to a halt. She whipped back her fiery, orange hair, smoothing out her dress as the breeze picked up.

"Hello," Ian said as he pointed to Joanna, who was holding a basket, gesturing for Isaac to take it. "What's she brought?"

"Oh, those? Just some cakes for your dad. She says he

deserves a thank-you since we've been coming so much lately. He must be getting pretty sick of us by now."

Ian nodded. They *had* been coming more and more, he realized.

"How many does she have today?"

"Lots. She barely slept at all last night. They kept coming, one after the next."

Ian sighed. He knew that more bodies to dig up meant more work for him. Usually, his father went about his business by himself, but when the workload grew to be too much, Ian tagged along, holding lanterns or helping to shovel. Bertrum was supposed to help, too, but *his* contribution usually consisted of sitting around with a pipe and listing off every mistake they were making.

"They'll probably be at it for a while," Fiona said as they walked the north side of the Yard, passing familiar spots. Nearing the path to the lake, Fiona paused, pointing far off in the distance, where a small meadow joined the forest. "Does the Yard go all the way out there?"

"Sure. It winds around both sides of the lake. The last grave is right before the trees."

"What's the name?"

"The name?"

"On the stone. You said you had to learn every name in the whole place, right?"

Ian was at a loss for words. He struggled to remember, but for the life of him, he couldn't recall the name. Thaddeus? No. Katherine? Was it a man or a woman? Young or old? It had been a long time since he'd gone out that far. Lately, Bertrum had been keeping him close to the manor.

"I . . . I don't know," he admitted, a bit embarrassed.

"Well," Fiona said, "I guess there's only one way to find out. Come on!" She took him by the hand and fled through the Yard, zigzagging between the tombstones.

When they reached the edge of the meadow, Fiona nudged him.

Ian turned and saw the book in her hands. "Another one? Really?"

Fiona grinned. "Nothing special," she said, "but I thought you'd like it. Here."

She placed the book in his hands. *Splints, Casts, Crutches, and Canes: A Guide.*

"One of the texts for Novices . . . I figured Bertrum could benefit. And you, if you ever hurt yourself around all those tools."

Ian clutched the book to his chest. "This is great! Did I tell you about Bertrum's ankle?"

She laughed. "I can't believe it's still attached."

Ian opened the book, peeking at some of the illustrations before gently packing it inside his satchel. "Thanks, Fiona."

"Hey," she said, "you need all the help you can get, right?"

"I feel bad," Ian said. "I never have anything for you. Nothing special, at least."

"You don't need to get me anything. Exploring the Yard is enough. Just show me that grave, and we'll call it even."

They continued through the meadow, closer and closer to the forest's edge.

"So," she huffed, "have you talked to your dad about studying at the Guilds?"

"Not yet."

Fiona had known for a long time that Ian wanted to be a Healer. Sometimes, Ian was surprised Bertrum and his father never caught on. Surely they'd noticed the countless books Fiona brought him, and Bertrum was basically a semi-alive test subject. Still, Fiona was the only person he'd ever confided in, the sole keeper of his secret.

In many ways, it was the exact opposite of Digging. Ian wanted to help the *Living*. He wanted to cure the sick. Fight disease. Beat back the cold grip of Death at all costs. Always, his thoughts drifted back to his mother. If only there'd been a Healer present . . .

"You'll have to tell him soon," Fiona said. "I know you have your life here, but there's so much more. And you can show your father what you can do! You've certainly got enough practice with Bertrum. How many times have you had to re-stich his fingers back on?"

Ian couldn't remember, really. And that didn't count the toes and ears. He felt the needle and thread inside his cloak pocket.

"It seems like always, these days," he told her. "His ear nearly fell off last night. I'll have to work on that later."

Whatever ailments befell his friends, Ian was prepared. He always had his satchel slung over his shoulder, filled with bandages and stitching, and his own special blend of herbs and salves.

But it'd take more than that to become a Healer. It wasn't something he could learn while Digging with his father and Bertrum. The training was intensive. It took years, and the professors at the Healer's Guild were tougher than most. The Healer's Guild had several schools. Some apprentices studied bone mending and surgery; others specialized in midwifery. But there was one school of Healing that Ian was most interested in: the Herbal school. There, he'd make medicines with his own hands, and see the look on his patients' faces when their ills were cured.

Ian felt the butterflies rumble in his stomach as he pictured the Healers' greenhouse. He could hear the chiming of the morning bells, clear as day, ringing out from the ramparts of the Guild Houses. He could see the robed students making their way down cobbled streets, entering the glass doors of the greenhouse to carry out their experiments. He imagined himself there with them, hard at work, running his hands through leaves and petals, dissecting branches and roots as he concocted his potions, the smell of pollen filling his nostrils like a cloud of incense.

"You'll love the Guilds," Fiona continued. "The buildings in their neat rows at the center of the Capital are so pretty." She gazed off into the distance. "There's tons of people our age there, too. And the Healer's Guild is the biggest building of them all. You can see its golden spires rising up from miles around. It's *beautiful.* You'd be such a good student, I just *know* it!" She was silent for a moment. "The Choosings are in a month, you know."

"The *Choosings?*"

"The tests to gain entrance to the Guild where you want to study. I hear they're hard, but I don't think you'll have a problem with the Novice tests." She nodded to his satchel. "You've basically done everything already."

"Have you taken them?"

"I never tried to get into a specific Guild." She shrugged. "I'm not really bothered. I'd rather study a lot of different things."

After their conversation, Fiona had suggested that he broach the topic with his father.

"And if you want to get in with the Healers, the Choosings are the only way."

Ian nodded. He still hadn't worked up the courage to say anything. It wasn't that he was afraid of his father. In fact, his father was the kindest person Ian knew. It wasn't scolding that he feared he'd receive. It was Isaac's disappointment.

After all, Ian was the only child. If he were to forsake the life of a Gravedigger, there'd be no one else to take his place. Isaac couldn't just hire some child from the village. A Digger's power was in his blood. And if House Fossor failed to uphold the Code, the balance between worlds would begin to crumble. With no one to guide restless spirits through the Void, the world of the Dead would grow even darker.

Ian didn't believe it would be easy to forsake his calling, but, deep inside, he knew that it needed to be done.

He just wasn't sure *how*.

He'd thought about it all during his lessons with Bertrum over the past couple of nights, going over how he'd break the news to his father, writing out his arguments in his head like a speech.

So far, he hadn't found the right words. He doubted he ever would.

And the clock was ticking. With only a month before the Choosings, Ian felt his time running thin.

Fiona and Ian reached the edge of the woods, stopping in the shadows of the tall pines and knotty elms that formed the boundary at the end of the meadow.

The grave lay just before the first tree, its weathered

stone cracked and lopsided by a root jutting beneath it. Ian crouched down, brushing his fingers over the inscription. The stone was so worn that he had to feel the curves of the letters.

Yoren Connors

"Yoren." Fiona sounded it out slowly, like she was trying to learn another language. "A bit of a weird name."

"It's old," Ian replied. "No one's had that name for a long, long time. There're a few more Yorens in here. Yorgas and Yornevs, too. This one's way older, though. He's been here for ages."

"I wonder why he's so far away from the rest?"

"Maybe he didn't want to be buried near anyone," Ian guessed.

"Sounds like a grouch to me. He probably wasn't any fun."

Ian would have to agree.

Fiona hummed softly to herself as she wandered along the edge of the woods, peering inside. Ian remained in front of the stone, trying to make out the date. He wished Bertrum were there. If anybody could decipher an ancient tombstone, it was he.

"Hey! What's this?" Fiona was pointing at the ground. As Ian edged closer, a cold chill ran up his spine. She'd found it.

The Pumpkin Trail.

Aside from the Fossor Crypt, it was the only other part of the cemetery that made him uneasy, and the reason he usually didn't venture out this far. At the edge of the forest sat a group of pumpkins, still bright orange, though they'd been sitting there for years. They were big and bloated, covered in thick, white bumps. Their stalks were long and thick, gnarled and twisted like evil horns. Ian peered deeper into the forest. The monstrous gourds grew in two rows, forming a winding, twisted trail that stretched back into the trees as far as he could see.

Fiona didn't seem to find anything ominous about the place. "Where does it go?" She leaned in closer, eyes narrowing as she gazed down the trail. "It's so *dark*."

"We should go back," Ian said. "Bertrum doesn't like when I come out this far."

Fiona eyed him curiously. "Why?"

"He told me the Pumpkin Trail is the one area of the Yard I shouldn't go to alone."

"The Pumpkin Trail," Fiona repeated, turning back to face it. "And why not? You're not alone, now."

Ian shook his head. "He says it's evil. 'Don't feel right.'"

Fiona reached out to the nearest pumpkin, her fingers hovering just above its wrinkled, orange skin.

"Don't!"

Standing alongside her, Ian felt his body grow cold. He wasn't afraid of the dark. Not usually. Pitch-black never bothered him. But the darkness of the forest was different. Even on a cloudless, sunny day, the trees here stood wrapped in shadows, everything under their branches enveloped in a murky shroud, as if under an evil spell.

"We should get back to the manor," Ian said, hoping Fiona would take the hint.

She stayed perfectly still, her body rigid as she stared at the trail. For a moment, it seemed as though her hair wasn't even moving in the breeze. The trees didn't rustle, nor did the blades of grass beneath her feet. Ian rubbed his eyes to make sure he was seeing clearly.

Finally, Fiona shifted her gaze and pulled herself away.

As she did, Ian saw a figure moving through the trees. Its shadowy form zipped behind the trunks of elms, slender and slight. Ian froze, listening to the *crunch, crunch, crunching* of leaves, the snap of twigs. The shade peeked out from behind a gnarled maple and, for a split second, Ian could make out a tangled mess of black hair outlining a pair of ruddy cheeks.

It was the girl.

He'd seen her before. She'd been watching him for months now, whenever he wandered too close to the edge of the forest. At first, Ian thought he was seeing things. But after the first few times, he knew she was real. He could feel her eyes on him, following his every move. And though he tried to see her, she was always just a flash, or a blur.

Before he could call out to her, she vanished into the brambles, scampering off through the vines and stumps, as fast and sure-footed as a squirrel.

"What was *that*?" Fiona asked, taking a few steps closer to the Pumpkin Trail.

"No!" Ian leapt over, clutching onto her arm before she took that first step onto the forest floor. "We can't," he said, trying to pull her away. "We need to go. *Now.*" He gave Fiona's arm one last tug, urging her to follow.

All during the walk back, she asked him about the trail. "Haven't you ever wanted to go in and see what it leads to?"

"No. Not really."

"Hmm. If I had something like that in *my* backyard, it would drive me mad! I'd have to discover what was in there or it would just pick away at me . . . like an itch I couldn't scratch."

"What if you did, and you found out that it was something bad?"

"*Is* it something bad?"

Ian shrugged. "There're people in there. Or so Betrum says."

Fiona narrowed her eyes. "What kind of people? What are they, wild or something?" She formed her hands into claws and feigned a lunge. "Rawr! Feral beastlings? Shape-shifters?"

"How should I know?" Ian said, swatting her hands away. "It's not like I've ever walked in there for a chat."

"Well, I'd want to find out. It'd be frustrating to keep guessing. I mean . . . they *are* your neighbors."

"I'm fine with guessing," he told her. "Believe me. Even if I wanted to go inside, I couldn't. Bertrum would kill me."

"That wouldn't be a problem," Fiona said with a grin, "Your father could always bring you back."

Ian shot her a glare. That was the last image he needed in his head. "Very funny."

Fiona frowned. "Don't you want to know *everything* there is to know about this place? Not just the stones and crypts, I mean, but the all the fields and rivers and ponds? This graveyard goes on for leagues!"

"I used to."

She wrinkled up her nose. "You need to be more adventurous, Ian." She grabbed a hold of his hand, squeezing it tight. "We'll go down the trail next time. Together."

Ian didn't know what to say. Her eyes were so serious.

She meant it.

He wanted to tell her how nervous those woods made him, but he was too ashamed to admit it. She was brave. It made *him* want to be brave, too.

29

"Bertrum doesn't have to know every little thing," Fiona went on. "We can always sneak past him. He's not exactly quick on his feet." She squeezed Ian's hand. "Trust me, okay? You always say how badly you want an adventure. To see the world outside, right?" She pointed back to the trees. "Well *there* it is. We could go. Bertrum doesn't need to know. It'll be our secret."

"All right," Ian said, trying to keep his voice from shaking. "We'll go, next time. Together."

Three

Clack!

The noise roused Ian from a deep sleep. He kicked around under the sheets, startled, flung from dreamland like a fish yanked out of its pond.

Clack!

Clack!

His eyes slowly adjusted to the dark.

Clack!

Something was banging against the window, the sharp sound echoing off the pane. He tumbled out of bed, tripping and falling against his nightstand. A glass of water fell to the floor, just barely missing his copy of *Itches, Bites, and Rashes: Curing with Prickle Pine*. Ian went to move the book but ended up falling and landing on the cluttered floor with a dull *thud*.

Clack!

Clack!

He got up and, drawing the curtains, found his window being bombarded by pebbles. They flew up out of the darkness, pummeling the panes like tiny fists. He lifted the latch and let a gentle breeze into the bedroom, trying to see out into the dark.

"Ian!"

He leaned a little farther, poking his head out into the night air. Fiona stood in the yard below, another pebble at the ready.

"Fiona? What are you doing here? What time is it?"

"It's late," she said, letting the pebble drop to the grass. "I need to talk to you."

"Is everything okay?"

"Just come down! Please!"

He threw on his cloak and bounded downstairs. When he reached the backyard, he found her pacing on the lakeshore, vigorously rubbing her hands together.

"What's wrong?"

"I got one."

Ian searched her face, trying to understand. "You . . . got one . . . what?"

"A Call." She sprang forward, wrapping her arms around his shoulders. "Ian, I got a *Call!*"

Ian squirmed out from her hug, watching as she spun around in excitement.

"Are you sure it wasn't just a dream?"

He knew how real those could seem. He wouldn't blame her for overreacting if it were. He'd always been told a Voicecatcher wasn't contacted by their first spirit until they reached adulthood.

Fiona shook her head. "I know what a bad dream feels like. This was . . . different. I felt myself losing control, like my mind was melting. Someone got inside of my head. Floating inside my thoughts. I could hear a voice. A *child's* voice."

"A child?"

"His name is Thatcher," she said. "I could see it on the headstone. Thatcher Moore. He needs help. I know that much, for sure."

"Maybe we should tell my father."

"No!" Fiona grabbed Ian's wrist, pulling him in close. "*We* should do it. Just the two of us."

"*Us?* But we can't. I—"

"Can't we at least *try?* I know you've been having second thoughts about Digging. But you're the only one who can help me, Ian. Not your dad. Not Bertrum. You. *Please.*"

Ian struggled to answer. Even if he did try to help, he wouldn't be of any use. He didn't have it in him to Speak. Not yet. Maybe not *ever.* Learning how to do it was bad enough. The thought of touching the Void sent a shiver down his spine, jolting his belly with a sharp, icy sting.

Fiona was so sure about it though. So sure about *him* . . .

"He Called *me,*" she said. "Not my mom. I don't know how, and I don't know why, but it happened. Our parents aren't the ones this spirit is reaching out for. We are."

Ian watched her eyes sparkle in the twilight, and for a brief moment he caught that wondrous twinkle of mischief. "Your mom doesn't know you came here?"

"No," she said. "I snuck out."

"Listen, if we do this, and things go wrong . . . like if I mess up, or it doesn't work—"

"It *will* work. I'll be there to help. I can *feel* it."

33

Speaking the Words wouldn't be easy. His stomach was already turning at the thought. "I can't," Ian said, his voice shaking. "I don't have my own shovel." He could feel sweat trickling down the back of his neck. "And I can barely remember the Words. I'm not a Digger, Fiona."

"You have training," Fiona said, her words charged with excitement, "and your father has a shovel. I've seen it hanging in the study. Please . . ."

"It'll go wrong," Ian said. "I'm telling you, Fiona. It's not going to happen the way you want."

Please, he begged silently. *Please understand.*

"I'm not asking you to become a Digger overnight. I don't want you to become one, anyway. I only want your help. Just this once. I need to know if the Call is real. I need *you.*"

Ian glanced back at the manor. No lights shone inside. His father was fast asleep, and Bertrum would be busy at work on the other side of the graveyard. It would be a long time until dawn. He and Fiona could try and be back before the first cock crowed. Ian looked up to the window of his bedroom, thinking of all the books inside. Books that Fiona had given him. Selfless gifts, all because she believed in him.

Would it be too much to believe in her, even if it scared him? A Catcher's first Call was supposed to be a splendid thing. A wondrous event. He couldn't take that away from her.

"Stay here," he said. "I'll fetch the shovel."

They crept through the cemetery, scurrying away from the

house, dodging moonlit stones. Ian struggled under the weight of the obsidian shovel, dragging it behind him like the sledgehammer from his nightmares.

He'd snuck back inside the manor while his father slept. Lighting a single lamp, he'd crept through the study, dodging the floorboards he knew would creak and groan the loudest. Heaps of dying embers cast a faint glow from the fireplace, giving off their last sparks of life as the wind swept down the chimney. The shovel hung just above, its obsidian even darker in the shadows. Ian took it in as he slowly approached, studying the twisted stone grip, the sharp edges at the top, the engravings along the shaft.

Taking his father's shovel felt wrong. A Digger's shovel was an extension of himself. Isaac Fossor's very spirit was etched into that black stone. Ian reached up to lift it from where it hung above the mantle, but hesitated. Though it was just a tool, he resented it. One day he would carve his own shovel from the obsidian mound. He would sharpen it, just as Isaac had. He would hew the midnight rock until the shaft was sturdy and the grip strong. Isaac would guide Ian's hands as he chiseled his own symbols into its sides. In doing so, Ian's fate would be sealed. He'd be a Gravedigger, through and through. The shovel would not be a tool, then. It would be his master.

There would be no way out. No Guilds. No Healing. Only the soil. Only the Dead and the Void and the endless expanse of the graveyard.

"Not yet," he whispered, feeling the anger rise as he gripped the handle. "Not *ever*."

He hoisted the shovel off the iron pegs, struggling as he toppled back across the carpet. It was a miracle he hadn't woken his father as he bumbled out of the house, *banging* and *clanging* against the walls, fumbling off with the family heirloom. He'd forgotten how heavy the shovel was. It seemed to fight against him, pulling him to the floor, unwieldy and unbalanced, as if it knew Ian was not its owner.

Fiona followed close behind with the oil lantern. Ian had told her to cover it with a hand, so it gave only a pale glow. Bertrum would be busy at work in his forge, far off in the eastern corner of the cemetery. The old corpse didn't need to sleep, and he kept himself occupied through the wee hours mending odds and ends, forging mattocks and spades, iron stakes and ax blades. Ian hoped the old grump didn't decide to take a midnight stroll.

"Are we close?" Fiona asked.

Ian pointed to a rusted iron gate. He motioned for Fiona to look up at the statues lining the walls, row upon row of smiling cherubs.

"In here," he said, pushing open the gate. It creaked loudly.

"What's this?"

"The Children's Yard."

Fiona lifted the lantern up to the nearest statue, gazing at the face of the cherub, its chubby, marble cheeks raised in a joyful grin.

Ian led her through the plots, pointing out the dates on the stones. Some of the graves were decorated with rotted ribbons. Others were covered under piles of ancient, wooden toys. One even had an old rocking horse alongside it, so weather-beaten and warped that it looked like a statue itself.

"It's all kids?"

"All kids."

Fiona's eyes grew wider with each grave marker they passed.

Amelia. Age ten.

Frederick. Age seven.

James. Five.

Anne. Nine.

Rebecca. Six.

George. Four.

Charlotte. Three.

"It's so sad," she finally said.

Ian led her farther in, stopping in front of a grave nearly overrun by wild hydrangeas. Pushing the blue bulbs out of the way, he examined the marker.

"You're sure this is the one?"

Fiona held the lantern up, nodding as she passed the light over the stone. "That's him."

Thatcher Moore. Departed from this World on the thirteenth year of his birth.

Ian hesitated, balancing himself on the shovel, staring down at the grave.

He felt Fiona's hand on his shoulder. "Just this once, Ian."

Moonlight gleamed off the sharpened head of the shovel. It no longer fought against him. It seemed to be alive, begging to taste the cold dirt, to dive headlong into the earth. It wanted Ian to use it. To Dig his way down into the midnight soil for the first time. The first Dig of what would be many. Countless. A lifetime's worth, if he couldn't find it in himself to break the ancient cycle.

"Well," he said, hoisting the shovel up over his shoulder, "let's get started."

Ian's hands were blistered and bloody by the time he unearthed the coffin. He was drenched with sweat, and his shoulders and back ached. Six feet was a long way to dig, he realized. His father made it look easy. Years of practice would make *anything* look easy.

Fiona sat with her legs dangled over the edge of the hole, holding the lantern low so Ian could see. She gasped when she heard the shovel *smack* against oak.

"There he is!" she cried, unable to contain herself.

Ian leaned the shovel aside. "*Not so loud!*" he whispered. He massaged the knots in his neck, then got onto his knees and swept away the loose dirt from the wooden box, clawing with his nails to dislodge the packed clay molded to the lid.

When it was fully uncovered, he paused, resting his back against the wall of dirt. He took deep breaths, pressing his head against the cool earth. Even though he hated to admit it, it felt good being so far down. He felt secure. Safe. There was something comforting about the open grave, the darkness, the coppery mineral smell of the soil.

Ian tipped his head back and gazed up at the stars. They were a spectacular sight. Usually, the view from six feet below wasn't much to wonder at, but that night the constellations swirled above his head like a billion diamonds shimmering in the dark.

He returned his attention to the coffin, preparing himself for the next steps. Bertrum's voice boomed inside his head, reciting the Digger's Code.

The Dead are not the Living. They shall not walk above ground, nor breathe the air of mortal men.

A Digger shall not grow attached to the Dead. Show

compassion for the pain of the restless souls, but love them not, for that is the path to confusion and danger.

The bones of the Dead must return to the earth, where they shall find rest.

The Dead are dead, and nothing can change that. Mortal life is a gift given only once. It cannot be lived eternally.

A Digger must not refuse a request from the Dead. He must do everything within his power to set things right, and guide restless souls to the Great Beyond, where they will find peace everlasting.

This is the sole purpose of the Digger. This, and no other.

As Ian repeated the words in his head, a rope came tumbling down. Fiona began to shinny her way into the grave, but lost her grip and landed with a *thud* on the coffin's lid. As she brushed the dirt from her dress, Ian gave the rope a tug to make sure it was secure.

"So," she whispered, "are you ready?"

Ian stood before the coffin for a long while, nervously clenching his fists.

"You've come this far," Fiona said. "That's half the battle, isn't it?"

Ian shook his head. "Digging is the easy part." He pointed to the coffin. "*This* . . . this is the battle."

Fiona nervously chewed her nails as she watched him grab hold of the lid. He gave her one last look before prying it open, then held his breath as he peered inside.

Thatcher Moore, or what was *left* of Thatcher Moore, lay peacefully before him. Fiona gasped. So did Ian, and for good reason.

Thatcher Moore was nothing but a skeleton.

Ian examined the shockingly white bones, all perfectly arranged, just like the pictures in his anatomy books. As he looked at the skull, he couldn't help but think that it was grinning. He stared into the empty eye sockets, losing himself in the deep, dark cavities. Even without eyes, Thatcher seemed to be staring right back.

Fiona crouched down beside Ian, nervously poking at Thatcher's shinbone.

"Now what?"

"Now we see if we can wake him up."

Ian got down on one knee and gently placed his hands on Thatcher's skull. It was time.

A warm sensation burned from the tips of his fingers as he brushed them against the bone. Ian could feel his own life force emanating from his hands into the corpse, a strange, comforting energy pouring forth like water. More than that, he felt the emptiness inside Thatcher. But as Ian held on longer, he began to feel another source of life pulsing in return. Something was stirring inside those skeletal remains.

It was working.

Ian cleared his throat, hoping with all hope that he wouldn't jumble the words.

"I have dug deep, and I have reached you. Hear me now, departed: I have heard your Call, and have journeyed down from the land of the Living." He leaned in closer, his face only inches away from the grinning skull. "With these words, I give you breath."

He waved his hands over Thatcher's eyes. "With these hands, I give you life. Speak now, friend." He'd never said those last words aloud. He'd studied the incantation, but that final phrase was never to be used until the actual ceremony marking the end of his training.

Ian was exhausted after his speech. His tongue felt

swollen inside his mouth, his jaw ached, and his head felt heavy and cloudy, like a boulder rolling through fog. The warm pulse in his fingertips grew stronger, and as he spoke the Words of Resurrection they burned like he'd held them over an open flame.

Then, as quickly as the process began, it stopped. One last burst of heat, one last wave of energy, and Ian's world suddenly seeped into a deep, penetrating black.

Ian drifted alone in the darkness. It enveloped him like a cold, inky cocoon, consuming him. He tried to see through the gloom but found he couldn't. He should have known it was impossible. The Void was darkness incarnate.

He felt his body floating through that cold, penetrating nothingness, and his ears rang with a *whoosh* as if he were a bird soaring through open air. He tried to move his arms, tried to swim through the blackness as the icy sting of panic clamped down on his chest.

Ian gathered himself, willing his breaths to become more even, his heartbeat to slow. He thought back to Bertrum's lectures among the gravestones, then searched his surroundings, hoping to make out something, *anything* in the deep, vast dark.

Almost as quickly as he'd been thrust inside, the Void spat him back out. Ian's eyes adjusted to the light of the stars as his body was thrust back into the world of the Living and he was, once again, back in the open grave, splayed out in the dirt and clay.

He could still feel the taint of the Void. A strange coldness stuck to his skin like droplets of ice. He raised his arm, studying the goose pimples. He longed for the fireplace, for the warmth of his own bed.

He sat back, drained and murky-headed.

Fiona remained crouched beside him. She kept her eyes fixed on the skeleton, waiting for something to happen.

The seconds ticked by, bleeding into minutes.

Still, they waited, unable to move or speak, paralyzed with equal parts anxiety and excitement.

After a while, the anxiety and excitement fluttered away, leaving only a strange, empty sense that something hadn't gone quite right.

"Did you see him?" Fiona asked, nervously wringing her hands.

"No," Ian admitted. He rubbed his throbbing temples.

She frowned. "Maybe it doesn't always work the first time," she said.

Ian shook his head. "No. It always works. *Always*. I've never heard of a Gravedigger who wasn't able to wake someone up." He sighed, slumping down farther into the dirt. He wished Fiona hadn't come along. Being *alone* and failing would've been embarrassing enough.

"Maybe you missed part of the speech?"

Ian knew she was just trying to make him feel better. He wished he could crawl into himself and hide from the world. Digging was the one thing he'd been trained to do, the only thing he'd been put on this earth for . . . and he'd failed at it. He never wanted to experience that again, the darkness and emptiness of the Void.

Yet failure worked in strange ways, and he was both relieved and frustrated that none of his training had seemed to do him any good.

More importantly, he'd let Fiona down.

"I said all the words right. And I *felt* them flowing through me. I don't know . . ."

"It's probably a good thing it didn't work."

"I guess so," Ian muttered. "Maybe this is the sign I needed. This isn't what I'm meant for after all."

"Only you can decide that," she said.

"Tomorrow, I'll talk to my father. He'll have to understand."

Ian took one last look at Thatcher Moore before gently setting the lid back into place. They climbed up out of the grave, breathing in the sharp night air. Ian already missed the smell of the dirt. It lingered in his nostrils, like a trail of perfume.

Though he'd never admit it to Fiona, the open grave beckoned to him. The soothing, dark place called to something in his blood. Something far deeper than he understood. Part of his soul ached for it. He rubbed at his temples as a headache began to pound.

It was well after midnight when they reached the manor. Fiona stopped by the gate and took Ian by the arm. "I'm sorry." She stared down at her shoes, slowly digging her heel into the grass.

"You don't need to be."

"But I am. If I didn't push you so hard . . ."

"No, really. It's all right. I'm not ready. That's pretty clear. But at least you made me *try*. There's nothing to be sorry about. *I* should be the sorry one. I couldn't help you. I know you wanted to see Thatcher, to hear why he Called. I . . . I wanted to help you. Even if it scared me."

She nodded. "It may be better, this way. Now you know what it's like to Speak the Words for real."

Ian shrugged. "I just don't know how I'm going tell my dad. What will I say to him?"

She smiled. "Tell him what's in your heart. Whatever you say, I'm sure he'll take it well. I have a good feeling."

"You'd better get home before your mom notices you're gone."

"You're right."

"Night, Fiona. Get home safe."

"Good night, Ian."

He watched as she made her way down the cobbled path, hesitating before she reached the gate. She wavered for a moment, then turned back to him. "Everything will look better in the morning."

Ian didn't know how to respond. He waved, watching as she disappeared into the dark. Sighing, he turned back to the house. All he wanted to do was collapse onto his bed and forget everything.

Maybe the morning *would* be better.

He just needed to get through the night.

After he cleaned off the shovel and returned it to its place above the fireplace, Ian quietly made his way upstairs. He shrugged off his cloak and crawled beneath the covers. For a long while, he stared up at the ceiling, back and shoulders aching. It was a blessing, he realized. The Digger's Code, the Words, the Void . . . none of it had worked. Maybe it *was* a sign that he truly wasn't cut out for that life. Maybe he *could* break the cycle. House Fossor had lasted a thousand years. Perhaps the Digger's magic hadn't rubbed off on him the way his father had hoped. Perhaps he *was* different from the rest.

Ian thought about the Choosings at the Guilds. One month to go. Thirty days. It wasn't much time.

Still . . .

The same unwanted thought always came back to plague him. There were no other sons of House Fossor. If he strayed from the path, that balance would falter. What would happen then was a mystery, but all his life, he'd been told that series of events could *never* come to pass. He racked his brain for the answer. Who would tend the Yard when Isaac grew too old and Bertrum eventually crumbled? Who would answer the Voicecatcher's Calls? If no Digger Spoke, the voices of the Dead would fall silent, and the Void would teem with despair. Ian's mind raced, his body sore and tired, and his head still feeling as if it were filled with lead.

He fell into a deep sleep, his dreams filled with the cold blackness of the Void.

Four

"Hey! *Psssssst!* You awake?"

Ian grumbled as he pulled the covers over his head. *Now* what?

"Hey!"

The whisper came from the foot of his bed. Ian tried to identify the speaker as he squirmed beneath the covers. It was too quiet to be Bertrum, *that* was for sure. Perhaps he was still dreaming.

"I know you're awake. I can see you moving, you know."

Frustrated, Ian kicked off the blankets. Why would no one give him a moment's rest? Angry and sleep-deprived, he sat up, rubbing his eyes.

When he opened them, what he saw sent a shiver down his spine.

There, at the foot of his bed, sat the skeleton of Thatcher Moore. His skull was tilted to the side like a curious dog, two rows of teeth gleaming in the moonlight pouring in through the window.

Ian edged away until he slammed against the backboard, knees up to his chest.

"Th—Thatcher?"

The bony figure nodded, shuffling a bit more onto the bed.

"You left before I woke, Digger. It takes a while for someone to wake when they've slept for so long, you know. You don't just spring up bouncy and ready to go."

Ian rubbed his eyes, pinching himself just to make sure this wasn't a nightmare. He pinched until his arm went numb and his eyes watered, but still the skeleton remained. "How . . . how did you get here?"

"*How?*" The voice was thin and rattling, like a whisper underwater. "I climbed out after you filled my grave back in. Thanks for *that*, by the way." Thatcher held up his hands, finger bones caked with dirt.

Ian stared at him, confounded. He'd done it. He'd actually *done* it. Even without his own shovel, without ever reciting the Words before.

The problem was, a Gravedigger usually put the Dead back to rest. It *was* part of the Rules, after all. A big part, really.

Very rarely did the corpse follow you home.

"This isn't possible," Ian whispered under his breath. "I didn't . . . I didn't see you in the Void . . ."

"You woke me up and didn't even have the decency to wait. Now how's that make *you* look, huh? What kinda Gravedigger runs off before the ritual's through?"

"I didn't know you were awake," Ian shot back. "I didn't think it *worked*."

"Well, I think an apology's in order."

Ian gritted his teeth. "I'm sorry."

Thatcher's jaw clicked. "Good. Anyway, Digger—"

"Ian. Call me Ian."

"All right then, Ian. I remember the Digger back in my day, the one who lived in this house. Iago. Nasty man. Bit of a brute, really. He used to chase us out of the Yard all the time. Hated it when kids would try to sneak in. Joke was on him, though. He was slow as molasses. And then the caretaker! That lumbering old corpse knew how to give someone a wallop."

"Bertrum. He's my teacher."

Thatcher's rib cage rattled as he laughed. "*He's* your teacher?"

Ian nodded. "He's all right once you get to know him."

"He may be. Couldn't say the same for Iago." Thatcher paused, catching himself. "Sorry. Don't mean to disparage your, what would he be? Great-great-great-great-grandfather?"

"Something like that."

Ian pictured old Iago's portrait: bulbous head, massive jowls covered with a thick beard, watery, shifty-looking eyes too close together. Bertrum rarely spoke of him, and when he did, he never spoke kindly. Iago the Disagreeable, he called him.

"Why did you Call Fiona?"

Thatcher scratched his chin. "I couldn't Call the other Voicecatcher. She's so *old*. I like Fiona better. She's young, like us. She understands."

"Understands what? What's the problem?"

"I'm dead. Was dead, mind you. Floating in that blackness.

But something's been happening. Something new. I've been seeing lights."

Ian leaned forward. "Lights?"

"Aye. Like stars, only not as bright. Just a few, at first. But they kept showing up. Before I knew it, I wasn't just drifting. I was awake. I was *aware*, thinking." Thatcher shivered, his bones clacking. "Being able to think in all that darkness isn't fun, and it got me remembering. Remembering life."

Ian struggled to understand. "Why would remembering life be a problem?"

"Why? Because things were just getting *good*, that's why. It was an early winter, the year I passed. The snowstorms started. Then the sickness came. It swept through the village fast. I caught it first. No more mischief. No more games. I was bedridden, tired, and weak."

Ian glanced at his pile of books. "You were sick?"

Thatcher nodded. "As I lay there those last few days, all I could think was . . . it was just getting good. Then it happened."

"What happened?"

Thatcher whipped his head up, and for a moment the empty eye sockets seemed to narrow. "What *happened*? I died, *that's* what happened. My fun was cut short. How is *that* fair? Hmm?"

"It's not fair," Ian agreed. "I wish there was something that could've helped you, back then. That's just the way things are. 'The Dead are dead, and nothing can change that.'"

"That's where you're wrong. You *can* change it. You *did* change it! I'm alive again!"

"I'm sorry, Thatcher, but that's not how it works. Wanting to be alive again . . . that's not, well, that's not something *I* can fix. It's not like a fever or a sprained wrist. I can't change the Rules."

"But you gave me my *life* back!"

"It was a mistake," Ian said, flustered. "I didn't even *know* I did. This wasn't supposed to happen. I couldn't even find you in the Void! I'm sorry, but I need to put you back to rest."

Thatcher sprang up from the bed and backed away, his bony feet *tap-tap-tapping* on the hardwood floor.

"You Spoke the Words, Ian. You can't go back on them. I know the Rules. How's that last one go? 'A Digger can refuse no request from the Dead. He must do everything within his power to set things right,' and so and so forth."

"I'm sorry," Ian said. His heart felt heavy. He wished the Rules *did* work that way. Things would be so much different if he could *give* life. He knew what it felt like to lose someone to the sickness. If only Thatcher could understand . . .

"Well, I'm not going back down there. I prefer it up here. I've missed this place."

Ian wanted to scream. "Now you listen to *me*. Tomorrow night, we're going back to your grave. I'll let you stay for one day, but after that, it's the Children's Yard. Got it?"

Thatcher held up his arms in surrender. "Fine. One day is better than nothing, I suppose."

"You can stay in here tonight. In the closet. I can't risk having anyone see you. If word gets out that I let you above ground . . . it won't be good for either of us."

"*What?* I have to stay cooped up in this room?"

"It's either that, or we can go back to the Yard right now."

Thatcher sighed. "Fine. Deal." He held out a hand. Ian took it in his own, wrapping his flesh around the cold, spindly bones.

As much as Ian disliked living by the Code, he couldn't very well break its Rules. He was already pushing things as it was.

The skeleton took a few steps over to the window, leaning on the sill as he gazed out. "Can't say I'm too happy about it, but I'll stay hidden. Looks like it's the better offer."

"Better offer?"

"Never you mind, Digger. You get some rest, now. I won't bother you till morning."

Ian lay back down, propping himself up on a pillow so he could keep watch over his guest.

He couldn't believe it. Just hours earlier, he'd thought he'd failed at reciting the Words. Now, he was having a chat with a skeleton in his bedroom. Events had gone from bad to worse. He thought of Fiona. She'd said everything would look better in the morning. Well, the sun was just beginning to rise. Something told him his problems wouldn't just vanish in the daylight.

Thatcher turned from the window.

"You're lucky, you know. To be alive."

The sincerity of the skeleton's words caught Ian off guard. He'd never thought about it, really. He'd spent so much of his time trying to *avoid* the thought of Death, dreaming of his mother in her tomb, of the mystery of the Great Beyond . . . "What does being dead feel like?"

"There's no feel to it, really. Not in a proper sense."

"How could there be no feel to it?"

"Did you *feel* anything before you were born? Did you have any sense of what life was before you existed?"

"No, I guess not."

"Well there you are. It's just . . . nothing. It's the Void."

Ian shuddered, pulling the blankets tighter around himself. He could still feel the effects of the Void.

"It's the same for everyone?"

"Can't say for sure. I know some people say they see lights or hear music or see their family and friends in the Beyond. Not me, though. Suppose I wasn't lucky enough to wind up there. But when you woke me up, everything came back."

Ian shifted uncomfortably, figuring it would be best to change the subject. If they kept up all that "what's it like to be dead" talk, he'd never get any sleep.

"What was it like when you were alive?"

Thatcher perked up. "It was wonderful!" he cried. "So many adventures, Ian. So many . . ."

"What'd your parents do?"

"Farmers. Everyone's folks were farmers. 'S all there was around here. Graveyard wasn't half as big when I used to run through it. Village didn't even have roads."

It'd been so long since Ian ventured outside the cemetery walls that he'd almost forgotten what the village looked like.

"And how'd you pass the time?" He suddenly found himself wondering if Thatcher was expected to travel a set path in life, as strict and firm as his own.

Thatcher snorted. "Farm, mostly. Ran the plow or tended the cows. Stuff so boring you could fall asleep standing up. Not a whole lot of fun. That is, until the sun went down."

"And when the sun went down?"

"Oh, we'd have a right good time. We'd meet every night after supper, all the kids from 'round the village, usually at my place, up behind one of the old barns. My folks didn't keep much in there, so it made a great little hideout. We'd build toys or play games or come up with something to do down near the shops and market square. Pranks."

"I've never done any pranks."

"No? You should try sometime."

Ian thought about it for a minute, then decided he probably wasn't the pranking type.

"What kind of pranks did you do?"

"Oh, you name it. Put toads in all the girls' shoes. Filled the watchman's coat pockets with butter. Sometimes we'd loosen the wheels on every carriage in town. When that got old, we'd file them down into squares. Made for a bumpy ride. The postman wasn't none too pleased. Neither were the coachmen."

"Didn't you get caught?"

"Oh, sure we did. It was worth it, though. Mr. Creetcher— he was the butcher back in my day. We'd sneak into the shop and take all the pork. And I mean all of it. Chops, bacon slabs, roasts." Thatcher clicked his jaw. "Nice and salty, I can still taste it. Creetcher knew how to slice up a sow better than anyone. He was better at butchering than he was at keeping his door locked, that's for sure."

"That's not a prank," Ian insisted. "That's just flat-out *stealing.*"

"Well, you didn't let me finish. Before we grabbed all Creetcher's meat, we rustled up all of Old Mrs. Buttersby's pigs. The whole lot. Walked them right into the butcher shop and tied them to the counters. So it wasn't stealing. Not in the proper sense. Just replacing the old with the new. We made the shop come to life, as it were. You should've seen the look on Creetcher's face when he came in the next morning and found his place filled with *live* animals. Old geezer nearly dropped dead on the spot. Never seen a man so shocked. He was too used to seeing them all sliced and diced. That was a good joke. One of my best, really. Got a real talking-to after school that day . . ."

Ian found himself laughing at the skeleton's stories. "I have to admit, that does sound like fun."

Thatcher slumped down, resting his skull in his hands. "It was. But it could've been so much more. There was so much left to do . . ."

"I know it's not fair," Ian said. "Life usually isn't. I'm starting to think it's not meant to be. I'm sorry, Thatcher. Death is never a good thing. No one is ever ready for it. But it sounds like you made the most of your life while you could . . . Not everyone can say that."

Including me, he thought.

"Aye," Thatcher replied. "Suppose they can't." He lifted his empty sockets. "You making the most of yours, Digger?"

Ian tried to answer, but found the words stuck in his throat. Could he confide in Thatcher? Would it be breaking another Rule?

"Suppose you can't know," Thatcher sighed. "You won't until the end."

With that, Thatcher entered the closet, gently shutting the door behind him.

Not sure if Thatcher was completely trustworthy, Ian kept his eyes open for as long as he could before falling into an uneasy sleep.

The next morning, after making sure Thatcher was still safe,

Ian went downstairs where he found Bertrum waiting for him, two axes resting over his shoulders. The old corpse handed one to Ian, wordlessly motioning for him to follow.

They marched across the cemetery, all the way through the north side to the edge of the forest, finally stopping at the exact spot he'd taken Fiona the day before. Bertrum paused by one of the maple trees, sighing as he dropped an ax from his shoulder. "Firewood," he growled. "This'll be a nasty winter, lad. Can never be too prepared, I reckon."

Ian nodded, wondering why they'd had to come so far just for some wood. There were plenty of other trees around the manor.

"Here," Ian said, producing his needle and thread, "before you do any more damage."

It took a while to get the old grouch to sit still, but Ian finally managed it, stitching up Bertrum's dangling ear as the corpse went on about the difference between burning maple and ash, oak, and cedar. Which ones burned longer, which gave off the most heat, and which were too smoky. Ian tightened the last stitch and gave Betrum's ear a sharp tug, testing the strength of the thread.

Bertrum reached up and gave it a tug of his own, grunting in approval. "Gettin' better at that every time," he said. "Maybe thisn' won't fall off any longer." He stood, hefting the ax. "Let's get to it, then. Might be ye'll have to stich up a finger or two by the time we're done."

After an hour of chopping, Ian had filled a whole wheelbarrow's worth. Bertrum nodded, throwing his ax to the ground.

With otherworldly strength, he pulled the boy close. His one eye bulged as he spoke in low, measured tones. "I was watchin' ye yesterday. I've warned ye 'bout venturin' too close to the trail. I know Fiona wanted to take a peek 'round there, but I'd thought you'd have enough sense to keep away. The trail's no place for young'ns. It's rotten. Reason why there's hardly a grave out here. If, for any reason, ye find it necessary to get this close to the trail again, ye make sure to tell either me or yer father, understood?"

"Yes, Bertrum."

The blacksmith loosened his grip. "Good. Didn't mean to be so rough on ye, lad. Suppose I just feel protective is all."

"I know," Ian said. "I saw her again. The girl."

Bertrum froze, his good eye narrowing as he growled, "That so?"

Ian nodded. "She was watching me, behind the trees."

Bertrum's knuckles cracked as he made a massive fist. "Aye. Well, if she knows what's good for her, she'll stay beneath them trees. No use worryin' yerself over her, lad. She has her place. You have yers."

"Who is she?"

Bertrum didn't answer. Instead, he turned back to the woodpile and began chopping. "Fill that other barrow," he said, over his shoulder. "And be quick. We still have to work on yer stone carving, if ye ever want a shovel of yer own."

Ian let the ax fall to the grass. "Bertrum . . . who *is* she?"

The blacksmith raised his ax high into the air and brought it down with a mighty *whoosh*, sending pieces of wood flying. "Someone ye shouldn't be wastin' a single thought on, boy."

Ian shrugged, trudging back to the wheelbarrow. He wanted to ask him why. But, no, everything had to be a mystery. One big secret that he couldn't be a part of. He hated the fact that he needed to be watched over. He couldn't stand being told what to do, and when to do it. He couldn't even show Fiona around the Yard without Bertrum's warnings. The cemetery was enormous, but Ian felt so confined, always watched over like a prisoner, judged and graded on every move he made. Even out in the open meadows, it felt stifling. He could look after himself. It's not like he was completely helpless.

He fought the urge to come clean to Bertrum, to tell him that he'd done it, recited the Words of Resurrection. *That* would prove that he wasn't some weak child. *That* would prove that he didn't need to be ordered about.

But, like the speech he wanted to give his father about enrolling at the Guilds, Ian knew that it would never happen. After all, children rarely won arguments with adults. Especially when they had you beat by four hundred years. If Bertrum and his father did find out, he'd just be that much closer to Digging. One step closer to that dreaded fate.

"Yer father's gone away on business," Bertrum growled, loading more logs into the wheelbarrow.

Ian nodded. He was used to Isaac's long absences. After all, the Gravedigger's work went far beyond shoveling and Speaking. The restless Dead had certain tasks they needed completed. The work varied. Some had messages they needed passed on. Some wished to come clean about past crimes or mistakes. Some had secrets that needed revealing. Others, apologies to give or truths to admit. Whatever the case, the Gravedigger was charged with setting things right. So, more often than not, Isaac would venture far from home, tracking down relatives, friends, enemies, or acquaintances of the

Dead. He had no choice in the matter. It was the Digger's Code.

These trips had become commonplace for Ian. As he'd grown, he learned to be fine with them. At least, he'd become pretty good at *pretending* to be.

"How long this time?"

"Might be gone more'n a week. Somethin' tells me it may be closer to a fortnight, but ye never know. He'll be a busy man in the comin' days. Joanna gave 'im a pretty long list. Longer'n any I've seen afore. Yer father's a smart man, and he don't dally, so I can't say for sure. Yer guess is as good as mine, lad."

Ian sighed. Being left alone with Bertrum was a punishment in itself. With *him* in charge, Ian knew the coming days would be filled with chores. His father had only been gone a few hours, and they were already chopping down trees. His arms were still sore from digging. Ian didn't want to think about the list Bertrum must have for him. He'd probably have Ian re-shingle the roof and weed every headstone in the graveyard by the time Isaac returned.

"Aye. Busy season, this. I remember some o' yer forbears would go for months without Speakin' at *all*. Actually, got a chance to put my feet up every now and then. There was an *order* to things. Not all willy-nilly, like it is now."

"Yes, Bertrum."

"Go stack the wood by the shed, lad." He tugged his ear. "And thank ye for the repair. Ye learn that in one o' them books?"

Ian nodded and lifted the wheelbarrow, the muscles in his arms burning as he struggled under its weight.

When Ian had finished stacking the firewood, he seized the opportunity to avoid his undead guardian, bounding upstairs to his room. He grabbed a quill and parchment and began writing a letter to Fiona, asking her to come as soon as she could.

It's urgent, he wrote. *I have something to show you.*

He raced outside just as the postman rode up to the gate, excitedly pushing the wax-sealed envelope into his hands. "Make sure she gets it today," he whispered, looking over his shoulder to make sure Betrum wasn't lingering around.

The postman nodded as he grabbed onto the reins and galloped away.

Ian wrung his hands nervously as he made his way back inside, thinking about Thatcher tucked away in his closet.

When he passed the study, he noticed an envelope sitting on the table.

He picked it up, examining the letterhead. It was his father's handwriting. Addressed to him.

Ian,

As I'm sure Bertrum's told you, I had to go away. I don't know how long I'll be. Perhaps a week. Perhaps a month. I don't want you to worry.

I know this is a difficult time, Ian. Your mother's anniversary is less than a week away. And it will be the first year that I won't be home to spend it with you. For that, I am truly sorry.

Please know that I love you very much, and that I grow prouder of you with each passing day.

I've left some flowers in the kitchen. Please put them with the rest when you go out to the lake. Give my best to Joanna and Fiona, should you see them.

Remember, Ian: The Yard is in your care, now. Try to listen to what Bertrum has to say.

Will write more when I get the chance.

Love,
Dad

Ian sighed. The anniversary. It'd be ten years since his mother had passed away. Almost his entire life. He'd always remembered when the anniversary was approaching. With all that was going on, he'd completely forgotten.

And his dad would be gone. That really stung.

It wasn't that they had much of a celebration, really. Every year, Ian, his father, and Bertrum would construct these magnificent bouquets. Ian grew them special in his garden, and only picked the most beautiful. At dusk, the three would walk down to the lake, where they'd place the flowers into small paper boats. And the current of the lake would always pull them toward his mother's island tomb. Year after year, the flowers would reach that distant shore, gently bobbing up onto the beach, leaving Ian wondering if his mother was the one guiding them.

Five

Fiona arrived late in the evening. Ian had waited for her all day, avoiding Bertrum and his seemingly endless list of chores. The hours dragged as he languished around the empty manor, barely able to contain his excitement.

He ran out to greet her the moment she wandered up the walkway, whisking her into the house before she could say a word. He led her up the candlelit staircase, bounding up the steps two at a time before tripping on the landing.

"What's gotten into you?"

Ian winced as he picked himself up, gingerly dabbing at the scrape on his knee. "I have something to show you." He took her by the hand, pulling her in close as they stopped in the hall outside his room. "The Call," he huffed. "It was real, Fiona. The Words worked. Thatcher Moore's here."

Fiona took a step back. "Ian . . ."

"Look!"

"Ian!" she said. He opened the door, motioning for her to follow. Fiona stayed out in the hall. She hadn't moved an inch.

"What's wrong?" Ian asked. "Don't you want to see?"

Fiona's eyes widened.

Ian felt his cheeks turning red.

"What? Do I have something on my face?"

"No," she said. "Ian, your hair! Look at it!"

Ian felt his heart lurch. *Oh, no,* he thought. *Not now. Please tell me it's not happening now.*

He ran his fingers through the tufts at his temples.

"Here?"

She nodded.

"It's *white*," she said. "Like snow."

Ian ran to the washroom, taking a deep breath before looking at his reflection in the mirror. He could barely recognize the face that stared back. The dusting of white above his ears made him look considerably older. Certainly older than he *felt*. Even his light-blue eyes seemed to have gone a little gray. He touched the hairs, then plucked one, examining it under the light, twirling the white wisp through his fingers just to be sure it was real.

It was. There was no denying it. He could feel the goose bumps rise on his skin as he stared at it.

"It's like your father's," Fiona said from the doorway.

Ian let the hair fall to the floor. *Like your father's . . .* He'd checked his head every night since he could remember. The one night he *did* Speak, and not a single glance in the mirror. "I don't understand," he said, "It changed so quickly. It must have been while I was waiting for you.

"I need to cut it," he said, panicked. "My dad can't see this. *Or* Bertrum. If they find out what we did . . ."

"If you cut it, it'll just grow back."

Fiona was right. Ian shook his head, pacing wildly as he stared at the white hair on the tile floor. "I should've known this would happen." He pounded a fist against the wall. "I should've seen this!"

"It's not so bad," Fiona said. "Maybe they won't even notice. Not at first."

Ian stared at his reflection, feeling like it might be the last time he'd ever look back at the face of a child.

"They will," he sighed. "They'll notice."

Soon, he'd look like those portraits in the study. It wouldn't be long before he joined them. Just another gloomy face in a frame. He shivered.

Fiona stepped out into the hallway. "Is Thatcher really here?"

Ian pulled himself away from the mirror. His problems had stacked onto one another, growing like a stone wall he'd never be able to climb.

He lifted a lamp from the dresser and slowly lead Fiona to the closet. "Now don't panic."

"Panic? Ian, this is a dream! I can't believe this . . . My first Caller."

Ian pulled the door open, allowing the light to pour in.

But inside, all he found was a pile of clothes and blankets. He stepped inside to get a better look, moving aside heaps of crumpled cloaks.

Nothing.

Thatcher was gone.

Ian stared at the mess. "He was . . . He was here . . ."

Fiona's smile faded. "If this is a jest, Ian, it's not very funny . . ."

"It's no jest," he said, rummaging through the piles to be sure. "He was here last night. I swear it. I saw him go into the closet. I was up all night *talking* to him."

Fiona frowned, her nose wrinkling. "You had a long night. You probably just had a nightmare."

"It wasn't a nightmare," he insisted. "Thatcher Moore crawled up out of his grave. He came into my room. He sat right there, on the edge of my bed! Fiona, the Words worked."

Fiona kept her eyes trained on the closet, staring at the piles.

"You don't believe me, do you?"

"I do believe you, Ian." She turned back to face him. "I'm just trying to understand." She crossed her arms, studying Ian's bedroom.

"He . . . he must've snuck out this morning."

"Out into the Yard?" Fiona clapped her hands together. "We have to go find him!" She grabbed the hem of his sleeve, pulling him to the door.

"Listen," he said, struggling against her. "Maybe we should just tell Bertrum."

Fiona froze. "What?"

"I don't know," Ian said, nervously rubbing the back of his neck. "I'm starting to think this was a bad idea. We're not ready for . . . for all *this*. I wanted to fail, Fiona. I didn't want to Speak the Words, to bring Thatcher back. I thought that if I couldn't do it, maybe I wouldn't be worthy enough to Dig. Maybe my father would see that it's not the right path. Now that it's worked . . . I just don't know what to do. It won't be long before Bertrum finds out."

"There's still time," Fiona said. "We find Thatcher and put him back. No one needs to know."

Ian slumped down against the wall. "What if we can't? Don't you see? When my father finds out what I've done, I'll be a Gravedigger in his eyes. I'll never set foot anywhere near the Guilds."

"You don't know that," Fiona said. She crouched down in front of him. "Listen. Thatcher is *alive*. He's out there somewhere, and we're going to find him. We *have* to. I can't just let him run wild. *I'm* the one who got the Call. I'm the one who started this, and *we're* going to set things right. You can't give up so easily, Ian. You're not like that. You're thoughtful." She gestured to the books littering the floor. "You're studious and generous, something my mother is always trying to get me to be. Now, we can give up right now, and you can say goodbye your dreams, or we can go out there and try to fix this. How will it look if we just backed down and told our parents? This was your first time Speaking, but it was my first Call. We need to handle this without anyone's help. Don't you see that? If we don't solve our own problems, how are we going to prove we're good enough to do anything ourselves?"

"If Bertrum finds out, it'll be the end," Ian muttered, almost to himself.

"Look," Fiona said, "You can tell him now, or you can *fix* it. And maybe that's best. Even if he finds out after, he'll see that you're capable of handling things yourself. Isn't that what you want?"

Ian gave her words some thought. "We need to be quick," he said, carefully. "If we don't find Thatcher by sunrise, that could be it for us."

"We'll find him," Fiona said. She offered him a hand. He took it, hoisting himself up off the floor.

Ian grabbed a pair of lanterns from the closet and handed one to her.

"Wait," she said, "I have an idea."

She darted over to the closet and grabbed a wool cap, red with giant earflaps. Ian sighed. He never really liked that hat. She fixed it over his head, making sure he was completely covered.

"There," she said, satisfied. "That should take care of your hair for a while."

Ian slipped his cloak over his shoulders, then adjusted the hat. He didn't even want to know how ridiculous he must look.

They snuck out of the manor and into the graveyard. The shadows were back, moving through the stones, evading the lantern light like mischievous midnight dancers. Every now and then, Ian would stop, freezing at the slightest sound or movement. But it was always nothing more than a shadow. Or a squirrel. Or the wind. Or his own ears and brain playing tricks on him. The night can do that, especially when you're stumbling through it in a panic, searching for a skeleton.

"What's he like?" Fiona asked.

Ian had to think about that for a while. Thatcher had seemed agreeable, at first. Fun, even.

But there was something off in the way Thatcher had acted. Something strange he'd said. He'd told Ian that his was the "better" offer. Ian had spent half the night wondering what the skeleton had meant. There was a piece of a puzzle that he was missing and that he'd been too tired to question. But maybe it was nothing. Thatcher was from another era, after all. Ian had to keep reminding himself of that. Might as well have been from a different dimension, really.

"He's different," Ian finally said. "Hard to describe. Not dangerous or anything."

At least he hoped not. Mischievous, maybe, but not a threat. Thatcher *was* a restless soul, after all . . . Probably a bit more restless than most.

"It's got to be such an odd feeling. You know, being dead for all those years, and then being awakened all of a sudden."

Ian thought of the Void. "It was an odd feeling for me, too. Thatcher didn't want to go back. He got upset when I even mentioned it."

Fiona shined her light at a crumbling ossuary, walking a little faster when she saw the pile of skulls neatly arranged inside. "Can't say I blame him. If you got a second chance, wouldn't you want to take it?"

"That's what he doesn't understand. It's *not* a second chance. You know what he told me when I asked him why he Called you? He said his only problem is that he's *dead*. You must see how ridiculous that is. That's not a *problem*. It's certainly not a good enough reason to contact you."

"Maybe it is for some people. Everyone's different."

"Still," Ian said, "you know the Rules. The Dead only reach out when they have problems. Real, *actual* problems." He patted his satchel. "If I could go back in time maybe . . . maybe I could have helped him. I can't give him what he wants. Not now."

"Are you sure he didn't need help with anything else?"

"No. That was it. He just wants to be alive. 'To have fun,' he said. 'Cause mischief.' 'Play pranks.' He kept saying his 'time was cut short.'"

"Well, it *was*."

When Ian gave her a look, Fiona bristled. "What? You don't think so? He's *our* age. How would you feel if you knew that *this* was it?"

She was right. Ian was a bit embarrassed. Sometimes he wondered why he even bothered arguing. Fiona was *usually* right. He, of all people, knew what it was like to have your time cut short. His dreams about his mother were proof enough of that.

"I'd feel terrible," he admitted, realizing he understood Thatcher more than he'd thought.

The pair continued on in silence, huddled in close, jumping over small streams and scurrying through moonlit clearings and meadows, eyes skimming the passing headstones. There were so many of them. Ian realized that they might never find Thatcher. The graveyard went on for miles. If he really wanted to, Thatcher could stay hidden forever.

Ian spied the dark outline of the Fossor Crypt as they neared the center of the Yard, its twisted spires menacing in the gloom and shadow.

"Spooky," Fiona said, shining the light under her chin.

Ian shivered. One day, his bones would rest there, deep down in the dark. The haunting exterior was scary enough, but that knowledge frightened him more than anything.

Fiona shined her light on the nearest gargoyle. Ian took a few steps back, gazing into the wild stone eyes, the jagged teeth protruding like daggers from its gaping maw. It was hunched over, wings extended behind hulking shoulders, crouched and ready to pounce. Fiona moved the light along the roof, pausing at every stone beast, each more terrifying than the last.

Ian saw something move out of the corner of his eye.

"Look!"

"What is it?"

"I don't know," he said, eyes fixed on the rooftop. "I thought I saw something."

Fiona clutched her lantern.

"We should keep moving."

Ian nodded, taking one last look at the sneering gargoyles before turning away.

"But you just got here!"

The voice flitted through the air, wispy and hollow as wind.

Ian froze. Fiona whipped the light around, wildly searching for the source.

"Thatcher," Ian whispered. "He's here."

"Of course I'm *here*. What are you doing out so late? It's past your bedtime. If I didn't know any better, I'd say you're up to no good. I see you've brought the girl along, too."

Ian scanned the surrounding headstones.

"Where are you?"

"What are you, blind? I'm over here."

"Over where?"

"Oh, you Diggers are no fun," the voice echoed. "Fine. I guess you need a hint. Look *up*."

Up?

Fiona gasped as one of the gargoyles rumbled atop the mausoleum. The stone monster seemed to come to life, inching precariously close to the edge of the roof. It teetered for a moment before finally falling, shattering against the ground with a loud *crack*! The head broke off, rolling across the grass before stopping just shy of their feet.

Ian edged back, stumbling over a tombstone as she raised her light to the rooftop once more.

Slowly, a skeletal figure crept into the space where the gargoyle had been, bones tapping against the granite as it leaned against a half-crumbled spire. It folded its arms, grinning, the light illuminating the empty sockets in its skull.

Thatcher nodded toward the demolished statue, shoulder blades arching as he shrugged. "Looks like I've made a bit of a mess. Sorry about that, Ian. Guess I don't know my own strength."

"I don't care about that right now," Ian said. "You need to come with us."

"Oh, I don't know about that."

Ian could feel his ears burning under the wool cap. He wished he could reason with Thatcher. He wanted to help him. But the skeleton was making that very, very hard. "Listen," he said. "I gave you one night. You went against your word, Thatcher. You're going back to the Children's Yard. Now."

"True. True. You *did* give me one night. Very generous of you, I might add. A whole *night*." He paused, glancing up at the moon. "And if I'm not mistaken, *that's* not the sun, so my one night isn't quite over. Wouldn't you agree?"

"No, no, no," Ian said, stepping over the remains of the gargoyle. "You've been above ground long enough. Come on. You know what happens next."

"One more hour," the skeleton pleaded.

"How about ten minutes?"

"Three-quarters."

"Fifteen minutes."

"Half an hour."

"Enough!" Ian cried. "Get down from there! You're coming with us, whether you like it or not. I'm not messing around anymore, Thatcher. This isn't a game."

The skeleton perked up. "Games?"

"Oh, no. Don't even think about it."

"I like games!"

"We're not playing!"

"Well I say we *are*. Here . . . how about this . . . If you can catch me, I'll go back. But if you *can't*, I get to stay above ground another day. Fair?"

"I'm serious, Thatcher. Don't make me come up there."

The skeleton snorted. "Don't bother. I'll save you the trouble."

He dropped down and hung from the edge of the spire, bones *clacking* like wind chimes as he swayed in the breeze.

"No!" Fiona cried. "You'll hurt yourself!"

Thatcher waved her off with his free hand. "Never you mind, Voicecatcher. I'll be fine. Just watch!"

"Thatcher, don't!" Ian cried.

Too late.

The skeleton let go, laughing as he plummeted to the ground.

Ian winced as a few of Thatcher's ribs snapped on impact, knobby knees twisting, and shinbones splintering with a *crunch*.

Thatcher lifted his skeletal frame from the grass, popping a few wayward bones back into place, then looked around. "See? Nothing to get so worked up about."

Ian moved forward. "All right. You've been above ground long enough. Let's go."

Thatcher's ribs rattled as he threw his head back and laughed. "Now? No, no. I'm afraid not. *We're* playing tag. Hope you two are good runners."

"Thatcher, stop!"

"Catch me if you can, Ian!"

Thatcher sprinted past the mausoleum, laughing as he rounded the corner. His skeletal legs carried him faster than Ian expected, *clicking* and *clacking* as he disappeared into a sea of tombstones.

"Let's go!" Fiona cried, taking off after him.

They raced through the northwest corner of the cemetery, charging up the rolling hills and down into the marsh, their shoes becoming caked in mud as they sloshed through the mire. Thatcher evaded them with an otherworldly speed. They came up out of the marsh and into Ishver's Yard, the rows of graves first dug by Ian's grandfather. Ian could see the lake come into view on his left. He squinted in the moonlight, just able to make out his mother's tomb.

"Watch it!"

He swerved out of the way, narrowly avoiding a felled oak.

"That was a close one!" Fiona called over her shoulder. "Keep your eyes forward!"

The way the undead mischief-maker bounded through the graves made Ian nervous. Thatcher didn't have lungs, so losing his breath wouldn't be a problem. As a mere mortal, however, Ian had no such luck. A surge of pain shot through his body as he ran harder, trying to catch up.

"How is he moving so fast?" Fiona gasped.

"I don't know!" Ian answered, his lungs aching for air. How *was* Thatcher moving so fast? Bertrum limped around slow as a snail, and he still had most of his meat on his bones. How could a skeleton move with such speed?

"Something's not right!" Ian said, wheezing horribly.

Fiona let out a frustrated grunt.

Every time Ian thought they were gaining, Thatcher darted in the opposite direction. Fiona kept up a good pace, and Ian found himself struggling to stay with her as the beam of her lantern guided him through the dark.

"We need to catch him before he gets to the north meadow!" he cried.

The meadow marked the northern boundary of the Yard. If Thatcher made it to the woods, they'd be in trouble.

Though there was no rule written about it anywhere, Ian was pretty sure a corpse wasn't supposed to beat a Gravedigger in a footrace.

Thatcher's feet dug into the dirt as he slid to a grinding halt, stopping just before the tree line.

Fiona raised her lantern to light his face. "Okay," she huffed, "that's *enough!*"

Thatcher turned to face the woods, taking a few steps toward the trees. He stopped and stared down at the ground. "I give up, Voicecatcher. You win."

"Good," Ian said. "Now, let's go." He looked up at the sky. Dawn wasn't too far off. If they headed back now, they could reach the Children's Yard before the sun rose.

Thatcher pointed toward the woods. In all the excitement

of the chase, Ian hadn't realized where the skeleton had been leading them.

"Wait. I remember this place," Thatcher said, standing perfectly still, staring into the dark. "Never got a chance to go down the Pumpkin Trail."

Ian paused mid-step. "What'd you say?"

"Was I not clear? I said I never got a chance to go down there."

"This was here when *you* were alive?"

Thatcher nodded. "'Course it was. The older boys used to dare each other to go in. They said it was bad. Said it swallowed people whole."

"What's down there?"

"Yeah," Fiona prodded. "Where does it go?"

Thatcher scoffed. "How should I know? I never took a look myself."

"Well, didn't any of the other kids?"

Thatcher shook his head. "Some *said* they did. Bragged about it around the village. But they were liars, the lot of them. Just telling tales to impress the girls, I guess." He swept his hand over plots behind them. "This whole spot was old Yoren Connors's farm. He used to come to buy feed from my father pretty regular. He was always grumbling about something or other. Most of it, just your average moaning and groaning. There was one thing he always went on about, though. The land near the woods was bad. Something was wrong with the dirt, he said. It went sour, like it'd been salted. No corn or barley or carrots or even potatoes would take root there. He said it was the woods that turned the ground sick. He was always warning the village about the trail. Said it caused the sickness. My folks ignored him. Most of the village did.

Everyone knew about the trail, but no one knew who where it led exactly.

"Yoren would come to my father's every few months and try out different seeds. None of them worked, that is until he tried pumpkins. They took to that soil like you wouldn't believe. Old Yoren's land was riddled with them They grew so quick and so close together, the whole field was a sea of orange. Only he couldn't sell them. People got sick of pumpkin pie pretty quick, and that's about all they're good for.

"Yoren said he was cursed. Couldn't even sell the land. He died alone and penniless, and after he passed on, the house just stood there. The pumpkins, too. No one would go anywhere near the old place. Too close to the woods." Thatcher paused, turning back to the trail. "Too close to *that*."

Ian remembered the lone gravestone he'd inspected the day Fiona found the trail. Yoren Connors. *That's* why he'd been buried so far away from the others. No one wanted him near them, even in death.

"That's terrible," Fiona said.

"Funny thing is, everyone *believed* him," Thatcher said. "They *did* think the land was cursed. Only nobody lifted a finger to help. No one had the guts to go into those woods."

"It can't be that bad," Fiona muttered.

"It may be true. May be it was all just stories, after all." He sighed. "Well, I suppose there's only one way to find out."

"Thatcher, no!" Ian shouted.

Without warning, the skeleton bounded into the woods, disappearing into the murky darkness of the trees.

"We need to go after him!" Fiona cried.

Ian froze, panicked. Adrenaline pumped through his body, ushering in a raw, crippling fear, unlike anything he'd felt in his life. Every fiber of his being told him to turn back. To *run*. But as Fiona stood waiting at the foot of the trail, Ian knew that he had to go on. He couldn't let her down. If Thatcher lost them in those woods, they'd lose him forever.

Fiona gave him an encouraging smile. "It's now or never, Ian. Are you ready?"

Ian smacked his lips, mouth dry as fear gripped his throat like an iron fist. "Ready," he croaked.

A Digger endures, he repeated in his head. *And a Digger fears no darkness.*

Well, not usually, anyway. . . .

Ian's feet felt heavy as he took those first steps onto the nettle-covered path. It was as if the darkness of the forest had its own weight, the sinister shadows bearing down on him. It was so thick he felt as if he could've reached out and touched it.

They crept down the trail side by side.

Ian strained his ears, listening as Thatcher kept a steady pace ahead of them, leading them along by the sound of bones crunching on dead leaves. "Don't know what all the fuss is about," the skeleton's voice called from the darkness. "It's just the woods. What's so scary about the *woods*?"

A lot of things, Ian wanted to reply. Mainly, not knowing what was in them. His mind raced as he thought of the girl he'd seen, the sound of her feet as she moved along the forest floor. He scanned the trees, searching for that shadowy figure that always seemed to be watching from afar.

But the girl was nowhere to be found. Only the gnarled

branches of the oaks and elms reaching out like spindly hands, waiting to grab him in the dark.

The pumpkins framing the path grew larger as Ian and Fiona trekked farther into the trees, orange bodies grotesquely out of proportion, their thick tendrils twisting along the forest floor like a tangle of serpents.

Fiona's palms were cold and clammy as she squeezed Ian's hand. "How far in does the trail go?" she asked.

"No idea," Ian replied.

Ian had never thought about how large the forest was. He only knew it as a place-marker, a border to the cemetery. The end of the known world.

Bones rattled several paces ahead. "C'mon!" Thatcher called. "Keep up, you two."

As Ian strained to make out the skeletal silhouette, his lantern dimmed. He shook it. It burned bright for a moment, then faded, the pale glow softening as the flame sputtered.

Fiona shot him a worried look. "You didn't bring any oil, did you?"

Ian shook his head.

She squeezed his hand tighter as the wick gave one last flicker and died out.

Ian tried to spot the moon through the branches above, scouring the pitch-black sky for signs of light. Anything to help guide them.

A thick fog rolled in, covering the ground like a blanket. The midnight air stung his cheeks as he trudged on and pulled his cap down more snugly.

Thatcher was nowhere to be seen, but they could hear twigs snapping as his bony feet plodded along.

"Wow! Would you look at *that*!"

Lights were glowing along the trail, flickering like orange fireflies. Fiona pointed to the pumpkins, then drew Ian over to examine the nearest one. He shuddered. A face had been carved into the flesh, a mouth twisted into a lopsided grin lit from within by a candle, causing the eyes to glow an evil shade of yellow.

Jack-o'-lanterns leered all along the trail, each with its distinctive smirk. Warped by the fog, the faces twisted into crouching demons waiting to snap at their ankles.

"Wonder what made 'em?" Thatcher asked, his voice growing faint as dead branches rattled overhead.

"Yoren never said?" Fiona called, stumbling in the mist until Ian caught her by the arm.

"Never," Thatcher said. "But he talked about evil. Never said what kind. People? Monsters? The pumpkins themselves?"

Ian felt a wave of dread. "Monsters" was the last thing he needed to hear. His skin prickled. He knew something was out there. He could sense strange eyes on him. Following. Waiting.

As they walked on, the air itself seemed to grow heavy, so thick he felt he could reach out and touch it. He felt himself slowing down. His thoughts drifted toward sleep, and he a sudden urge to lie down and close his eyes, even though he was afraid.

Fiona yawned, stretching her hands over her head. "Why am I getting so tired? Ian? Do you feel something?"

Ian heard himself agreeing. His legs wobbled beneath him, thoughts drifting to dreams. He kneeled in the path, rubbing his eyes as exhaustion swept over him.

Fiona slowed a few paces ahead. When Ian came closer,

she dropped to the ground, her legs giving out beneath her. Panicked, Ian knelt down beside her. Her breathing was slow and measured, her eyes closed, a placid smile on her lips.

Ian grabbed her shoulder and gave her a shake. "Fiona, wake up!"

It was no use. Fiona rolled over onto her stomach, softly snoring.

The fog grew thick around the edge of the trail, swirling closer, closing in like a ghostly drape. Strange animal howls pierced the ever-encroaching silence, echoing out in the distance.

He shook her again. *Please*, he thought. *Please, don't leave me alone in this place.*

The fog began swirling around his ankles. He strained his ears, listening for Thatcher's footsteps ahead, but heard nothing.

Ian bent down to turn Fiona over, gently cradling her head in his hands as he shifted her body.

He turned her face.

A pale skull grinned back.

Ian screamed, dropping her from his arms as he staggered back against a tree. The fog grew heavier, following him, pulling at his limbs like chains. He fought against it, his eyes never leaving Fiona's skeletal face. Her body lay perfectly still, rigid like a corpse in a coffin.

"This isn't happening," he told himself.

Suddenly, Fiona sat up. The bare teeth of the skull seemed to smile.

"Oh, but it is, Gravedigger." The voice that hissed from Fiona's lipless mouth stabbed into Ian's eardrums like knives. *It wasn't her*, he thought. It couldn't be.

81

The thing that looked like Fiona stood up, tall and impossibly thin, body contorting like a puppet on strings, moving in jagged and disjointed strides in the light of the jack–o'–lanters.

"Come, Gravedigger," it said, reaching out a slender, clawlike hand. "It's time for us to rest, now. Sleep."

Ian kicked against the fog tightening around his legs. His body felt so heavy. He gritted his teeth, pushing with all his strength. With one last desperate shove, he broke free. The fog recoiled, moving back across the trail.

He backed himself up against a tree, closing his eyes.

"This isn't real," he said. "A dream. That's all. Just a dream." He was sick with fear, but the strange urge to sleep was stronger than ever, muddling his thoughts.

When he opened his eyes, the pumpkins were waiting. They gathered around Fiona, floating in the air, their long stalks dangling like tentacles. Ian felt the heat from the flames burning behind their eyes.

"Gravedigger," they cackled in unison, floating ever closer. The stalks reached out to him like twisted arms, their smiles wreathed in flame. "Another Digger for the tomb."

Ian found he was too exhausted to move, his body leaning helplessly against the tree. It took everything he had not to give in to the heaviness he felt growing inside his chest.

"I," he croaked, "am not . . . a Gravedigger!"

The fire-eyed pumpkins laughed. It was a cold, wicked sound.

"Don't fight it," Fiona said. "You wear the cloak. You walk the Yard. *Digger.*"

"You're . . . you're not her," he whispered. "You're a dream. A nightmare."

The skeletal figure cocked its head, studying him with deep, lifeless pools of black. "No," it said with a deep, rumbling voice. "But I can change." The skull collapsed in on itself and fell off the body, landing on the ground in heap of ground bone. Ian turned away, finding it harder and harder to move, to think.

The jack-o'-lanterns floated in circles around the pile, stalks waving wildly. "Change!" they bellowed. "Change!"

The pile of broken bone began to tremble. Ian watched in horror as a hand of stone shot out from the rubble. A hideous figure lurched up from the ground. Ian's eyes widened as he recognized it. The gargoyle from the Fossor Crypt. It let out a burst of steamy, putrid air from a pair of granite nostrils, baring its fangs in the light of the jack-o'-lanterns. With a great heave, it spread its stone wings.

"You must sleep," it said, pointing a gnarled claw to the ground. "Join the others."

Ian looked down. The trail had become thick with broken bones. They covered the ground, ribs and skulls and fingers scattered like clay shards in mounds and heaps.

He struggled to stand, feeling his legs go soft. He could hardly keep his eyes open.

"Sleep," the jack-o'-lanterns echoed. "Sleep and dream of the cold dark. The deep grave. Sleep like the ones you send to the Void."

Ian's legs gave out from under him. He fell forward, knees landing hard on the shattered bones. He couldn't move his arms to break his fall. All he could do was look up at the floating horrors gathered around him, regarding him with eyes of bright fire.

His body went limp as the fog returned, blotting out the

faces and the flames, curling around him like a blanket of icy mist.

"Fiona," he groaned, feeling his heartbeat steadily slow, his eyelids grow heavy. "Father. Bertrum. I'm so sorry . . ."

The fog consumed him, and Ian surrendered to a dark and dreamless sleep.

Six

Unfamiliar voices floated through the dark.

"Will he wake?"

"He's still breathing. He'll wake."

A soft rustling.

"No!" another voice snapped. "We're not to touch him! You know that."

"I know," the second whispered. "I just wanted to be sure."

Ian drifted in the darkness, listening to the sound of feet crunching through leaves.

A sharp stab of pain woke him with a start. Almost blinded by daylight, Ian found himself face-to-face with a strange girl. She recoiled, clearly as shocked as he was, and backed a few steps away.

Ian tried to stand, but hit his head. Panicked, he realized he was in a wooden cage barely large enough to hold him. He gripped the bars and tried to make sense of his surroundings.

The girl edged closer. Tangles of black hair outlined a face of warm olive skin, her green eyes glowing like slivers of jade. A light brown dress hung loose from her shoulders, simple-looking, like a burlap sack, almost as if she'd sewn it herself. Charms of twine, feathers, jade, and coins hung from a long necklace and several bracelets that clattered when she moved.

Her fingers curled around the bars as she leaned in.

"Digger," she said softly, "can you hear me?"

Ian scuttled back as far as he could to the opposite side of the cage. It wasn't far enough. Her eyes widened as she studied him. Ian felt like a bug in a jar.

"Ian," he said, still wiping crust from his eyes as he regained his bearings. "My name is Ian."

"Ian," she repeated, as if the name were somehow familiar. "I'm Olivia. The spell you were under was a nasty one. We feared you wouldn't come out of it."

Ian thought of the pumpkins floating along the trail of bones, the gargoyle from the Crypt snarling its cruel, stone snarl. Fiona . . .

"Where is she?" he demanded.

"Your friend? She's safe," Olivia gestured over her shoulder. "She woke not long ago. My sisters are keeping her company."

Ian tried to stand once more, hitting his head even harder on the wooden ceiling. He winced, rubbing the swelling bump on his skull. "What did you do to us? Where am I?"

Olivia regarded him for a moment, almost as if she

didn't understand the question. "You're in the woods," she answered. "Where else would you be?"

Ian felt his breath tighten as he quickly studied his surroundings. They were in a clearing, the forest floor thick with moss. His eyes drifted down to a group of tiny houses huddled beneath ancient trees. They were so overgrown with brush and vines that they seemed to blend in to the trees. Tendrils of thick black smoke curled from a few of the dilapidated chimneys. Ian inhaled the stench of damp woodsmoke.

It was strangely quiet. No wind rustled through the leaves. No birds chirped in the branches. Even the insects were silent. All he could hear was his own heart pumping. He tried to calm himself as the rapid, shallow beat pounded in his eardrums.

The stories were true. There *was* a village in the woods.

"Grandmother cast the spell," Olivia said, "not us. We're too young to work spells that strong. I'm . . . I'm sorry if it was too upsetting." Her dark cheeks blushed even darker. "Grandmother's spells are nasty sometimes." She bent to a crouch. Ian watched as she rummaged through something on the ground. His satchel.

"What are you doing?" he snapped. "Give that back!"

"These tools are strange," she said, holding up a small, handcrafted finger splint. "You must have a lot of such things, in that big, stone house of yours. Grandmother always warns us about Digger magic. How does it work?"

Ian watched her twirl the wooden splint in her hands, studying it like it was an object of great importance.

"It's not magic," he said. "It's a splint."

Olivia cocked her head. "Splint?"

"It heals bones," he said. Olivia looked to be about his age,

87

but he suddenly felt like he was talking to a much younger child.

She placed the splint back inside the satchel, then lifted up one of his books. Ian read the cover: *The Healing Properties of the Common Nurnroot*.

"I . . . I don't know what you want," Ian said. "Please, if you'll just let me go, I won't say anything. I'll never come back, I swear."

Olivia didn't seem to hear him. She placed the book on the ground, slowly turning the pages. She frowned. "What kind of book is this? The writing is so strange."

"It's a book on Healing," Ian said, confused. "You can't read the title?"

Olivia shook her head.

"You don't know how to read?"

Olivia bristled at that. "I know how to read," she said, stuffing the book back into the satchel. "Grandmother has me read her books. They look different from yours. You Diggers make strange markings on your pages. Is that part of your magic, too?"

Ian didn't know how to respond. There was so much he wanted to ask her, but he didn't know where to start. He felt like he was in the middle of a bad dream.

"You keep talking about magic. I don't have any magic. I'm . . . I'm not even a Digger. Not truly."

Olivia grabbed the hem of his cloak, pinching the black cloth between her fingers. "You say you're not a Digger, yet you wear their clothes. Black as a moonless night, black as your black souls. That's what Grandmother says."

"I don't know what your Grandmother's been telling you, but she's wrong."

Olivia flinched. "Keep your voice down, Digger!" She shot a worried glance up to the surrounding trees.

Ian looked around the clearing, finding it still empty.

Olivia came a few steps closer. She peered into his eyes. "Hmm," she muttered. "They don't look as black as they do in the books."

"My eyes aren't black," Ian answered. "They're blue."

Olivia nodded. Suddenly, she reached into the cage, grasping Ian's jaw. He struggled against her, but her grip held firm.

"I won't hurt you," she said. "Just open your mouth."

"What for?" Ian asked, completely at a loss. He tried to edge back, but there was no room in the cage.

"Open," Olivia repeated. "I want to see."

Resigned, Ian opened his mouth. There was nothing he could do, trapped as he was.

Olivia peered into his mouth, biting her lip as she studied whatever she was looking for. After a time, she released her hold. Ian leaned back on the bars, massaging his jaw.

"Odd," Olivia said, "Did you file your fangs down, or do they sprout as you get older?"

"Fangs?" Ian didn't know what to say. Olivia stared at him, waiting for an answer. "I don't have fangs. I don't know why you'd even think I would." He opened his mouth and placed a finger on his canine tooth. "See? This is the sharpest tooth I have. Everyone has them. Check for yourself."

He watched as she dabbed the tip of her tooth. As she did, he realized he'd seen her before. That dress. The black hair, the dark complexion.

"It's *you*," he said.

Olivia quickly took her finger out of her mouth, stiffening.

89

"It *is* you, isn't it?" he said. "The one who's been watching me at the edge of the forest."

Olivia wrung her hands, glancing wildly around the clearing.

A crow cawed overhead. Olivia gasped, watching wide-eyed as the black bird shifted on its perch. It looked down with beady, glistening eyes.

"I . . . I shouldn't be talking to you alone," she said, voice shaking as she kept her eyes fixed on the crow.

"What is it?" Ian asked. "Just tell me, what am I doing here?"

As if in answer, the crow cawed again, lifting off the branch and flying into the woods. Olivia watched it until it disappeared into the trees before turning back to Ian.

"Grandmother had us bring you here. She wanted to watch you . . . to see what you would do."

Ian's mind was spinning. Nothing Olivia said made sense to him, and he couldn't get a clear answer out of her, no matter how hard he tried.

"Fiona," he said. "I want to see her."

Olivia nodded. "Very well," she said, and turned to face one of the cottages. "Bring her out!" she called.

Ian watched the cottage door. He could hear a rustling inside. A scuffle and *thump*. The door swung open, and Fiona stepped out into the light. She was blindfolded and flanked on either side by two girls who looked like smaller versions of Olivia.

They shoved Fiona forward, giggling as she stumbled over rocks and roots. Ian sensed something was off about them. The way they laughed. The dagger-like quality of their smiles. The fire behind their eyes.

One let go of Fiona and skipped over. Her chubby cheeks were marked with dirt. "Here's the Seer, Olivia!" She twirled across the grass, stopping before the cage. When she saw Ian, she stepped back, eyes wide. "He's awake? You should have told us! He could have hurt you!"

Olivia placed a hand on her shoulder. "Don't worry, Clara. I can watch out for myself." She gestured to Fiona. "Take her blindfold off."

"Hey, watch it!" Fiona snapped as Clara yanked the sash off her eyes.

"Fiona!" Ian said. "Are you okay? Did they hurt you?"

"Silence!" the littlest one thundered. She stomped over to him, feet barely visible under her oversized dress, her hair so long that it trailed on the ground behind her, decorated in multicolored feathers and strings of beads.

She stopped in front of Ian, glaring at him with dark, serious eyes that seemed far too old to belong to someone so young. She couldn't have been older than six, but she had a commanding quality.

"Digger," she sneered, "yours is an unclean magic."

"Nora," Olivia said, "I don't think so." She picked up his satchel and offered it to her. "I've looked at his things, I even examined his—"

"Enough!" Nora snapped. "You shouldn't have done anything, big sister. Grandmother said so. I *heard* her say it."

Olivia sighed, cradling the satchel in her arms.

Nora planted herself in front of Ian, who had to crane his neck down to look at her. The tiny girl stood with her hands on her hips, her face etched with a deep frown.

Ian swallowed, feeling like he had a stone lodged in his

throat. "We . . . we came with someone else," he said to her. "A friend."

"Yes," Nora said. "Your skeleton. You followed him into the wood." She smirked. "And Grandmother sees *everything* that happens in the wood."

Grandmother again. Ian felt his chest tighten.

"Nora," he said, "please, why are we here?"

Nora adjusted the sleeves of her oversized dress, which had fallen down over her hands. "Because that is what Grandmother wished. She's been preparing for this for a long time. She invited you, Digger." She paused, jabbing a finger at Fiona. "But *this* one was trespassing. She doesn't belong."

"Don't hurt her!" Ian yelled. "We followed the trail. We were just trying to find our friend, that's all."

"So you did," Nora said. "You followed the path. The path was laid long ago, Gravedigger. Laid to wait in silence, until the right soul was chosen to follow it. A few were said to have taken it, but their souls were lost. The path was not for them. It didn't call to them. It called to *you*."

Ian tried to wrap his head around what she was telling him. It didn't make sense. *She* didn't make sense. He closed his eyes and pictured home. He thought of the books in his room. His father in his armchair. The dusty portraits. The fireplace in the library. The flowers growing in the neat rows of his garden.

It all felt so far away. Home was a distant dream. Shivering in the wooden cell, Ian found that he even missed Bertrum, with all his chores and lessons. Raking leaves and reciting the Code would have been a pleasure compared to the trouble he now found himself in.

Why couldn't he just have told his father about wanting to join one of the Guilds? What was he so afraid of? Hurting his father's feelings was surely better than being trapped in a cage. How hard would it have been to just admit that he never wanted this life? If being kidnapped and imprisoned was part of a Gravedigger's lot, then he didn't want anything to do with it. He couldn't even protect his friends. None of this would ever have happened if he'd just told his father how he felt.

He looked to Olivia. "Is that why you watched me all those times? Were you leading me to the trail?"

"I . . ." Olivia's voice faltered.

Nora shot her a warning look. "Olivia . . . ?"

"I didn't lead him. I just wanted to watch him. After Grandmother told us about the Diggers . . . I wanted to see if they were real."

Nora shoved a finger at Ian's face. "Looks real enough to me. Grandmother *also* said to stay in the woods. Grandmother says you're the oldest, and so you're the smartest." She shook her head. "I wonder what she'll have to say about *this*!"

"But I stayed in the trees!" Olivia countered. "There wasn't any harm in it. I just wanted to see those carved stones in the meadow, the big stone house with its stone gates and walls. Grandmother talks so much about the Diggers and their magic. I was curious." She turned to Ian with a pleading look in her eyes. "I wasn't leading you anywhere. It was Grandmother."

Ian found that very hard to believe.

Nora crossed her arms. "Grandmother won't be pleased when she hears what you've been doing." She huffed. "I'm certainly not."

"Well, I don't blame Olivia," Clara said, her tiny voice squeaking as she skipped closer to the cage. "He *is* rather fun to look at! Did you check for fangs?"

"All right," Ian huffed, "who *are* you people?"

Olivia exchanged a look with the other girls. "We're . . . what would you call us?"

"A brood!" Clara squeaked.

"That's nonsense," Nora said.

"Fine. A gaggle!" Clara chirped.

Olivia shook her head.

Clara mussed her hair as she thought. "A tribe? A sect?"

Nora shushed her with a finger. "No, no, no. A *coven*."

Ian bristled. "A coven? Like witches?"

"I suppose," Olivia shrugged. "I don't like that word. *Witch*. It's like a curse. Doesn't roll nicely off the tongue. It's *ugly*."

"We are Those Who Weave the Threads," Nora said proudly.

"The *forbidden* Threads!" Clara added.

"*Weavers*!" Ian gasped.

"Quite so," Nora said.

Ian's head was pounding. He'd read about Weavers before—practitioners of black magic. Witches who tapped into the darkest regions of the Void. It was said that they communed with the creatures of the Underrealm to work their spells. Ian studied the three girls. They looked like forest-dwellers, but *Weavers*? Weavers were old crones with hooked noses and warts. They stole children from their beds and cooked them in cauldrons like stew, sprinkling in bits of toad and bat wings to make their evil potions.

But those were only stories parents threatened their

children with when they didn't do their chores or finish all of their supper. No one could use magic like that. Not *really*.

"Nonsense," Fiona said, speaking up for the first time.

"You don't believe us?"

Ian wasn't sure. He had no reason not to believe them, but still. He could only shake his head, afraid to answer either way.

"I believe you're *mad*," Fiona said, "but not Weavers."

Olivia pursed her lips. She joined Clara and Nora a few paces away, huddled in hushed conversation.

As they spoke, Fiona edged her way over to the cage. "Don't worry," she whispered. "I'll think of a way to get us out of here."

Ian nodded, eyes fixed on the trio. Olivia finally turned back to them. "All right," she said, "how about a demonstration?"

"Demonstration?" Fiona asked.

Nora watched her with narrowed eyes. "What are you worried about, Seer? There's no such thing as a Weaver, *right*?"

Fiona swallowed.

The girls formed a small ring in the center of the clearing. Olivia looked at Ian, hesitating a moment before joining them. "Which one should we do?" she asked.

"Let's make the sun go away!" Clara said, excitedly.

"No, no. That's a boring one," Nora said. "A *cloud* could do that."

Clara's face scrunched in thought. "Let's make the animals talk!"

"Too bland," Nora countered

"What if we turn the Digger into a toad?"

Olivia seemed to ponder that. "Something . . . something nicer, maybe? How about a butterfly?"

Nora looked like she'd just sucked on a lemon. "A butterfly?" she asked. "What's the fun in that?"

"A cabbage!" Clara said, beaming.

"We could make it rain bones," Olivia offered. "A small shower," she added, "nice and quick."

"I'd rather set the wind on fire," Nora said, with a smirk.

"Nothing that serious," Olivia said definitively.

"Let's make him forget how to talk!"

"The Gibberish spell?" Nora scoffed. "But that's so *easy*."

"We could always shrink him," Olivia said. "Just for a few moments."

"Or make him taller!" Clara said. "Eight feet! No, *thirty*!"

"Why would we make him thirty feet tall?" Nora snapped. "He'd be able to crush us under his boot."

Clara tapped a finger to her chin, deep in thought.

Olivia perked up. "I know!" she said. "Let's turn the leaves! That's an easy one." Her voice lowered for a moment. "And it doesn't hurt anyone."

Clara clapped her hands together. "Yes! Perfect!"

Nora shrugged. "Very well."

Ian and Fiona exchanged a worried look.

Nora turned back to Fiona. "All right . . . watch now, Seer. And tell me you don't believe."

They began to move clockwise, humming softly, spinning around like a three-headed top. One by one, they lifted their arms. Ian watched as Threads of light sparked to life at their fingertips, glowing purple and gold. The Threads grew larger, more complex, as they worked their magic, tracing odd, swirling symbols in the air like chalk on slate. The Threads glistened as they took the shape of three webs. The girls sang louder, and the webs joined until the entire clearing was encased in a spiraling cocoon of light. Their eyes rolled back as they chanted, voices melding like a choir:

Now we join to sing the song of Autumn Everlasting
All the trees grow sick and gray
With all their branches passing
The leaves are burnt to gold and brown
The water frozen to the ground
In death and toil
Souls are bound
Through Autumn Everlasting

The winds will howl
Their gusts will bite
While summer skies
Turn black as night
In ghostly palls
And deathly dreams
Those twilight terrors
Gain in might
Through Autumn Everlasting

The creatures quiet
The flowers die
As children scream
And mothers cry
The doom of mortal man is nigh
Through Autumn Everlasting.

The song burrowed into Ian's head, burning his brain like fire. He held his hands over his ears and tried to block it out.

He couldn't explain it, but something deep inside told him that this melody was bad. It wasn't just the words. It was how the girls sang them.

In a single, precise motion, the girls threw up their hands, and the giant web of light shot up into the air, slowly disappearing in a shimmering haze like gold dust.

The forest fell silent once more. Ian looked around, confused. Nothing had happened. He was expecting . . . well, he wasn't sure what, really, but *something*. But the Weavers just stood there in the clearing, stiff as boards. All was as quiet as it had been before. Olivia was the first to snap out of her trance.

Fiona stood her ground, defiant. "What? Was a *song* supposed to scare us?"

Olivia seemed almost saddened at that. "Not a song, Seer. Look." She gestured to the branches overhead. Fiona and Ian looked up. They both felt something in the air . . . some invisible force moving on the wind. Ian felt a slight charge run up his arms, making his hairs stand on end.

Fiona wrinkled her nose.

"Just wait," Olivia said. The wind picked up, rustling softly through the treetops.

And then the leaves began to change.

It was slow at first. The color of the maple leaves gradually faded, growing lighter and lighter as the deep green seeped to yellow. Some trees blushed bright red, others burst orange. In a matter of seconds, the canopy that had been a vibrant green was awash in golds and crimsons.

A few of the larger leaves fell, fluttering and spiraling gently to the ground. Fiona reached up and plucked one out of the air, holding it close to her face. She slowly twisted it between her fingers, examining it.

Ian trembled in the cage. They were in the presence of Weavers. Real-life, actual *Weavers*. He didn't want it to be true. *This is wrong,* he thought. *All wrong. We shouldn't have come here. I shouldn't have let this happen.* Something terrible had been unleashed.

He decided he'd strangle Thatcher the first chance he got for leading them into this mess.

A crow cawed overhead. The Weavers looked up, watching as it swooped in slow, wide circles over the clearing.

"We've wasted enough time," Nora said. "Grandmother's eager to see him."

Seven

Ian stretched when Clara released him from the cage, rubbing his cramped neck, touching his feet with the tips of his fingers. He felt like a coiled rope being unfurled.

Nora dragged Fiona along. Clara skipped beside them, humming to herself. As Ian struggled to keep up, the tiny Weaver grabbed onto his hand, squeezing tight with her little fingers. He looked down and saw she was smiling knowingly at him.

Stranger and stranger.

"This way," Olivia said, leading the group through the clearing, past the cottages, and into the forest, ducking under a willow branch as she stalked down a narrow, twisting path. She carried Ian's satchel slung over one shoulder. He kept pace just behind her, not wanting the bag to leave his sight.

"Your grandmother doesn't live with you in the village?" he asked.

Olivia shook her head. "Grandmother's been busy lately. She doesn't leave the house unless she needs to."

Ian glanced around. "Where's everyone else?"

"You mean our parents?"

"They have to be around somewhere, right? You three don't live out here by yourselves."

"And why not?" she asked. "We're able to manage on our own."

"Of course," he said, catching himself. "It's just, well . . . strange, is all. Sorry. Not *strange*. Just *different*."

Olivia slowed until they were walking side by side. "This doesn't happen outside the wood? In the town with the stone houses?"

Ian hesitated, unsure of what to say. "It . . . it could."

"Yes," Fiona added, seeing him struggle. "Sometimes it does. But usually children without parents get sent to a boarding home."

"A boarding home?" Olivia asked. "You mean a house of wood?"

"No. They're stone houses, too. Big ones, with a lot of beds for all the children, and people to feed them. Almost like parents."

"Mother died," Olivia muttered, stomping through the bracken.

"Long ago," Clara said sadly.

"I'm sorry," Ian said, making sure to keep his eyes trained on his shoes.

Nora snorted. "I'm sure you are."

"Mine did, too," he said. "She was very sick . . ." A long silence followed. "How . . . how did it happen?"

"Magic," Olivia answered.

Ian struggled to keep up as she spun her way through a mess of vines.

"It was a spell. A bad spell. A *killing* spell. The kind they don't teach you in books. She made a small mistake and it backfired. That's what Grandmother says. No pain. Which is good, I suppose."

"What about your father? Is he still alive?"

"Yes. Somewhere, I think."

"You think?"

"He's not around anymore." She paused, shooting Ian a look. "Not that he abandoned us or anything. One of *his* spells went wrong, too. Turned himself into a skunk by mistake."

"A skunk?"

She nodded. "He was trying to turn a copper mug into a golden one. For Clara. She always wanted him to turn stuff to gold. But he wasn't very good at it. It only worked about half the time, and whatever he transformed would always turn back after a while. He never learned the full spell. He got it mixed up in his head and said the words in the wrong order. And his hands were never too steady when he Weaved. The Weave to turn things to gold and the one to turn people into animals are very similar, you see. Clara still catches him running around the garden sometimes. He can't talk, though. Just makes little squeaks. I hear him, every now and then. It's a shame he can't stay around."

"He tried to spray me once!" Clara said, pinching her nose.

"We shoo him away," Olivia said sadly.

Clara sighed. "Poor Father Stinky Spray."

Ian shook his head, stunned. "Are there others?"

"We're the only ones left now," Nora said stiffly. "Grandmother says it's our duty to stay. She says the others gave up too easily. *We* don't give up."

"And you don't leave the woods?"

Olivia shook her head. "It's against the rules."

"We're never to leave," Nora said, sneering at Olivia. "Grandmother made that *very* clear."

The trees grew taller as they ventured deeper into the woods. Roots clawed up from the dirt like the tentacles of some ancient, hideous monster. Ian trod carefully, watching his every step as he struggled to follow Olivia. She didn't seem to have any trouble navigating the thickets and brambles. She'd been raised among those trees, after all. She'd spent her whole life playing in their shadows. It was her home.

Ian felt less like a prisoner and more like a trespasser as he followed her down the path. He'd stumbled into a world where he didn't belong. Branches slashed his cheeks, caught on his cloak.

Nora pointed to Ian. "Why don't you tell him *why* Grandmother says we're never to leave, Olivia?"

"Nora, please. Do I have to?"

Ian watched them stare at each other, still amazed that Nora, little as she was, seemed to command such power over her sisters.

"I'll say it if you won't," Nora huffed. She glared at Ian. "Because your kind are dark sorcerers. You kill people and trap them under those stones, then feed off their bones. You should be ashamed."

Olivia nervously wrung her hands. "Nora, please . . ."

Ian tried to edge back. "What? Gravediggers help people."

Nora scoffed. "Help? You cast tortured souls into the Netherworld. You banish them to the Underrealm. You call that *help*?"

"*The Underrealm*," Clara echoed.

"You don't know what you're talking about," Fiona shot back.

"I don't know what your grandmother's been telling you," Ian said, "but whatever tales she's spinning, they're wrong. Diggers don't work in the Underrealm. That's where evil souls go. Where *demons* live. Everyone knows that. We help the restless ones reach the Beyond."

Nora scowled. "Grandmother warned us that you'd lie."

"Ouch!" Clara stumbled as she walked into the waiting branches of a pricker bush. She jumped back, almost into Ian's arms. "It got me!" she cried, lifting up the hem of her skirt to look at the thorn stuck in her knee.

Ian kneeled down and examined her leg. "Olivia," he said, "could I have my bag, please? I have salves in there, good for cuts and stings."

Olivia paused, clutching onto the satchel. Before she could take a step, Nora swatted it from her arms.

"What do you think you're doing?" she yelled, spinning to Ian. "We won't have your black magic done here."

Ian bit his lip, stifling a scream. "I'm trying to help her. She's hurt. I was looking for an *ointment*."

"He's studying to be a Healer," Fiona told them.

Nora pointed at Clara's bleeding knee. "*Poisoner*, more like. She doesn't *need* your help. We know your Digger's tricks. Your devious ways."

"You don't know what you're talking about!" Ian shouted.

"You fill that graveyard of yours with corpses," Nora shot back. "You *kill* people!"

"It's . . . it's true," Olivia said quietly. "Grandmother says that Diggers won't be happy until the whole world sleeps beneath the soil."

"The whole world!" Clara echoed, her eyes tearing as she dabbed at the cut on her knee.

"This is ridiculous," Ian said, shoving his way past Nora. He picked up his satchel and pulled out a vial.

As he did so, Nora held out her fingers, tracing a small line of light that quickly ignited and grew, taking the shape of a viper. Ian edged back as the golden apparition slithered through the air, stopping just short of his face.

"Be very careful, Digger," she warned. "Very. Careful."

"Here," he said, gently tossing the vial at her feet. "This will help her. It's not a trick. It's *medicine*. Calendula. A *flower*. See?" He pointed to the orange-yellow poultice. "It's used for cuts."

Nora narrowed her eyes. With a wave of her hand, the golden viper vanished, retracting back into her fingertip. "Come, Digger. I'll not have you distract us anymore with your trickery. And you, Clara. It's only a prick. Toughen up!"

Ian considered arguing with her, but realized it would be useless. She had it all so wrong that he didn't even know where he'd start.

The group continued down the trail in silence until the bracken grew so thick he wasn't even sure if it *was* a trail anymore.

"Here we are," Olivia said, batting her way through a cluster of bushes. "Come along."

The hut sat by a river, surrounded on all sides by birches. They stood like silent sentinels, blindingly white in a sea of gold and brown foliage. A murder of crows watched from the branches, hundreds of beady eyes staring down.

Olivia watched the crows with a wary eye. "Grandmother doesn't see many visitors," she said. "*None*, actually. You should be honored."

"*Very* honored," Clara said.

Black smoke billowed from the roof. Ian could see candles flickering inside through the soot-covered windows. A stinging, acrid smell filled his nostrils as they made their way closer.

Olivia pounded on the front door. "Grandmother's very particular," she warned. "Speak up when you address her. And stand up straight."

"She likes that," Nora said.

"Slouching's *disrespectful*," Clara added.

"Look her in the eye, too," Olivia said. "She gets upset, otherwise . . ."

Fiona scoffed. "You don't have to do anything they tell you, Ian."

"Quiet!" Nora snapped. "Best behavior, Digger. *Or else.*"

Ian nodded, though he didn't know why he had. Who cared what some old Weaver thought?

Olivia knocked on the door.

"Enter, child!" a voice called.

"Please, Ian," Olivia whispered, "best behavior, okay?" She gently opened the door.

Candles burned on every surface, wax dripping onto the floor in goopy puddles. Baskets hung from the ceiling, each filled with an assortment of herbs, some in large bunches tied with twine, others packed in small jars. He recognized a few of the plants from his botany books. Demon's mint and pixie blossom, hound's tongue and mistflower. It was a dangerous assortment. All of them were poisonous.

Ian could hear motion behind one of the doors. He tried to keep calm, knowing that this "Grandmother" was close by. Trying to steady himself, he continued to gaze around the room.

There were other specimens he didn't recognize. Huge mushrooms with oily black skin, veined with red. Bulbous gourds that looked like they were rotting away, sickly green and putrid yellow. He sniffed at a sprig of spiky leaves before turning his nose away, nostrils flaring as if they were on fire.

"Flameroot," Nora said with a smug grin. "One flake of those leaves dropped into your drink and . . . well . . . let's just say your insides won't be on the inside for very long."

"It *burns*," Clara said.

"They call it Flame Tonic," Olivia added. "Best you keep away from that."

Ian wiped his nose as he took in the rest of the hut.

Every wall was lined with shelves filled with glass bottles, their mysterious contents glowing in the candlelight. A table was covered in an odd assortment of knickknacks; butterfly wings, frogs' legs, rabbits' feet, and crows' feathers were arranged in precise, orderly piles like a strange buffet.

Embers burned in the stone fireplace, sizzling and glowing like the eyes of a demon while a black cauldron bubbled over the dying flames. Ian poked his head over its edge, watching the greenish-brown liquid sputter and swirl, wondering what kind of slop the old sorceress was conjuring. It smelled like wet socks and rotting cabbage.

"Oh, supper!" Clara exclaimed. She and Nora climbed up on footstools next to the cauldron and began stirring with spoons almost as big as they were.

Olivia sat herself down in a rickety rocking chair and folded her hands in her lap. "Interesting things, yes? Grandmother's collected a lot of curiosities through the years."

Ian held up a jar of eyeballs. "What are these for?"

Olivia made a sour face. "You don't want to know."

Suppressing a gag, he placed the jar back on the table. An eyeball floated up to the surface and stared back at him. Ian shuddered.

Shards of crystal carefully arranged on a folded cloth sparkled, drawing him closer. "What are these?" he asked, reaching out a finger.

"Seeing stones," Olivia said. "I wouldn't touch them, if I were you."

Ian quickly moved his hand away. As he examined a vial of sizzling potion, a loud *thump* came from the next room.

"I'll only be a moment!" the voice he'd heard earlier cried out. Ian put his ear to the wall. It sounded like a fight had broken out.

He stumbled back as a white shape came bursting through the door. Ian watched the old woman, mesmerized as she scurried about.

"I'll be right with you, dears," she said over her shoulder. "Just looking for my bone saw. Time is of the essence, you know." She reached into a cupboard, plates and cups clattering to the floor as she blindly felt around. "Aha!" she exclaimed, holding it up in triumph. She turned, startled, as she laid eyes on Ian.

Ian was startled, too. She didn't look anything like he'd

imagined. She had snow-white hair looped together in intricate braids, through which a few crows' feathers stuck out, haphazard and frayed. Though her dark face was weathered and wrinkled, he could tell she'd been quite beautiful in her youth. She wore a white robe, loose-fitting and light as silk. Where was the black hat? The hooked nose covered in warts? The rotten teeth and yellow eyes? Her teeth were a bit crooked, but she wasn't exactly the menacing, vile creature he'd heard about in the stories. Ian met Fiona's eyes across the room. She seemed just as shocked as he was.

"Ian," the woman said, breathless, "it's so nice to meet you."

The old woman smiled, brushing his cheek with a soft and tender touch. "Shorter than I imagined. Skinnier, too. What are they feeding you in that graveyard? Birdseed?"

"No, ma'am," Ian said, finding it difficult to look her in the eye.

"Ah, well, you're here now."

She looked at Olivia. "The other one's nearly ready, dear. Please go keep an eye on him."

Ian swallowed. *The other one?*

He watched as Olivia lifted herself from the rocking chair.

"Take this," the old woman said, handing her the saw. "We just need a little bit. Right off the shin. Oh, and take the Seer, as well. What's one more?"

"Yes, Grandmother." It was only a split second, but Ian noticed Olivia cringe as she took the saw in her hands, before quickly gathering Fiona.

"Ian, be careful!" Fiona cried before Olivia took her by the arm, disappearing into the next room.

The old Weaver turned back to Ian, smiling once more. "It's good fortune that you've come."

"Good fortune?"

"Yes. It's a sign. My visions foretold your arrival. They can show you a great deal, you know. Just last night, I saw a white horse. It was galloping across a black field, so bright and pure in all that . . . darkness. It was *you*, Ian. I could sense it. Some folks say I've lost my edge, but old Dehlia can still tell a *vision* from a *dream*. Dreams can lie. Visions are truth. It came to me the moment you stepped foot in these woods. A white horse galloping. Yes, I can still move through the Void. I can travel through it as a spider moves along its gossamer thread. Tell me, Ian, do you know which way the wind blows?"

Ian didn't know how to respond. "You've . . . been to the Void?"

The old woman laughed. "Of course. How do you think we Weave the Threads? They lie in the Void. In the murk and the shadow. The glorious dark! Don't tell me you thought Diggers were the only ones who traveled in the rift, heh!"

"There's no magic in the Void," Ian countered. "Only the dark. Only the lonely souls."

"You're wrong, Ian. Your Digger blood makes you blind to the wonders of the rift. There are layers deep inside. Layers like an onion, ripe for the peeling."

Ian trembled, unsure whether he should believe her. He took a few steps back, trying to edge his way to the door. "What do you want?" he demanded, voice shaking. "Why am I here?"

The old Weaver's eyes narrowed, and the warmth she'd shown only moments before vanished. When she spoke again, her voice was harsh. Acidic. It crept from her throat like a hiss.

"You're here to help me with my Weave, of course. I need

you. Well, *part* of you." She leered. "Just a few drops of blood. That should do it."

Ian's breath caught.

"Yes. Just a little. It's an old Weave. Very old. I've been waiting a long time to cast it. *Much* too long. Ten years goes by slowly when you spend all of them waiting. But the hour draws near. I'll not lose another to your Digger ways." She produced a long, slender knife, twisting the blade as she lifted it into the air. "That graveyard of yours can use a bit of . . . life."

She leaped forward and ripped the wool cap off of Ian's head, gasping as she ran a spindly hand through his hair. "So, it's true . . ." she whispered, almost to herself. "You've done it. You've touched the Void."

"Not really," Ian replied.

"Nonsense! The hair tells it all, Ian. You've traveled. You've bathed in the deep, cold black."

"Listen," he said, "I don't know what you're trying to do here, but—"

Before he could finish, the air was squeezed from his lungs. He tried to move, but his legs wouldn't work. Some invisible force held him still, turning his muscles to stone.

The Weaver laughed as she grabbed him by the hair. "Hush, now!" she barked. "I'll not have you screaming your head off when we're trying to *work*! We must be silent. We must be *calm*."

Ian struggled against her as she led him to the door, his feet dragging against the floorboards. The old Weaver just chuckled.

"*No!*" he shouted.

"No? Oh, Ian. We don't like that word in this house. Such a nasty word. Such a *mean* word. Calm. Calm, now . . ."

With her other hand, she brushed his cheek. A soothing energy instantly flowed through his body. His stomach warmed. His muscles relaxed. He felt himself drifting away, just like he had on the Pumpkin Trail.

The last thing he saw was the smiling face of the Weaver as the world around him seeped to black.

When Ian woke, he was hanging in chains. The room was dark, lit only by the flickering light of a candle. He opened his eyes slowly, careful not to make a sound. He didn't want them to know he was awake. Not just yet.

Cages and spiked contraptions, menacing boxes and coffin-like enclosures lined the walls. Ian saw whips and chains, daggers and pincers, leather straps and fireplace pokers, and a myriad of other tools of pain. It looked like the bowels of a castle dungeon—a torture chamber.

"Ian? That you?"

Thatcher was on the other side of the room, dangling upside down from shackles around his ankles.

"Thatcher!" Ian was relieved to see him. The skeleton was a sight for sore eyes. "How did you get here?"

"Oh, Ian . . ."

"It's all right," Ian replied, trying his best to put on a brave face. "What did they say to you, Thatcher? Do you know what this is?"

Thatcher rattled in the chains. "The old one, Dehlia, she's been talking to herself. The same thing, over and over: 'She's trying to leave.'"

Ian looked around the room for something he could use

to break the chains. His legs ached as he tried to swing himself over to the wall. If he could get up against one of those blades . . .

"Who's trying to leave? Thatcher, what is this?"

"Ian," Thatcher croaked, "I'm sorry."

A muffled shout came from the opposite corner of the room. Ian swung himself on the chains to get a better look, horrified to see Fiona tied at the wrists and ankles, her mouth stuffed with a rag.

"Fiona, it'll be all right," he said, trying to calm her as she fought in vain against the restraints. "We'll get out of here."

Fiona said something, though Ian couldn't make it out.

The door flew open, and Olivia and Dehlia entered, dressed in long, black robes. The candle's flame wavered, sending their long shadows dancing across the wall.

Dehlia clutched her hands to her chest. "Oh! You're awake! Splendid!"

Ian winced as the shackles dug into his wrists. Dehlia smiled, tugging on the chains.

Olivia stacked some kindling under a cauldron in the center of the room. She flicked her fingers, setting the wood alight with a *whoosh!* The liquid bubbled and hissed, an acrid smell filling the room.

"Take the saw, child."

Olivia stepped back from the flames, looking wide-eyed at her grandmother.

"*Now,*" Dehlia barked. "Do as I say, child. I'll not tell you twice."

Again, Fiona shouted through the rag, though Dehlia paid her no mind.

Olivia picked up the curved blade from the table and approached Thatcher.

"A few more shavings should suffice," Dehlia said. She handed Olivia a silver chalice. "Here, collect them in this. Don't drop them, now. We need them pure. Untainted."

"Yes, Grandmother." Olivia said, meekly.

"Hey, hey, hey!" Thatcher cried, trying to squirm away. "What do you think you're doing, Get away from me with that thing! This wasn't part of the offer!"

"Hush!" Dehlia snapped.

"I will not! It wasn't supposed to go like this! You said I'd be safe. You said *Ian* would be safe!"

Better offer.

The words rang out in Ian's brain like an alarm bell. Thatcher had spoken of an offer, the night they made their pact.

Olivia placed a hand over Thatcher's mouth, simultaneously silencing him and holding him steady as she sawed away on his shin. Ian could hear the blade rubbing against bone. He watched as chalky, white dust fell into the chalice. Olivia sawed faster, gritting her teeth as the jagged metal sank in deeper.

"What's he talking about?" Ian asked. "What offer?"

Dehlia smiled. "Ian . . ." she cooed. "Poor, foolish boy. You didn't think *you* were the one who woke this wretched creature, did you?" She laughed. "The Words you Spoke were only whispers. *I* found Thatcher in his slumber. *I* urged him to Call the Voicecatcher. I knew what kind of soul he was. I knew he'd agree to my terms."

Ian's stomach turned sour. It couldn't be true.

"What terms?"

"The simplest ones, really. He leads you here, I give him what he wants."

"And what's that?"

Dehlia cocked her head, lips pursed. "Why . . . *life*, Ian. Mortal life restored, in full. Something you Diggers could never grant him. Not when you blindly follow that 'Code' of yours."

Thatcher swung wildly on his chains, freeing himself from Olivia's grasp. "What's the matter with you people?" he shouted. "Ian! Look at me!"

They locked eyes. Ian tried to read the empty sockets in the dim candlelight.

"I'm sorry," Thatcher said. "Please believe me, Ian. I never meant it to go this way. She said she'd fix me! Said she'd make it better if I just brought you. Please, you have to—"

"Olivia, silence him! The sound of that creature's shrieks hurts my ears."

Olivia hesitated. Ian saw the faint gleam of tears in her eyes.

"Now!" Dehlia screeched. "I will *not* have you disobey me!"

Olivia put her hand against Thatcher's skull, softly caressing it until he stopped convulsing. His bones went slack as he swung silently in the dark, sent off into a deep sleep.

Dehlia rubbed her temples. "All that racket hurt my head." She crouched down, her eyes level with Ian's. "I've no use for him any longer. He's served his purpose." Her eyes narrowed. "He's brought me my prize."

She beckoned Olivia closer, taking the chalice from her hands. Producing a pestle from the folds of her cloak, she began grinding up the bone shavings to a fine powder, humming to herself. "Bone shows us who we are, Ian. It tells us where we have been. Bones are like paintings and books. They show us the past. All we ever were. They are history and roots, solidified and strong. But the blood, you see . . ."

She stopped grinding, setting the pestle down on the table. Ian winced as she picked up the curved dagger again. She brought it up to his arm, lightly grazing the skin with the tip of the blade. It felt so cold it burned.

"Blood shows us what we cannot see. It shows us what is known and all that can *be* known. Bone is blind while blood sees all. The future runs in this red liquid like a river runs over the horizon. It's a key, this blood. A key that can open infinite doors. And what's behind them? Unfathomable things, Ian. Things you or I scarcely dare to dream. The Digger's blood, most of all. Yours is an ancient line. A strong line. The blood of House Fossor is steeped in power, in mysteries untold. Hold still."

Ian cried out as everything went red, his mind blinded by searing pain as the blade plunged into his arm. Dehlia's lips curled in a cruel smile as she twisted it deeper into his flesh. Beside her, Olivia shuddered.

"No!" Ian cried.

He watched as the blood ran down his arm, snaking around his elbow, dripping down his forearm, and gathering at his wrist before falling like raindrops into the waiting chalice. He shut his eyes, listening to the *drip, drip, drip* as it splashed into the silver cup. *It's too much*, he thought.

His vision dimmed. Soon, the room was spinning and all he could focus on was the candle burning in the corner. He watched as the flames danced against the blood-smeared walls, swirling round and round until his stomach turned and he wondered how much time he had left on this earth. *This could be it*, he thought.

He'd pondered Death all his life. He'd been raised to do so. But for the first time in eleven years, he began to think about his own. Was this his time? It couldn't be. There was still so much he needed to do. So much he *wanted* to do.

Yet, as Dehlia drove the dagger deeper into his skin and the pain seared his brain like the coals of a blacksmith's forge, he wasn't sure if he'd make it. He'd once read about how much blood a person could lose before it was too late . . .

The Void was approaching. As the blood trickled from his arm, he could almost see it—the swirling, black vortex, opening in the sky like a tear in a sheet. The cold air froze him, his weightless body floating, floating, floating ever so gently, light and lithe as a feather in the wind. He could feel himself swept up in the Void's dark embrace, not as a shepherd guiding others through, but as a lost soul, himself.

No, he thought. *You can't go. Not yet. You can't let it take you!*

He closed his eyes, trying to collect his thoughts, but all he could concentrate on was the pain of the Weaver's dagger. She pushed it in deeper, and Ian opened his eyes wide and cried out in agony.

He heard Fiona gasp. "What are you doing to him?" She'd managed to get the rag out of her mouth and was rolling along the floor, fighting wildly against the ropes.

Dehlia didn't take her eyes off the blade. "Be *silent*, Seer. And observe . . ."

"Don't watch," Olivia said to Fiona, taking her by the arm. "It's best you don't see."

"Get off of me!" Fiona spat. She tried to roll away, but Olivia held her still.

"Just a little more," Dehlia said, forcing the dagger in deeper. Ian could feel the blade graze muscle.

He'd never felt more helpless as he hung there, trapped in a room so dark, in a house so hidden away in a forest so vast, so far from everything familiar and good.

"Look, now."

White smoke plumed from the chalice. Dehlia poured it carefully into the cauldron. Ian heard his own blood bubbling and hissing and popping as it mixed in with Thatcher's ground bone.

"Breathe, Ian. Breathe deep. You must take it in."

His eyes watered as the smoke filled the room. It smelled of putrid iron—some kind of strange alchemy that wasn't meant for this world. He could taste it as it drifted into his mouth, seeping deep into his lungs, enveloping his brain.

It carried him back to his early childhood, filling him with memories of nightmares and old fears. It twisted his mind, sucking out all hope and comfort like a cold, black vacuum, leaving him lost and frightened and alone. He tried to fight against it, tried to block out the smell, the sense of dread and dark magic. But to no avail.

Dehlia dipped a ladle into the sizzling ooze, pouring its contents onto the dirt floor. It burned into the soil, black smoke curling up to the roof. She closed her eyes and stood on the burning patch of ground.

"Blood and bone sprang from earth, and to that earth they shall return. Hear me, Netherworld! Hear me, Underrealm! Blood has been shed and bone has been broken! Bask in the glory of these gifts and bring about the Dark to overtake the Light! Blood of the Digger, bone of the Dead, mix them together and skies will turn red. Heart of the Digger, soul of Dead, together they boil and bring about dread!"

She paused, wafting the smoke to her face.

"Don't try to fight, Ian. There's no point in that. You won't be able to, anyway. Give in. Yes. That's the best way. The only way. It will all be over soon." She smiled. "I've been trapped in these woods for far too long. A decade of waiting. Watching. Plotting. *Festering*. But this"—she held up the blade—"*this* will set me free. I suppose I should thank you, really. Your blood is the key that will unlock these chains of mine. A special blend, indeed." She turned to Olivia, "And you . . . you will no longer disobey me. Never again. You will see just how cruel the outside world can be to Those who Weave the Threads. Do you hear me?"

Olivia nodded sheepishly, staring at the floor.

The remaining mixture sizzled inside the cauldron. Ian's blood began to glow. It filled the room, casting everything a horrible shade of red. *This is a nightmare*, Ian thought. *What else could it be?*

Dehlia held the chalice under her nose and breathed deeply, sighing with delight. "Ah, do you feel it, Ian? The barrier between worlds thins . . . The rift grows. Living and Dead . . . the two are becoming one. All thanks to you, my child. Rejoice!"

Eight

BOOM!

The blast echoed through the chamber like a thunderclap. The cauldron shattered into a thousand pieces, shards of molten lead flying through the air, the smoking mix of blood and bone splattering across the room. Olivia ducked behind Thatcher's hanging bones, crying out as the liquid burned through the floor.

The door flew open as if a hurricane had rolled through, slamming against the wall with a loud *crack!* Brilliant sunlight flooded in. Ian squinted, struggling to make out the figure looming in the doorway.

"Who *dares* disturb my sanctum?" Dehlia shrieked, cupping a hand over her eyes to get a look at the figure.

"Heh! Some sanctum, ye got here, Dehlia. 'S far's I can tell, 's nothin' more'n sticks and moss. Same as it ever were."

Ian couldn't believe what he was hearing. That voice.

Bertrum limped into the room, though he walked a bit straighter, Ian realized, his bulky shoulders squared and stiff. Like a soldier on the march. His one good eye scanned the room like a bulbous, yellow lantern, widening as it passed over the three captives still in chains, then narrowing as it fell upon the Weavers. "I've come for the young'ns. Unhand 'em. Now."

Dehlia remained still.

Bertrum reached down to his belt and loosed a wicked-looking throwing ax.

"I won't repeat meself. Release 'em, or the next one won't miss." He raised the blade, elbow and shoulder popping as they slid in and out of their sockets. "Weaves are nice for a lark, I suppose. But it's *steel* that does the real damage. I can promise ye that. Don't think there're many potions to put a Weaver back together once she's split in two, eh?"

Dehlia cackled. "True. But there's only one ax. And *two* of us."

"May be so," Bertrum growled. "Still, I think I can handle meself well enough."

Dehlia took a few steps forward. "Tell me . . . how does it feel, being a slave to those corpse-whisperers? Must grow tiresome, waiting on them hand and foot. How many years, now? Three hundred? Four? Obeying like a dog. Such *toil*. No better than a death sentence, really. How does it feel to fail yet *another* you've sworn to protect? I've heard the tale. Can't say I'm surprised."

Ian saw Dehlia's gaze flicker to Olivia. The younger

Weaver nodded and sprang out from behind Thatcher, running toward the door at the far end of the room.

In one heaving motion, Bertrum flung the ax forward. Ian watched as it screamed through the air, sinking into the wooden frame an inch from Olivia's face with a *thunk*! She went pale as she eyed at the blade against her nose.

"I wouldn't go out that way, lass," Bertrum said, readying another ax from the strap on his back. "Got plenty more, here. Next one'll be more'n a warning. Sharp, these. Take that pretty head 'o yers clean off."

Olivia stepped away from the door, wide eyes fixed on the steel gleaming from the oak.

"Now," he grumbled, "what's say we loose those chains?"

The old Weaver just stared at him. She unclenched her fists, letting them fall to her sides.

Bertrum stepped forward. "What? Did I misspeak? I said release 'em! *Now!*"

Dehlia did as ordered, keeping an eye on the ax as she loosened the leather straps around Ian's wrists. He dropped to the floor, body limp like a rag doll. The Weaver went to lift him up, but Bertrum lurched forward before she had the chance.

"*DON'T TOUCH HIM!*" he thundered. "Don't you *dare* touch him! Back, now. Back!" He gestured to Thatcher. "That'n, too. Release 'im."

"But . . . but what do you care about this one? He's just bones, after all. Surely he's of no concern."

Bertrum scoffed. "I don't need to give ye a reason, Weaver. Yer not worthy of *reasons*. I came for all of 'em. The Living n' the Dead."

Olivia unlocked the shackles from around Thatcher's

ankles, wincing as he collapsed onto the floor, a heap of bones. Bertrum lifted Thatcher off the ground and threw him over his shoulder like a sack of flour.

He waved his ax. "Up against the wall wi' ye. Stay there until we're out of the woods. Understand?"

Dehlia crossed her arms over her chest, sneering. "How long do you think you can keep them safe, hmm? Not forever, Bertrum, I assure you. There are great things at work. Things that can't be beaten or *hacked* away. Things that cannot be stopped. The spell over these woods is lifting like a shroud. The Void is weakening. The sleepers are waking. Soon the Fossor Yard will teem with chaos. You won't be able to protect the boy forever."

"Mm," Bertrum grumbled. "Remains to be seen, I reckon. Close your eyes, Weaver. And don't open 'em till our footsteps fade. 'Cause if I hear so much as a peep followin' us through them trees, I'll go back to that village o' yers and tear the whole place asunder. Ye hear me?"

Dehlia smiled slowly, yellow teeth glowing in the pale afternoon light. "As you wish."

Ian sucked in the fresh air as he stepped out on the front porch. He gazed up at the trees, up to the blue sky and white clouds hovering above the branches. A warm wave of relief washed over him. Chained in that hut, he'd wondered if he'd ever see the light again.

Thatcher was still snoring on Bertrum's shoulder as he cleared a path through the brush. Ian watched him, deep in slumber.

How had he been so blind? Ian couldn't believe what he had heard. He thought back to the night before when he Spoke to Thatcher—that horrible feeling he'd felt in the pit of his stomach when the skeleton didn't wake. The black emptiness of the Void. The look on Fiona's face when he'd failed. The smell of the dirt as they reburied the boy in his coffin. The aching he felt as they trudged home.

But when Thatcher came later that night . . . Ian had never felt more excited, more filled with a sense of accomplishment. Proud that he'd conquered his greatest fear, even while knowing it wasn't something he'd ever want to experience again.

But it had all been a lie. A trick. Weavercraft, dirty and secret.

And it was all his fault. He'd had a choice that night. They didn't *have* to dig Thatcher up. He could have told Fiona to go home. But he'd wanted to help her. He'd have done *anything* to help her, because that's what friends are for.

Bertrum remained silent. Ian followed close behind, his hand entwined in Fiona's. Bertrum trudged and trampled through the underbrush, his massive body creating a trail of its own. Ian had never seen him move so fast. Not that he was complaining. He wanted to get out of the forest more than anybody. He'd already worn out a welcome that was never warm to begin with. Ian struggled to keep up with the blacksmith's pace, fighting his way through pricker bushes and past dead branches.

As he walked alongside the blacksmith, Ian suddenly realized the trouble he was in. Bertrum had caught him out. The blacksmith knew about Thatcher. He knew that Ian had recited the Words of Resurrection. To top it all off, the old grump had risked his *own* hide to come to their rescue. That part really stung. Ian felt the guilt rise up in his stomach like nervous, ice-covered butterflies.

He could make out the meadow ahead of them—the boundary of the graveyard. Off in the distance, Ian could see the faint outlines of the headstones, shimmering under the pale sun. Fiona broke out into a run, pulling him along behind her.

His heart sank as they came to the edge of his garden. The vegetable stalks were blackened and brittle, covered in the unnatural autumn frost of the Weaver's spell. The flowers lay withered and dying, the once bright petals now gray and sickly. His heart sank as he watched his beautiful, blooming creations dying before his eyes. Everything was lost. The honeysuckle was crumpled and dry, strung out like discarded ashes from an urn. The lady's slippers, once so brilliantly purple and yellow, were blackened and putrid. He walked up and down the rows, eyes welling up as he took in the destruction. Nothing had survived the Weavers' spell. All gone. The thyme and carnations, daffodils and tulips, orchids and spray roses and geraniums, all withered and crushed, their petals and stems frozen.

For so long, that garden had been the only place in the entire graveyard that truly mattered to him. It was his *home*, even more so than the manor. As long as he could remember, Ian had always known that no matter how bad things got, how frightening the future seemed, how real his nightmares felt, the garden was always there, waiting for him. The flowers and herbs weren't just a project. They were his children, raised with his love and care.

Winters had come and gone. Ian had lived through ten of them. It was natural for the frost to gather on the grass in the meadows, for the trees to shed their leaves, for the flowers to wither as the snow came to bury them like a blanket. But he'd also lived to see ten springs and summers. He always knew how long it would be before the snow melted and the air turned warmer, and the flowers would bloom once more.

But now, as he took in the blackened remains, he wasn't sure if spring would ever return. Ian gagged as he breathed in the unnatural odor of magic mixing with the smell of dead leaves and petals. "Gone," he whispered as he scanned the ravaged rows. "All gone."

He clenched his fist as the sadness slowly boiled to anger. How could the Weavers have done this? *Why?* Just to prove a point?

And then he realized, they didn't care. He doubted they even knew about this place. They didn't know the hours he'd spent tilling the soil, the research he'd done to make sure each and every plant grew just right. Even if they did know, they wouldn't have cared. He looked down at his empty hands, lost.

Fiona pursed her lips, then took Ian's hand in her own. "It will be all right," she said. "We'll fix this. There has to be a way. There's *always* a way."

Ian nodded as a lump formed in his throat. He caught himself before the tears worked their way down his cheeks. He couldn't cry. Not there. Not in front of Fiona.

He kneeled in front of the dying bed of river lilies—his mother's favorites—the one thing he felt he could still share with her. Hands trembling, he took one bloom by its black-ened stem, delicately plucking it from the frozen ground. He couldn't hold back his emotions any longer. Tears streamed down his face, warm and salty in the bitter air. The river lily's petal was dark and twisted. He ran a finger along its curves, the tears hitting his lips as the flower crumbled at his touch.

He felt Fiona's hand on his shoulder.

"Come on," she said softly, leading him away from the garden. "Bertrum's waiting. We need to get home."

Ian swallowed and wiped the tears away, letting the decaying lily drop to the ground as he followed after her.

Bertrum was waiting for them just beyond the garden, an unconscious Thatcher still slung over his shoulder. With a nod of his head, the old grouch beckoned them to follow. Ian fell in line, trudging behind the corpse, looking back one last time as the dying garden faded in the distance.

After a long silence, he worked up the courage to ask Bertrum a question: "How . . . how did you find us?"

The old corpse gave him a blank look. "The leaves, lad. I was out splittin' wood by the house when I saw the maples turn red. Only black magic could bring autumn six months early. And there's only one place where folks use such trickery." He leaned in. "Figured somethin' was wrong when ye didn't come down fer breakfast yesterday. Gonna have to try a bit harder to pull one over on me."

"I'm sorry," Ian said. "Really, Bertrum. I should've told you what happened . . ." He nodded to Thatcher, still snoring on the blacksmith's shoulder. "I should've told you what I did."

"Aye, lad. Ye shoulda. But I suppose I can accept yer apology. Yer a good lad, Ian. Maybe a bit too headstrong for yer own good, maybe a bit daft, at times, but a good lad, nonetheless." The old corpse grinned wide as a jack-o'-lantern. "Surprised ye had it in ye, if I'm bein' honest. Didn't think ye wanted any o' this Gravediggin' business. I've had to fight tooth 'n nail just to get ye to recite the Code. Now yer *Speakin'*?" He pointed a bent finger at Ian's satchel. "I'm dead, boy, not blind. Healing is in yer heart, not Diggin'." He gave a gap-toothed smile. "And without yer help, I'd be a pile o' bits in a wheelbarrow."

"You know her . . . the woman in the woods?" Ian cringed unsure whether or not he should have asked.

"Aye," Bertrum said after a while. "I know her. Or *used* to, anyhow. Still as ugly as I remember."

"She wasn't really that ugly," Ian said.

"Ugly on the inside, lad."

"Who is she?"

Bertrum bristled. "She's a *Weaver*. Didn't ye pick up on that earlier?"

"I know that," Ian said, "but how do you know a Weaver?"

The blacksmith stopped for a moment, wavering slightly. He propped himself up on a tombstone, lost for words.

Finally, he said, "I've been around a long time, lad. When ye've been kickin' round long's I have, ye run into all kinds o' people. Some more disagreeable'n others. 'S part of it, I suppose. Let's just say we're old acquaintances. *Very* old."

"How old?" Ian asked. "Old as you?"

"No one's old as me."

It wasn't much of an answer, but Ian knew he was in no position to demand more.

"Look," Bertrum said, kneeling down in front of Ian. "I know ye've got questions. And I'll answer 'em all in due time. But right now, we need to fix this little mess ye've brewed up." He nodded to the skeleton draped over his shoulder.

"Okay," Ian said, cheeks blazing in embarrassment.

Bertrum stood. "Let's see it."

"See what?"

"Ye know *what*. Take that cap off yer head. Let's see the white."

Ian lifted the wool hat. Bertrum stepped forward, cautiously looking over his matted scalp.

"Mm," he grumbled. "Yep. There's a few. White as snow. Ye should've told me, lad. Should've told me the moment it happened."

"I know," Ian said quietly. "I was scared. I didn't think it had worked." He sighed. "I was *happy*, thinking it didn't work."

Bertrum shook his head. "Well, looks like that didn't exactly go as planned, eh?" He shrugged. "Now ye've Spoken the Words to wake him, so I'm sure there'll be no problem Speakin' the Words to put him back to rest, right?"

"Right," Ian said, staring down at his shoes.

Bertrum mussed his hair. "Good. Now let's get the lass back home. Then you 'n me'll get to work."

Joanna arrived at dusk. Ian watched as she and Bertrum spoke in hushed whispers in the library. Ian and Fiona waited on the stairs, struggling to make out what the blacksmith and the Voicecatcher were saying. Joanna gasped as Bertrum gestured wildly, and her face went pale as she listened to Bertrum's story.

"Think we're in trouble?"

Ian shrugged. "If I had to guess, I'd say yes." He caught himself. "No. *Definitely*."

Fiona leaned forward, resting her head on his shoulder. "I'm sorry," she whispered.

"You don't need to be," Ian said. "I wanted to help you. We're friends. That's what friends do for each other."

"I know. I just hope Bertrum takes it easy on you."

Ian didn't want to think about it. He'd made more mistakes than he could count. Serious ones. It wasn't even Bertrum he was worried about. It was his father. Ian's only solace was the fact that Isaac was away. If he'd been around to witness that whole mess . . .

"I hope your mom does, too."

Ian didn't imagine that she'd take the news well. She'd always been a worrywart. If she knew the number of times Fiona had snuck out, she'd have worked herself into a fine frenzy. Ian had always assumed that the Calls had made her so anxious. He supposed he'd be on edge, too, if he was awakened each night by the screams of the Dead, echoing deep from the Void.

"All right, lad," Bertrum said, limping over to them. "Say good night to Fiona. Ye've had a long day."

"Let's go, young lady," Joanna said, ushering her daughter toward the door.

The friends exchanged dour looks as they parted. Ian remained on the steps, hugging his knees to his chest as he watched Fiona slowly march to the door.

Bertrum bid the Voicecatchers a good night as he saw them out. He waited at the doorway for a moment before reaching into his shirt pocket for his pipe, then struck a match on his cheek and took a few puffs before turning to Ian. "Had a lot of explainin' to do," he growled. "Gave me a right talkin' to. I suspect Fiona'll get the brunt of it when she gets home, though. Eh, she can take it. She's a tough little lass."

"Yes," Ian said, "she is." *Tougher than I could ever be.*

Betrum tapped the pipe against his chin. "Now, I think it's time we put that friend o' yers back to rest, eh? Got to see things through, lad."

Ian nervously rubbed the back of his neck. He didn't want to touch the Void. Not again. He reached deep inside of himself, searching for some flicker of courage. Just an ounce would be nice.

One last time, he told himself. *Just to put Thatcher to rest. This mess will be all over soon. Then Dad will be home and things can be set right. Maybe he'll see you're not cut out for this.*

"Mm," Betrum growled. Ian saw his good eye bulge as he took a long, hard pull, the embers in his pipe burning bright orange.

"You're going to tell my dad . . . aren't you? Or Joanna will."

Bertrum scratched his chin. "She won't. I had to beg and plead on that one. But I haven't decided, yet. Might. Might not. All depends on how ye handle this, lad. Can't very well lie to the man. We'll see what comes when it comes."

It was not the comforting answer Ian had hoped for.

Bertrum gathered up Thatcher and returned to the door. "Go fetch a shovel."

Digging.
　　Digging.
　　Always digging.

And just when Ian thought he'd dug enough, he had to dig more.

He grunted as he unearthed Thatcher's grave for the second time, arms aching as he slung dirt over his shoulder. The wound on his arm burned like hot wax, numbing his fingers.

"Thatta boy," Bertrum said encouragingly, watching his technique. "Bend those knees, lad. Takes the pressure off yer back. It's all in the shoulders. And the waist. *Twist!* There ye go. Slow and steady, now. Slow and steady. No need to rush. This un's got all the time in the world."

Ian gritted his teeth, jabbing at the soil like a miner trying to pound through bedrock. The autumn spell that the Weavers had cast had worked its way into the soil, turning it hard as stone. He was a puddle of sweat by the time he got down to the casket, all blisters and cramped muscles. And cold. It was nearly the end of spring, and he was *cold*. Cold and cursing Weavers under his breath.

"Good. Hop outta the way there, now."

Bertrum lowered himself down into the pit. Thatcher's bones rattled as he placed him in the oak box.

"There," he said, slapping his hands together. "Comfy cozy. Just like before."

Ian stared down at Thatcher's face, searching the empty eye sockets for any sign of life.

Bertrum stood over him, the oil lantern swinging from his hand. His one eye gleamed in the light, wide and watchful. "All right, Digger. Time to recite."

Thatcher awoke from his sleep, groggy and slow. He reached out a bony hand, waving it blindly through the air.

"Wha—Where . . . where am I?"

A skeletal finger brushed Ian's cheek.

"Ian? That you? Wh-what am I doing in here?"

Ian gently moved Thatcher's hand from his face and laid it back down at his side. "You're home," he said.

"Home? Oh, no. I'm in the Children's Yard. In the ground, aren't I?"

"Yes."

"You're putting me back?"

"Yes."

Thatcher clicked his jaw. "I'm sorry, Ian. I should never have listened to that old crone."

"No. You shouldn't have."

"She promised me things. Things I couldn't get anywhere else."

"She's evil," Ian replied. "She'd have cursed you. *Destroyed* you."

"Well, I know that now," the skeleton said. "If I'd known that then, I never would have agreed. I didn't realize it'd be all daggers and cauldrons. Please, Ian . . ."

Ian watched Thatcher's face. Try as he might, he couldn't help but believe him. The boy had just gotten in too far over his head. A Weaver's treachery was boundless. He knew that, now. Thatcher couldn't be held entirely responsible. He just wanted to live. Surely, Ian could forgive that. He would want that, too.

"I believe you."

Thatcher let out a deep breath, sinking down into the coffin. "All right, Ian. I'll go quietly. It was good while it lasted, though. Thank you. I don't suppose any other Diggers would've let me spend so much time above ground."

"No. I don't think they would have."

Ian closed his eyes, preparing himself to recite the Words of Rest.

"Ian?"

"Yes?"

"It . . . it won't hurt, will it?"

Though he couldn't understand why, Ian found himself fighting back tears. Thatcher was shaking. "No. It'll be like falling asleep. That's all. A nice, long sleep."

"Long? Forever, more like. And dark." He reached up toward Ian, clutching onto the drawstring of his cloak. "It's dark, you know. I told you."

"I know you did. But it won't be this time. You're going to the Great Beyond. I *promise*. Even if I have to drag you there myself. Now, try to think of something good. Something happy."

"I'll try."

"Goodbye, Thatcher."

"So long, Ian. It was nice being back. Caused a right bit of mischief. The most a kid could in one day, I suppose." He crossed his arms over his chest and waited, resigned to his fate.

Bertrum cleared his throat. "All right, lad. Ye've said yer goodbyes. I'll leave ye to it."

Ian waited until the blacksmith hauled himself out of the open grave. He took a knee by the casket and rubbed his hands together, trying to warm them up in the frigid night air. As before, he placed his palms on Thatcher's skull, concentrating on the life force oozing from his fingertips.

"Friend, the time has come," he began. "You have been lifted from your slumber, and have spoken to me of all your troubles. Now, I bid you rest. May your mind be at ease. May your spirit be cleansed. I wish you safe travel, departed to the Great Beyond, where we shall all one day rest as one. Sleep now, and dream the dream that never ends."

Ian felt his skin burn as he held onto Thatcher. The corpse let out a sigh, his rattling breath leaving his body for the last time.

Ian found himself shaking. A salty tear ran down his cheek and into his mouth as his fingers went ice-cold. He felt Thatcher's energy dry up as everything became quiet.

Ian went limp as the world faded to black. Cold, now, as he floated in the dark.

The Void swirled around him, wrapping about his body like thick smoke. He looked over and saw Thatcher beside him, and gasped.

Thatcher was no longer a skeleton. Flesh covered his bones, and the face that peered at him through the darkness was that of a child. Thatcher's blue eyes were sparkling in the dim light of the Void, his wavy, red hair tumbling down over his freckly, dimpled cheeks.

"You're right," Thatcher said. "It does feel different, this time."

As he spoke, a light glittered in the distance. It was small at first, no bigger than the head of a pin. But its brightness cut through the Void's darkness like a beacon, growing larger as Ian clutched onto Thatcher's hand and waded farther.

As they approached, the light shone brighter, and Ian saw a massive pair of gold and crystal doors.

The Gates.

He shuddered.

They'd made it to the entrance of the Great Beyond.

Thatcher stopped, gazing up at them in wonder. "This . . . this is it?"

"This is it," Ian echoed. "One step through those doors, and you'll be home."

Thatcher shied away nervously. "What's it like in there?"

"I don't know. That's something only you can find out."

Thatcher slowly released his grip on Ian's hand.

"You can do it," Ian told him. "Be at peace. There won't be darkness, anymore. Trust me."

"I *do* trust you," Thatcher said. He gave Ian one last smile before he swam away, and the Gates slowly opened to let him squeeze inside. Ian tried to peer in, blinded by the searing flash of light, trying to get a glimpse of the Great Beyond before the Gates closed, and the darkness of the Void returned, closing around him like a giant, black curtain.

It was done.

Thatcher was at rest.

Finally.

Ian waded there in the Void, feeling the coldness wash over him, goose bumps prickling his arms as he floated back to the world of the Living.

Sleep well. Maybe we'll see each other again, one day.

Maybe.

Nine

"There. I think she'll like this un."

Bertrum placed the last flower into the bouquet, positioning the petals until they lay perfectly. "Good thing you cut these early. Blasted Weavers. Nothin' beautiful will grow in this cursed autumn." He sighed. "Yer Mum was fond o' carnations. *You* were, too, though I doubt ye'd remember. She used to take ye out to the gardens when ye were a wee lad and pick 'em with ye." Bertum grabbed a lone blossom from the table, twirling its stem between his fingers. "She'd put one up to yer chin and tickle ye with it, and ye'd laugh and laugh. Never saw a baby smile wide as you."

Ian racked his brain, but those memories didn't exist in his mind. *Other* people remembered, but not him. He could never grasp the whole picture. Only snippets. Bits and pieces.

A sound or an image. It was strange to hear stories about yourself, like eavesdropping, the specifics always just out of reach. Still, it was nice to hear Bertrum talk about it.

He looked down at his own bouquet. It paled in comparison to his teacher's. The flowers stuck out this way and that, a mess of stalks and leaves and bent petals. It looked like he'd stepped on it. Ian had only managed to save a few blooms. The meager offering would have to do.

"I wish mine came out a little better."

Bertrum looked up. "She'll like it just fine. It's not the flowers that matter, you know. It's the thought. Always the thought. The fact that they came from *you*. She'll know."

He folded the sails of one of the paper boats, grunting in approval as he ran a sausage-sized finger across its stern. Ian began coloring his in. Purple. Her favorite color. Or so he'd been told. When he finished, he placed the flowers inside, making sure they held in the circular opening Bertrum folded, nudging the stems firmly in place. A calm lake could be surprisingly dangerous terrain for a paper boat. The slightest gust of wind could send their tiny armada adrift. But Bertrum took his time with the construction, as he always did, year after year. And year after year, as always, he was confident they'd reach their destination.

Flower boats in hand, they trudged out to the lakeshore, a funeral procession of two. Ian cradled the paper boat in his arms, his mind swimming. He thought of Thatcher in his grave, an unwitting player in the Weaver's plot. He thought of Olivia, deep in the wood, and Fiona, who at that moment was probably getting the scolding of her life. And he thought of his father, totally (and thankfully) oblivious to what had occurred. It hadn't even been a full day since Bertrum had rescued him from the Weaver's cabin, but to Ian, it felt like a lifetime ago. The event had been too strange. Like a waking dream.

His head was still filled with images of the dungeon. Of Dehlia's sharp eyes. The smell of the cauldron fumes, the rank iron stench of his blood as it ran into the chalice like crimson syrup. He felt dirty. Soiled by an ancient and evil spell, covered with a magical stink that the hottest water and strongest soap could never wash away. The birch trees. The twisted path. The village of thatched huts at the base of the trees. There were reminders of his ordeal everywhere. They followed him like a shadow.

He looked up at the trees with their gold and red leaves, and inhaled a lungful of crisp, autumn air. The spell that the girls had cast was a strong one. He didn't think it would go away any time soon. Fall had fallen, and it had fallen too fast.

Ian pulled his hood down as golden beams shimmered over the lake's surface, making it sparkle like liquid silver.

They stood side by side, watching the water lap against the stony shore. The tomb stood in the distance, sun reflecting off of the marble spires like a burning torch.

"Always looks better in the light," Bertrum whispered.

Ian thought about his recurring dream: the hammer, the dark, the cold. Pounding away on the casket.

Thatcher had told him that there was nothing beyond

death. Only darkness. Not darkness, really. More like the absence of light. Nothingness. Like the flame of a candle after it's blown out.

His mother couldn't have been lost in the Void. She believed in laughter and love and cherished flowers and gentle spring days. She believed in family and kindness. Surely, she wasn't wandering around in darkness. Surely, she'd found her way to the Great Beyond, where the sun always shone. A place of calm emerald pastures and gentle sapphire rivers. A place of warmth and cheer, where no one ever felt sad or alone.

"Are ye ready?" Bertrum asked, bending down to place his boat on the water.

"Not just yet. Let's wait a little longer. We don't need to rush."

Ian found himself thinking of that dungeon in the woods. The old woman's words echoed in his ears, so clear he would have sworn she was standing right behind him: *The balance between worlds thins . . . The rift grows wide. Living and Dead . . . the two are becoming one.*

The sky began to darken over the woods. A black storm cloud rose, seemingly up and out of the forest itself. It lingered in the distance, casting a long, creeping shadow over the north end of the lake.

"The Weaver in the woods, how did she know who I was?"

Bertrum gently set his flowers down on the grass and stared out at the water, fists clenched. He didn't move for a long time. Finally, he sighed, kneeling down in front of the boy. "Ian, I'm not sure how to say this. In truth, I'd never thought I'd have to. Maybe I'm just a stupid old man, but I honestly never thought it would come to this. Figured ye'd go yer whole life not knowin', and I figured that'd be just fine. Some things, we're just better off without."

"What things? Bertrum? What do you mean?"

The blacksmith stared into Ian's eyes, before placing a hand on his shoulder. "There's a reason why yer great-great-great-great-grandpa decided to keep me around. I've been in wars, lad. Seen the dark side o' humanity. Things that'd shake a man to the core if he let 'em. I've done things I ain't proud of, but that came in handy when the stakes was high. May be comin' apart at the seams, but my aim is still sharp, and my hands are still strong. Now, yes, I'm a gardener and a handyman and a teacher, but they ain't the only parts to my job. Part of it's keeping *them* away. Them and their black magic. I'm here to protect ye, Ian. Guard ye 'gainst evil of all sorts. Especially the evil that's in them woods."

"You're talking in riddles again."

"No, Ian. No riddles. There's a threat livin' in that forest. One that hasn't been a problem in a long, long time. But that don't mean it ever went away. That Weaver. The old one . . ."

"I don't understand," Ian said. "Why hasn't anyone done anything about her?"

"Not an easy thing to answer." Bertrum hesitated, tugging gently on his newly-mended ear. "Because, lad . . . she's yer grandmother."

Ian felt his chest tighten, like he'd been socked in the gut.

"Didn't think I'd ever have to break it to ye like this," Bertrum continued. "Never thought it'd fall on me to tell ye. Yer father and I . . . we hoped ye'd never have to know. But there it is. Cold and Plain and simple. Ain't gonna sugarcoat it for ye. Reckon ye deserve more than that."

Ian's legs buckled as he struggled for words. "How . . . ?"

"Yer mother lived there. In that forest, that village. They were Voicecatchers, once. A whole village of 'em. But somewhere down the line, things went bad. They started workin' the black magic. Usin' the Voice to tap into the Underrealm. The old Fossors caught wind of it, and they were none too pleased. The Diggers and Catchers made a pact. A pact that they'd each go 'bout their business in peace. Before long, the Catchers weren't much Catchers anymore. They *changed*. Wasn't much contact for a long time. No reason for there to be. Till the graveyard grew and got closer to the woods. Happened when yer father was around your age. We were runnin' outta space. Had to move closer to the trees. Yer granddad and me were clearin' out the brush by the edge of that meadow. Isaac was helping—well, as much as a young lad could, I suppose. He was runnin' along the forest's edge, exploring, right near that Pumpkin Trail. Somethin' caught his eye in those woods, and he came runnin' over to us, beet red and covered in sweat, grinnin' from ear to ear. He said he saw someone walkin' through the pumpkins. A girl. Yer *mother*, Ian."

Bertrum thumped himself down on the grass with a loud grunt, hands shaking as he pulled some sweetleaf out of his pouch and plugged it into the pipe. Once he sparked it up, he continued. "Now, I always figured yer father would end up with Joanna. They grew up together, same as you and Fiona. But all that changed when he saw that girl in the woods. He was smitten—beside himself. Courtin' her took a long time. She was afraid of us at first. Couldn't blame her, I s'pose—I ain't the easiest thing to look at—and she'd never left them woods before. Yer father was patient, though. He left notes for her at the edge of the trail. He'd stay up all night writin' her sweet nothings at his desk in the library. Yer granddad was none too pleased with the whole affair, but he kept his opinions to himself. It was love at first sight, so there was nothin' to be done about it, anyway. Yer mother was beautiful—graceful—even as a young girl. Ye could tell there were somethin' special about her. Somethin' in her eyes. She had this warmth, ye see. It was her soul. Ye could see her soul shinin' on the outside."

"Then, she was one of—"

"The Weavers? Aye, she were. But she didn't have an ounce o' her mother's darkness in her. Suppose that's why she chose to leave the forest. Dehlia, that *lovin'* gran o' yers, she wasn't havin' any of it. Banished the poor lass from that village, made her renounce all her old Weavery. Which wasn't so much a problem, as yer mother never used her powers, for good *or* evil. She blocked 'em out, tried to pretend like that whole part o' her life were just some bad dream. She felt at home here in graveyard with me and yer father and granddad. It was like she'd always been here. We never spoke of her time in the coven, seldom even looked to them woods. It was like we all chose to forget where she came from." Bertrum's eyes narrowed. "But *they* didn't. Weavers have long memories, Ian. They don't forget things easy as you 'n me. They'd hold onto a grudge for a thousand years if ye let 'em. *Grudge* ain't even the word for it. More like blood feuds. Yer mum's sisters didn't take kindly to her leavin'."

"Her sisters?" The more Bertrum spoke, the more Ian realized he didn't know anything, really.

"Now them sisters were the complete opposite of yer mum. They loved the magic, loved the dark and vile things that go along with Weavery and conjurin'. So they came here, on the anniversary o' the day yer mum left the woods. You were just a wee babe. Yer grandmother led yer aunts and a few other Weavers to this here spot, right on the lake, and yer mum and dad and I came out to face 'em together. Them Weavers wouldn't leave, ye see. And they wouldn't listen to reason. They were here for blood, and they weren't goin' nowhere till they spilled some."

Ian looked down and saw his skin was ghostly pale. His fingers had gone numb.

"Yer mum didn't want to use magic against her own kin. Hadn't played around with it since she left the village. But yer aunts gave her no choice. They cursed her for turnin' her back on her own kind. They cursed yer father, too, for drawin' her away—figured it was his fault. And they cursed her for havin' *you*. Said it was unnatural for a Weaver to have a child with a Digger. They came here for you, Ian. To use ye in a sacrifice. They wanted to get rid of yer parents and every trace of yer existence.

"Well, yer mum and dad were havin' none of it. Yer aunt was the first to make a move. She sent a wave o' lightnin' crashin' down on yer mum. I tried to dive in its path, but I was too slow. Didn't make it in time. All I remember is the flash, brighter than anythin' I'd ever witnessed in my life. She was powerful, yer aunt. More so than even yer gran. Yer mum was hit—hit bad— and then the other Weavers over-powered us. I tried to cut one down with an ax, but my aim weren't true that night. We were helpless. They had yer mum cornered. She . . . she . . .

"It were the worst moment o' my life, Ian. Layin' on the ground, helpless, watchin' 'em close in on her, black magic weaves thick in the air. Screamed my head off, rippin' and hollerin' and cursin' those soulless creatures. If only I could've reached 'em. If only my strength hadn't failed me . . ."

Ian put an arm around his teacher's shoulder. "It's okay, Bertrum. You tried to protect her. You did all you could."

The blacksmith shook his head. "Yer mum got the last laugh, boy. She waited till the rest of 'em got up real close—they were cacklin', the lot of 'em. I'd turned away by then. Couldn't stomach the savagery about to happen. They were almost on top of her, reachin' out ready to wring her neck." He clenched his fist. "Laughin'—they were actually *laughin'*. I thought for sure she was gone. Until I felt the blast. Yer mum unleashed something that night. Something so terrible and powerful that none o' her kin were left standin'. Truth be told, me and yer dad were lucky to be alive. But it was too much for her, casting a spell on her own mother to keep her trapped in them woods."

Betrum and Ian sat in silence. Ian clutched the flowers on his lap as the wind froze the tears to his cheeks.

"She got sick," Bertrum said. "The black magic the Weavers fought with seeped into her veins like poison, and she couldn't fight it no longer. She grew weaker by the day, horrid fever risin' and risin' . . . Yer father called on every Healer he could find, but in the end, none of 'em could save her."

Ian bit his lip, struggling to fight the oncoming tears as he pictured her lying there, wasting away while Bertrum and his father could only watch helplessly. "I wish I could have been there to try," he said.

Bertrum clasped Ian's shoulder with a heavy hand. "Even

with that bag 'o yers and all them books, ye couldn't have saved her. Like I said, lad, I didn't want to be the one to tell ye. But I suppose that wasn't right o' me. Or yer father. Ye should've been told a long time ago. Yer father thought tellin' ye sickness got her was the best way—less painful. We thought we were protectin' ye."

Ian shook his head. "I can't stand that."

Bertrum eyed him curiously. "Can't stand what?"

"That I need to be protected. You're always saying that."

The old corpse bristled. "Well it's true, lad. Ye *do*. I know ye want to be on yer own. I even know that Gravediggin' ain't where yer heart lies. That's been plain for a while, now. Written on yer face, clear as day. But there's a reason yer ancestors brought me back, and there's a reason yer father put ye in my care. The world outside is dangerous. Truth is, it's more dangerous for you than most other children. I think ye learned that lesson."

"It *is* dangerous," Ian said, "but it's not fair to keep things from me. Knowing about the Weavers could have helped me. It could have helped Fiona. You have to see that. I should know about my own family. We can't keep things from each other, Bertrum."

The corpse blew out a long plume of smoke. "Aye," he said. "We shouldn't. Like ye shouldn't have kept the fact that ye Spoke from *me*. I coulda helped ye."

"I know," Ian said. "But I . . . I just couldn't. Fiona was so determined. She wanted us to do it alone. To fix everything ourselves. I couldn't let her down. I didn't know what to do."

"I know, lad. I know." Bertrum studied the paper boat in his hand. "It's hard, growin' up. I'm goin' on four hundred 'n fifty years, and even *I* feel like I'm just pretendin' at it, sometimes. Still feel like a lost little boy, more often than not. And I can guarantee that yer father feels the same way. So don't think yer the only one. Remember this: growin' up don't mean that ye suddenly *know* everything. Ye just get better at *playin'* like ye do. Everyone needs help at some time or another. Ain't no shame in it. That's just the way o' the world. We need to depend on each other, if either of us's gonna make it out o' this world alive." Bertrum chuckled. "Come on, what's say we send yer mum her gifts, eh?"

Ian looked down at the boats. The flowers seemed to glow against the approaching storm clouds, bright as colored crystals.

"Sure."

Together, they placed the boats onto the water. Ian held onto his as it bobbed on top of the ripples, hesitating before letting go.

Bertrum allowed his to float away, crossing his arms over his chest as he watched it drift off on its journey. Ian anxiously stood at the water's edge as his boat struggled on the waves.

The gathering clouds brought a harsh wind sweeping across the lake, turning the placid ripples to choppy waves. Ian clenched his fists, silently cursing his grandmother. "If she doesn't let those boats across . . ."

"Don't worry, lad." Betrum said. "They'll sail against the wind. Yer mum will guide 'em along. Watch, now."

They met back in the dining hall, where Bertrum had prepared the traditional feast. Ian felt uncomfortable as he sank

into his chair at the head of the long table, gazing down at the blacksmith seated at the other end. Between them lay platters and bowls of every imaginable food. Bertrum had, as he did every year, outdone himself. Ian didn't know why the caretaker had gone to such lengths for just the two of them. The old grouch shrugged and muttered "tradition."

That word again, back to haunt him. Ian looked out at the cakes and muffins and crumpets, then the pheasant, the roasted pig, the turkey legs, and steaks.

After hearing Bertrum's story, he didn't much feel like eating.

Bertrum hadn't said a word since they'd returned to the manor. Now, he stared at the food in front of him, every now and then stabbing at a slab of meat. Of course, he couldn't eat any of it—what corpse could? Still, he'd take a bite and chew for a while. "At least I can still *taste* it," he said.

After Bertrum had his fill, he thumped a load of throwing axes down onto the table and began sharpening them one at a time with a whetstone.

Ian watched him work, his rough, gray hands moving the stone back and forth across the steel's edge.

Betrum looked up and noticed Ian staring. "We need to be careful, now," he grumbled. "Can't count yerself safe, not even behind these walls."

"I know," he said. "They're watching us, aren't they?"

Bertrum shrugged. "Can't say for certain. Dehlia . . . she's powerful. No tellin' what she'll do."

"I wish—" Ian caught himself before he could finish, feeling his cheeks redden. *I wish Mom was still here*, he wanted to say. *She'd protect us.*

It was strange. Her memory seemed . . . different, now. Tarnished . . . Everything he'd known about her had been a lie. Or was it? He still remembered the sound of her voice—the sweet, lilting, harmonious tone like a lullaby, even when she wasn't singing. That had been real. And even if she *had* been a Weaver, she wasn't the bad kind. Bertrum had said so. She wasn't like that old woman in the woods.

That old woman.

He had to stop calling her that. His stomach twisted into horrible knots at the very thought of her. She wasn't just some woman . . . She was his *grandmother*. While most kids' grandmothers were kind, knitting them mittens and baking sweets and telling stories, his was a murderous old crone who made potions from little boys' bones.

He kept returning to one question: why? Why had his grandmother done what she had? She'd spoken of revenge. Revenge for his mother? His aunt? The other Weavers who'd descended on the graveyard and fallen in the fight? Maybe Dehlia's grudge had nothing to do with his mother or himself. Maybe she wanted revenge for something far older, something that happened long, long ago.

Whatever her reasons, Ian couldn't help worrying. Something had been set in motion when his grandmother drew his blood and spoke those awful words. Something evil had been loosed. He had felt it as he walked out of those woods. He felt it in the graveyard, swirling in the autumn breeze. It followed him like a shadow, dark and menacing.

He put down his fork and ran his hand over his arm, stopping at the slash the dagger had carved. It stung as he prodded it with his finger.

"Don't mess about with it," Bertrum called from the other end of the table. "Let it heal on its own, lad."

Ian nodded, giving it one last poke before letting his

hands fall into his lap. He stared at the plate in front of him, concentrating on the stinging in his arm.

The food was still warm when Ian excused himself. He trudged up to his room in a fog, shrugged his cloak off onto the pile, and crawled into bed. His gaze settled on the open closet. He hoped Thatcher was all right.

Ian tried to relax, but as he sank further into the mattress, the wound on his arm burned. He'd dabbed it with every ointment and poultice from his satchel, but nothing seemed to ease the pain. Ian tossed and turned, unable to find a comfortable spot. He kicked off the covers and rose, pacing around the room like it was his prison.

A glimmer of pale light drew him to the window. He peered through the glass. The moon glowed strangely, casting everything in a pale shade of green, as though Mother Night, herself, had grown sick. Ian rubbed his eyes, sure he must be seeing things, but when he focused again, he still saw only the green pall. Just a hint, really, but enough to set his heart pounding in his chest.

A green moon.

What has Grandmother done?

Bertrum appeared below, stomping out of the manor's backdoor and into the Yard. He carried a torch in one hand, blazing bright against the sickly night sky. An ax rested on his shoulder. Ian watched as he lumbered to the lakeshore and halted, planting the torch in the ground beside him. The corpse remained motionless, the ax hefted in both arms, his gaze trained on the distant forest, waiting.

Ian watched him until his eyelids grew heavy, knowing Bertrum would keep his watch until dawn.

Feeling safer, Ian made his way to bed.

Ten

Again, he'd dreamed of his mother. Again, he'd rowed out to her tomb. He couldn't decide if having the same dreams over and over was comforting or terrifying.

It felt as though he'd been in his nightmare world for an eternity, though he'd only slept a few hours.

The dream started off in the same way it always had—alone in a rickety old rowboat, he'd panted, muscles aching, as he'd pulled the oar through the water, propelling the tiny craft along. But this time, the boat wasn't moving fast enough. He crawled along like a slug, struggling to inch forward. The tomb wasn't getting any closer, no matter how fast he rowed. The water was thick like molasses. For a while, he wondered if he was moving at all.

When Ian finally reached the tomb, the sledgehammer

was nowhere to be found. How could he have forgotten it? He never had before. He checked every inch of the rowboat, just to be sure.

Knowing that he'd never reach his mother without it, he turned the boat back, but the trip wasn't any easier as he slogged back through the ever-thickening water. By the time he reached the opposite shore, he was exhausted. Now, the water was completely still. He poked it with his finger to be sure, and it bobbed and jiggled before resettling to solid mass. He dropped a rock in, watching for the ripples; it landed on the surface with a dull *thud*. He watched, perplexed, as the stone was slowly swallowed down into the depths.

He retrieved the sledgehammer from the shed, loaded it into the boat, and began the journey back across the lake. He was anxious now—anxious and frustrated and quickly losing his strength. The longer he stayed on the lake, the longer his mother would stay in the tomb.

After what felt like an eternity, he reached the island again and tied off the boat. Tired, angry, and sore, he stepped onto dry land and turned back to the vessel.

The sledgehammer was gone.

And so the nightmare had continued: Ian would travel back across the lake, find the hammer, place it in the boat, and row back through the muddy, sludge-like water, only to discover the hammer had vanished when he arrived on the other side. Back and forth he struggled across the lake, cold and miserable and tired, trapped in an unbreakable cycle.

Ian woke to the sound of hammering.

He found Bertrum out by the toolshed, banging away on a large slab of carved slate. The caretaker grunted as he worked the chisel into the stone, sparks flying with each pound of the hammer. A new grave marker. Every few minutes, Betrum would stop chiseling and consult the piece of paper on the worktable. Ian walked over to examine the freshly cut words:

HERE LIES JACOB TANNER
BORN

The inscription ended there. Ian ran a finger along the smooth, cold surface.

"Had to check the death date," Bertrum said. "Can't mess that up. Family would have my head if I did. Be a good lad and fetch my pipe, eh?"

The blacksmith was just finishing up, wiping away the last bits of stone dust off the marker, when Ian returned from the toolshed, pipe in hand. Bertrum took a step back and sized up his work, slowly nodding in approval. "Think I'm gettin' a pretty good handle on this."

I should hope so, Ian thought. *You've been at it for a couple centuries.*

"Did you see anything last night?" Ian asked.

Bertrum took a long pull. "Nothin'. Patrolled round the manor till dawn. Just some crows flyin' round."

"That moon . . ."

"Weaver trickery," Bertrum grunted. "They can make ye see things that ain't there."

Ian nodded, but Bertrum didn't sound all that confident.

The old caretaker gestured toward the stone. "You'll have to give me a hand with the plot, lad. Mourning party's comin' tomorrow at noon."

It was the first new burial in a long time, Ian realized.

He found the ceremony exciting, in a way. Mournings were one of the few chances he had to view the outside world. The processions would make their way through the graveyard, grief-stricken friends and acquaintances clad in black. It was always interesting to watch as strangers solemnly enter the cemetery, listening as a holy man said a few carefully chosen words over an open grave. Ian had realized long ago that their experience was much different from his own.

To Ian, the graveyard was home—a place of adventure and warmth and mystery. But to those who visited, it was associated with great sadness. A place where they would never wish to stay for very long. Ian wondered if they noticed the true beauty of the land as he did, or if they just saw a dark, dismal dumping ground for sad memories.

"Wish yer father would hurry up 'n get back here," Bertrum said. "Ground's hard as a rock. 'Twould Would be nice to have three on it. We'll have to break out the pickaxes. Try'n soften it up."

As far as digging went, Ian would rather burrow down into an already-existing grave than carve out a new one. With *new* plots, you had to be very precise. Six feet deep. Three feet wide. The measurements had to be perfect, and so did the digging. It took a lot longer to prepare the ground for a fresh corpse. It was out respect, really, but there was also a good measure of pride mixed in. His father had once told him, a Digger who Digs well never has trouble falling asleep at night.

Ian and Bertrum began loading a wheelbarrow with their tools. Ian fetched a pair of pickaxes from the shed, dragging them along the grass, like the hammer from his dreams, struggling as he lifted them up and into the cart. With one fluid motion, Bertrum picked up the newly-inscribed tomb-stone and loaded it into the wheelbarrow single-handedly. Ian retrieved the shovels, mattocks, spades, and measuring tools, wrapping them in a grimy canvas cloth before following Bertrum to the plot.

Bertrum prodded the grass with the tip of a spade.

"Ground's frozen," he muttered. "Blasted Weavercraft. She couldn'ta just turned ye into a toad, eh? Had to go 'n make everythin' more difficult."

"Hey!" Ian retorted.

"What? At least if ye were a toad, ye'd be easier to look after. And I reckon ye wouldn't talk back near as much." Bertrum winked, mussing Ian's hair. "Ye could smile, at least. Bit 'o humor could do us both some good."

Ian frowned as he grabbed a ball of twine from the wheel-barrow. Carefully, he outlined the perimeter of the grave, pounding the twine into the ground with wooden stakes. Bertrum raised his mattock, gritting his teeth as he sank it into the frozen dirt. It took the better part of an hour before it was soft enough to dredge with the shovels. Ian joined the blacksmith in digging, and once the grave was deep enough, lowered pails for Bertrum to fill with dirt, using pulleys to lift them when they were full for dumping.

Bertrum sang as he worked, an old tune written by Ichabod Fossor centuries before:

Dig a hole for them
Six by three

And deep in the blanketed dark they'll be
To slumber till doomsday
To dream through the night
To ease all their worries
Abandon all fright
Fill it back in, now
Pack it down tight
And mark them a grave so you'll know them on sight.

On and on he sang, bright and jaunty, relishing in the work. Ian listened, losing himself in the tune. Bertrum's gargling, booming song seemed to take his mind off things. For a brief moment, Ian was at peace, away from woods, Weavers, and autumn spells, lost in digging.

Once they'd reached the six-foot mark, Ian went around with the flattening tool, packing the walls of the hole, smoothing them out, then carving out the sharp, ninety degree angles like a sculptor working a block of marble. He breathed deeply, filling his nostrils with the soothing mineral odor of the dirt.

"Come on up, lad."

For a moment, Ian found it hard to pull himself away. It was actually warmer down in the ground. Comforting. Homey. When he finally snapped out of his trance and climbed up, the autumn wind sent a chill down his spine.

Bertrum walked the perimeter of the grave, carefully measuring every inch. "Looks about right. Ye did a fine job."

With the inspection complete, they began the processing of setting the stone. Ian took a hoe and cleaved out a small indentation in the soil, not too wide and not too deep. Then he and Bertrum picked up the newly-inscribed marker and plunged it into the ground. Once it settled, Ian packed dirt in around the sides and gave it a final push to make sure it was secured.

"Excellent," Bertrum said. "Don't reckon that's goin' anywhere."

Then the pair carefully packed their tools into the wheelbarrow, and set off back toward the house, dirty and tired—the good kind of dirty and tired that comes from an honest day's work.

All Ian wanted to do was get into bed and crack open a book. It had been too long since he'd had a chance to do nothing but study.

Bertrum stopped abruptly as they neared the manor gates. His eye narrowed as he peered at the house. Ian paused beside him. "What's wrong?"

The corpse just growled.

Then Ian noticed someone standing on the front steps.

"Looks like we got us a visitor," Bertrum said.

Fiona raised her head when she heard them approaching, rubbing her forearm across her cheek. As they drew nearer, Ian could see she'd been crying. Something was wrong.

Bertrum cleared his throat. "I'll leave ye to it. Gotta put the tools back, anyway. Ye need me, just shout."

Ian waited until his instructor was out of earshot before continuing to her side. "What's the matter, Fi?"

She tried to smile, but her lips quivered so much that eventually she just gave up. "Can we go in?"

"Of course," he said, offering a hand. Her skin was as

cold as ice. She faltered before following him inside and up to his room.

"It started last night," she said. "The Calls."

Ian cringed at the word.

"They didn't stop, Ian. The entire night, they just kept coming, one after another." Her voice seemed close to breaking. "They weren't like Thatcher's, either. They were . . . desperate. *Angry*. A thousand voices *screaming* in my ears at the top of their lungs. My head is still pounding. When I woke up this morning, it felt like someone had driven a spike through my ears. I could barely walk. It *hurt*, Ian. Mom says it's not supposed to *hurt*."

Ian opened his bedroom door. He peered down the hallway just to make sure Bertrum hadn't followed them.

"Maybe the Dead were trying to tell you something."

"What?"

They both jumped at a loud *smack* against Ian's window. A yellowed piece of paper was pressed up against the glass, fluttering as the wind held it in place.

Ian turned to Fiona, who was staring out the window as if she were in a trance.

The wind picked up, howling as Ian grasped the window latch. The paper seemed to dance on the gusts, calling to him.

He lifted the latch, expecting the strong wind to rip through the room. Instead, it died down as soon as the window was propped open. The paper peeled itself off the glass and fluttered in, drifting like a feather as it gently landed on Ian's bed.

"Careful," he said as Fiona walked toward it.

When Ian got closer, he saw that it was a note.

The paper was old-looking. Ian feared it would crumble

in his hand if he so much as touched it. The handwriting was elegant, carefully painted onto the page like the writer had used a brush. A girl's penmanship. But while the writing was beautiful, the message was ominous:

Beware what the Moon brings.
—O

Fiona sidled up beside Ian, peering at the note over his shoulder. Her fingers dug into his arm as she read the message.

"*What the Moon brings,*" she whispered.

Ian didn't know what to make of the note. He stared at the last letter, the single *O,* a delicate perfect circle. His heartbeat sped up as he stared into it, as though if he kept his eyes focused on the letter, a hidden message might appear.

"How did they get it all the way up here?"

"Olivia must have snuck into the yard when Bertrum and I were out digging," he said, uncertainly. For all he knew, she was still in the house, hiding in a closet or behind a chair. She could have blended herself into the walls. She *was* a Weaver, after all. Maybe she'd made herself invisible and was watching them at that very moment. It wasn't that difficult to imagine. The past few days had taught him that anything was possible. Ian let go of the paper, watching as it slowly drifted back down onto the bed.

"Didn't they say they couldn't leave?" Fiona asked.

"They did. But that was then." Ian studied the note once more.

"*Beware what the Moon brings,*" he repeated.

"The Calls last night," Fiona reflected, frowning, "Could

it be the Weavers? Did Olivia mention anything to you, when you were alone with her?"

"No, nothing about the moon. Olivia was . . . different from the others. You saw that, too, right?"

Fiona furrowed her brow, trying to remember. "She wasn't as nasty as that little one, Nora, if that's what you mean. Still, Ian. She's one of *them*."

He hesitated. "Bertrum told me something, though. About the Weavers."

"He *knows* about them?"

Ian nodded. "It's complicated."

Fiona's green eyes suddenly seemed to ignite with emerald fire. "Tell me everything!"

Ian hesitated, remembering how hurt he'd been about Bertrum and his father keeping him in the dark about so many things. How could he do the same to Fiona and still call himself her friend?

She folded her arms. "You're really terrible at lying. Come on. It's *me*."

Ian hesitated for a moment. He hadn't even yet sorted out his newfound knowledge in his own head yet, never mind having to explain it all to someone else. Still, Fiona always told him about the things that hurt and scared her. It was only right for him to trust her enough to do the same.

And so he told her everything. Every ounce of the terrible truth. With each word, the sharp sting of memory burned. He envisioned his mother, the Weavers, that terrible scene on the lakeshore.

When he finished, Fiona remained perfectly still, perched on the edge of the bed. The room was silent, save the creaking of the old manor.

She shook her head in disbelief. "How could they have kept a secret like that?"

"Bertrum said he was trying to protect me. That things would be better if I didn't know."

"That's a foolish thing to think."

Ian's eyes went wide. She'd never talked about Bertrum like that.

Fiona noticed, shaking her head slowly. "I'm sorry," she said. "Bertrum isn't foolish. But that wasn't the right thing to do, either." She pinched the bridge of her nose in frustration. "I just can't believe they'd all do that. Your dad. My mom . . . They all knew, this whole time. It's not right."

"They didn't mean for it to end up like this." *We have secrets of our own,* he thought. "And, no. It's not right."

"At least Bertrum finally said something." She pointed at the note. "Now we know who we're dealing with. Those Calls, Ian . . . something is very, very wrong."

Ian looked at the paper again. "I don't know what to make of it." *What is this, Olivia? A warning? A threat? A promise?*

His grandmother's voice echoed in the depths of his memory.

The rift grows wide . . .

He crumpled up the paper and tossed it in the corner. In truth, he would have preferred to burn it. Things touched by the hands of Weavercraft were better off destroyed.

The next afternoon, Ian stood dressed in his finest ceremonial Digger's garb beside Jacob Tanner's grave. Bertrum had prepared his special burial cloak for the occasion, black as moonless midnight, with a pointed hood and embroidered symbols of green and gold, the same runes that decorated Isaac's obsidian shovel.

Ian stood two paces away from the open grave, resting his leather-gloved hands on the handle of his shovel. Luckily, he didn't need to use his father's for a simple burial, so he took an average wood-handled one from Bertrum's toolshed. It felt so light in his hands. Fiona watched from beneath a willow tree at the far end of the Tanners' family plots. Ian felt a bit strange with her looking on, but she'd insisted.

Bertrum stood a few paces behind Ian, his face hidden in a cowl so his appearance wouldn't upset any mourners not used to seeing a corpse walking aboveground.

Betrum leaned forward, whispering into Ian's ear as the mourning party made its way into the Yard. "You'll do fine, lad."

Ian nodded. While he'd stood beside his father at many a graveside, this was the first time he'd ever had to oversee a burial on his own. Since he wasn't even a full Gravedigger yet, he felt like an imposter. Of course, the Rites of Burial had always been a part of Bertrum's lessons, so Ian knew what to do. But as he stood there, watching the Tanner brood approach, he felt small, as though he were walking in his father's shadow once again, a child playing dress-up in his parent's clothes.

The Tanners bore the coffin on their shoulders, the oak freshly painted in glistening white and gold. Conflicting feelings tore at Ian, threatening to pull him apart. Here he was, about to partake in one of the most sacred rights a Digger could provide, and all he wanted was to set down the shovel and call the entire thing off. He wanted so badly to tell these people that he wasn't the person they thought he was.

But he couldn't let the Tanners down. They needed a Digger, and Ian was as good as they were going to get. He flexed his gloved fingers around the shovel and tried to stand a bit taller as they approached.

A Digger endures.

The family formed a large circle around the open grave. The men stood like solemn statues, their hands clasped behind their backs. The women dabbed at their faces with handkerchiefs, clutching on to one another. There were a few children present, most of them hanging on to their parents' sleeves, all bundled up for the abnormal autumn chill.

The crowd parted, and a holy man moved to the headstone, stopping for a moment to rest his hand on the newly-cut granite. He smiled at Ian, then took a book from his coat pocket and began the reading. Ian stared at the open mouth of the grave, not paying much attention to the words. He'd been hearing the blessing of the Dead almost as long as he'd heard Bertrum reciting the Code.

Ian remained silent, watching as a few of the women placed roses on top of the casket, sobbing as they turned back and joined the rest of the family members around the circle. The holy man finished his speech, bowing to Ian before joining the circle himself.

"All right, lad," Bertrum whispered behind him. "It's time."

Ian nodded, resting his shovel against Jacob's headstone.

Together, they grasped the ropes at either end of Jacob's coffin. Ian walked to one side of the grave, Bertrum to the other, and with great care, they slowly lowered the oak box into the earth.

As Bertrum gathered the rope, Ian retrieved the shovel.

He plunged it into the pile of soil beside the grave and gently poured a shovelful onto the coffin. In the Rites of Burial, this act was known as the First Embrace. He stepped back and knelt before the headstone.

"In the sight of the ones you've left, I, Ian of House Fossor, welcome you to your resting place."

He stood and faced the family. "It is done," he told them, hoping his voice wasn't trembling too much. "Here, Jacob will lie in peace, under the watchful eyes of my most ancient House. Here, we will guard him. Here, we will guide him. Here, we will give him the gift of sleep eternal." Ian ended the speech by touching a hand to his forehead, signifying the end of the ceremony.

The mourners returned the gesture. As was customary, they watched from farther away as Ian and Bertrum filled in the grave with soil. Ian knew they wouldn't leave until the last of the dirt was packed, and Jacob's resting place was officially sealed.

When the grave was halfway filled, Ian paused, taking a small break to wipe the sweat from his brow. As he did, he peered into the distant crowd of mourners. To his shock, he found himself staring at three familiar faces.

A girl around his age stood with two younger ones on either side, all dressed in black, olive-skinned and raven-haired. He squinted, unsure if he was seeing things, until one of the little ones turned in his direction. Her green eyes were glowing over a pair of rosy cheeks as she frantically waved to him. The older girl whispered something in her ear and grabbed her hand to stop her.

Ian paused to rub his eyes. When he looked back up, they were gone.

It couldn't have been them . . .

His arms shook as he finished filling in the grave. As the Tanners made their exit from the cemetery, the sun dipped below the trees.

"Well," Bertrum said as he slapped Ian on the back, "ye did well."

Ian watched the black-clad mourning party disappear out of the south gates.

"They were here," Ian said.

Bertrum stiffened. "They?"

"The girls. Olivia, Nora, and Clara." He pointed to where the Tanners had been standing moments before. "They were there, with the Tanners. I saw their faces clear as day."

Bertrum swung his eye in the direction Ian was pointing, issuing a low, rumbling growl.

"Out of the forest," he said. "No . . . this won't do." He swung back and took Ian by the shoulder, his grip hard as iron. "I want ye to take Fiona inside and stay there. Lock the doors, lad."

"What will you do?" Ian asked.

Bertrum's gray face formed a deep snarl. "Patrol the Yard," he said. "A line's been crossed today."

A murder of crows flew overhead, cawing loudly, the mass of black wings blotting out the setting sun. Ian cringed as he watched them pass, feeling the weight of a hundred black eyes looking down as they swooped over the graves and out toward the lake.

Bertrum pulled Ian close. "Inside," he said. "*Now.*"

Eleven

Ian and Fiona did as Bertrum said, gathering in the study as dusk fell over the graveyard. Ian tossed a few logs into the fireplace, using the bellows to fan the flames. He sat, peering deep into their orange glow, watching as they licked around the wood like serpent tongues, bright and searing and dangerous.

After a while he began to see things in them. He saw Olivia's face, her piercing eyes boring into his soul. He saw his grandmother, dagger in hand, smoke pouring from the blood-filled chalice she clutched. The images leapt from the embers like spirits calling out from another world.

You're seeing things, he told himself. *Just like that night on the Pumpkin Trail. That wasn't real. Just in your head.*

He ran a hand through his hair, trying to make sense of it all.

"It's getting dark," Fiona called.

The pair had built a tent in the middle of the room, a lop-sided hut of quilts and blankets, held up with broomsticks and end tables. Ian pulled himself away from the fire and crawled inside, suddenly feeling a bit safer.

Fiona was reading from a large, leather-bound book enti-tled *A Compendium of Fossors Past.* It had been written by Ian's ancestor, Isaiah the Scribe, detailing the lives and deeds of every Gravedigger since time immemorial.

Fiona curled up, skimming the page with her finger as she read aloud: "'And then there was Ignatious Fossor, son of Ibsen and Magda Fossor, who was the fourth Digger to exhume the earth. Ignatious holds a special place in Gravedigger lore, for he was the first and only among the Fossors to forsake the Code. One fateful night, he happened upon Rosalind, a distant daughter of a distant king. She had died at the height of her beauty, and even in death, her grace had not diminished. Upon seeing her, Ignatious was smitten. He Spoke the Words and brought her to life, but in his foolhardiness, refused to put the fair princess back to rest. Even at the behest of his father, and the king, himself, Ignatious would not listen. He turned his back on his duty, refusing to abide by the second rule of the Digger's Code: *A Digger shall not grow attached to the Dead.* While few records remain of Ignatious's fate, it is believed he lived out the rest of his days exiled on a distant shore, outlived, most likely, by his corpse-bride, forever roaming the earth in shame and solitude, shunned by House Fossor for all time.'"

Fiona turned the page and studied the illustration of

Ignatious, young and bright-eyed, standing beside a beautiful girl in a crown. Her face was pale white, brighter than Ingatious's hair.

"It's not the best ending," she said, "but Ian, have you read this? Fossors have abandoned the Code before. This book is proof that it has been done."

"And look at what happened," Ian answered. "Ignatious was shunned. He's the only Fossor whose portrait was burned. No one speaks of him."

Fiona pondered that. "But you're not Ignatious. He was rash. You're thoughtful. Surely, there's a way."

"Maybe," Ian said.

"Gravediggers have had daughters," she said, pointing to a picture of Isabelle Fossor, Ian's great-aunt. "It's strange, I always seem to forget that. They never dug?"

Ian shook his head. "Speaking only passes to the males," he said.

"That seems unfair," Fiona countered.

None of it seems fair, Ian thought. *The power to Speak isn't a gift. It's more like a curse.*

Fiona tapped a finger on the book.

"One day, someone will add *you* to this book."

Ian took it from Fi's lap and casually turned the pages, gazing at the engravings of Ingmar, the first of his line, taller than any man Ian had ever seen, clad in obsidian armor, being honored by the king outside the royal crypts. Ingmar had been a great warrior before being granted the power of the Digger's Speech by an unknown sorceress at court. Ian wondered if *he'd* ever do anything worthy of being written about. The more he read from the book, the more helpless he felt.

His forefathers were great men. Greater than he'd *ever* be. With all these wondrous tales of the Diggers of old, how could he ever hope to earn a place among them? He'd just be Ian, the Digger who messed up. Ian, the Digger the Weavers trapped. Ian, the Digger who wasn't really keen on Digging.

When Ian thought of his future, he pictured two rivers running alongside each other. One would lead him down the path of Digging, the path everyone expected of him. The waters of that river were calm. Familiar. Easy to navigate. He could see where that river ended, and he wanted no part of it. Even if he did, he knew in his heart that he'd never live up to the Code. Never live up to his family's expectations.

The second river was wild and raging, twisting and tumultuous, the river that led to the world outside the graveyard. The river that led to his future. He couldn't see where it ended. The horizon was murky, cast in a shadow of uncertainty.

Always, he felt the pull from the dual rivers, standing on the shore, a shovel in one hand, his satchel in the other. Family and duty. Freedom and dreams.

He pushed the book aside.

"So," Fiona said, wiggling into her slippers, "I've been thinking . . . Olivia's note. There has to be something we can do. This study is filled with books. One of them has to have an answer."

Ian thought of the woods. The snarling jack-o'-lanterns on the Pumpkin Trail. A burning sensation flowed up his arm as he pictured his grandmother holding the dagger. "The Weavers," he said, "They were at the burial today."

Fiona shot up from her nest of pillows.

"They were *here?*"

"I . . . I think I saw them. Clara waved to me. It all happened so quick, and then they were gone. Vanished."

"They're trying to tell us something."

"Look," Ian said, a bit frustrated. "After what happened, after what they did to me . . . after what they did to *you*, I . . . I just don't know if we can trust them. Maybe they were just taunting me. Showing me that they can leave the woods, that nowhere is safe."

"She *waved*, Ian. They didn't cast a spell, or attack. They wanted you to see them. Why would they want that?"

Ian struggled to for an answer.

"Whatever Olivia wanted us to know is in that note."

Fiona wrinkled her nose. "It's not much to go on."

"It's not. But it's all we've got."

"Come on," she said, pushing her way out of the tent. "No use hiding in here all night."

Ian hesitated before following her.

Fiona frowned. "What's the matter?"

"Nothing," he said. "It's just . . . you saw what they were capable of. It's still *autumn* outside. If they can do that just to prove a point . . ."

"They forgot one thing, though."

"What's that?"

"It's not like they were showing off to a couple of normal kids from the village, right? Whatever they're cooking up, you need to remember that you're *one* of them. Even if you don't feel like it, it's true."

Ian wanted to believe her. He watched her as she stood there, fearless like some warrior queen from a history book. It reminded him of the day she'd found the Pumpkin Trail. He'd been so scared of it his entire life, but the minute Fiona saw it, all she wanted to do was follow the path and see where it led. She hadn't hesitated when Thatcher ran into the woods. She followed right on his heels. She had more bravery inside her than he could ever hope to possess. She'd thrown herself into danger without a moment's hesitation. Once again, he wondered what she found to like in him. Where she succeeded, he failed. Where she thrived, he faltered. Ian was little more than the reluctant sidekick on her adventures. Still, she'd drag him along, ignoring his protests. Even if Ian didn't want to join her, Fiona would never leave him behind.

"That girl is bold," Fiona said. "I'll give her that. Leaving the woods in broad daylight."

Ian shrugged. "You say that like it's a good thing."

"Maybe it is. Ian, none of what she's done is making sense. If she wanted to hurt you, don't you think she would have done it already? Maybe she's starting to see she's on the wrong side."

Fiona's words made Ian pause. It was true. Olivia was different. She'd been more timid than the others. More curious. Even when they'd cast their spell, he noticed that Olivia didn't want them to do anything that would bring him harm. She was scared of the world outside the woods, but she didn't seem to hate it the way her grandmother did.

"You were right. She wasn't like the others," Fiona continued. "I noticed that. Surely you did, too."

"I did," Ian admitted. *Maybe she* is *on the wrong side.*

Fiona crossed the room to the window, then leaned on the ledge and pressed her face against the glass. "Umm . . . Ian? I think you'd better come see this . . ."

When Ian looked outside, the entire landscape was bathed in a bright shade of green. The moon loomed above the tree-tops, pale and huge. He could see the craters in its surface, and when he looked closer, could almost make out a rolling, green fog swirling over it. The fog swept off into the night sky, polluting the clouds and stars, shining down over the gravestones, draping everything in an eerie glow.

Fiona swallowed hard. "What's happening?"

"I don't know," Ian whispered, unable to take his eyes away. "The moon . . . I saw it change the night after Bertrum rescued us. Green, like this. But the fog . . ."

He reached out, as if he could touch it. He extended his arm. He winced, cradling it back against his chest. The dagger wound burned more terribly than it had before.

"Ian!" Fiona was beside him, studying the arm.

"My grandmother," he said, gritting his teeth through the pain.

"She's doing this?"

"It has to be her."

Fiona looked to the window, clenching her fists tight as the green fog swirled up around the manor.

"It's like the fog on the Pumpkin Trail," she said.

"*The balance between worlds thins . . .*" Ian said, echoing his grandmother's words.

"We need to get Bertrum." Fiona moved to the study door, but Ian grabbed her arm before she could take another step.

"He told me to stay inside. For us to stay in and keep safe. That's what I'm doing." Ian glanced at the fog. It swirled outside the window, curling in on itself like a serpent made of mist.

The balance between worlds . . .

Twelve

They huddled inside the tent. Ian had to practically force Fiona inside. She'd protested the entire time, eager to go out and explore the fog.

"Please," he said. "Bertrum gave me an order, and for once, I'm going to listen to him. You should, too." He felt silly, hiding inside a tent of blankets, but the fear was so strong that he couldn't think of a better place to go.

Resigned, Fiona hunched over a stack of books, wildly flipping though the pages. Ian was afraid to close his eyes. He looked outside and saw the study awash in green light pouring in through the windows, casting itself on the walls, creeping along the floor, even infecting the flames of the fire so they burned a sickly hue. Ian felt safe inside the tent. It was a refuge untouched by the dark magic.

But he knew he couldn't hide in there forever. He knew this wouldn't just blow over in time. He wished his father was home.

"I can almost feel it," Fiona said as she rubbed her arms. "And it has a *smell*, too. Musty. Heavy. Like old smoke."

Ian looked down at the pile of books splayed out in front of Fiona.

"What are you looking for?"

"A mention of Weavers. Black magic. Something like that. Your family's library should have something about them, but so far I can't find anything." She held up a book, its leather cover so worn Ian could barely read the title: *Touching the Void: Rites and Incantations.* "I grabbed anything that seemed at all related. Not a single mention."

"I hadn't even thought of that," Ian admitted. He peered at his satchel, stuffed with medical texts. He wouldn't find any answers in those pages.

Bang! Bang! Bang!

They jumped, startled by the heavy pounding on the door.

Ian untangled himself from the blankets he'd been curled in. It was close to midnight. He had a feeling this wasn't some casual visitor. The moon had risen higher, and he realized it appeared even closer, gazing down like an enormous eye.

"We should answer the door," Fiona said, nodding her head toward the entry hall. "It could be Bertrum."

Bang! Bang! Bang!

The beating shook the walls like an earthquake. A portrait of Imbert Fossor dangled from its frame above the bookcase, threatening to crash down at any moment.

"That's not Bertrum," Ian said. "He never knocks."

"We can't hide in here all night," Fiona said, lifting the blankets from the entrance of the tent.

"What are you doing?" Ian asked.

"Looking," she answered as she crawled out.

Crouching, they stalked through the library, careful to keep away from the windows.

Bang! Bang! Bang! Bang!

Faster now. The pounds were frantic. Ian positioned himself next to the door, holding his breath as he peered through the small peep hole. A man stood on the front porch, pressing his entire body into the door.

"He might be in trouble," Fiona whispered.

"What if he's dangerous?"

A low moan came from the other side. The stranger was throwing himself against the surface, his palms slapping hard against the wood.

"If that fog is the same stuff from the Trail, it's evil," Fiona said. She pointed to the door as the banging continued. "And that sounds like someone panicked. Someone trying to get out of it. Just like we were."

"Fiona, please."

"If he's in trouble, we need to help. We can't leave him out there."

Ian was frozen. Again, he peered out of the peephole, mind racing. Something had this unknown visitor terrified.

"Oh, this is ridiculous!" Fiona shot up from her hiding place, marched over to the door, and threw it open.

Before Ian had a chance to protest, the figure came flying into the foyer, followed by a gust of bone-chilling wind that slammed the door shut behind him. Fiona dove out of the way as the lanky stranger tumbled across the floor, catching himself at the bottom of the staircase.

He looked wildly around the entranceway. The man was tall, dressed in black finery. Ian noticed the bird-like features of his face: the angular jawline; the hooked, beaked nose; the furrowed brow; the thin but fearful eyes darting about the room. When he registered Ian, the man swallowed, his large Adam's apple bobbing up and down. "Oh, my. I'm . . . I'm frightfully sorry, young man." The stranger's lips quivered as he backed himself up against the staircase, casting fearful looks at the door.

Ian grabbed a candlestick from a nearby table, brandishing it in front of him like a sword. Even if Fiona was set on helping this man, they couldn't be sure that this wasn't some Weaver trick.

The stranger dabbed his forehead with his sleeve, trying to calm himself. "I . . . I'm not quite sure what's going on, you see. It's all . . . it's all very curious. I saw a light in the window, and as it's the only house among these dreadful gravestones, I was wondering if you could h-help me."

"It's all right," Fiona said. "Just go slowly."

The man forced a smile. His other hand nervously picked at the handkerchief sticking out from his breast pocket. He saw Ian with the candlestick and took a few awkward steps back.

"Slowly . . . yes, yes. Well, I'm not quite sure where to start, really. You see, I've just . . . woken up. And I'm not at all sure that I know where I am. I'm quite lost, you see."

Fiona and Ian's eyes locked as they listened to him stutter along with his story.

"It's strange," he said. "One minute I . . . I was fine. At least, I *think* I was fine. . . . In bed, safe at home . . . all very comfortable. I remember I was reading . . . can't recall the name of the book." He shook his head. "Anyway, that's beside the point. It's just . . . I can't remember falling asleep. It . . . it all went black. And when I awoke, it was still black. And *cold*." He shivered and wrapped his arms around himself. "I found myself unable to move. Unable to *breathe*, really. It . . . it took me a long while to get out of there."

Ian took a few steps toward the stranger, trying to get a better look at him in the moonlight. "Get out of where?"

The man cocked his head to the side, struggling with the question. "Where? Why the ground, of course." He patted the sides of his pants. Ian watched clumps of dirt fly off the fabric. The man pointed to the candlestick in Ian's hands. "I trust you won't strike me with that, my boy. I'm quite harmless, I assure you."

"Just tell us what happened," Ian said.

"When I reached the surface, everything was green," the man said, pointing to the window. "That dreadful moon. All I could see were stones. So many stones. I . . . I feared I'd be walking out there forever . . . until I found this place."

Fiona brushed his arm. "Don't worry. You're safe here."

"Thank you, my dear. I . . . I'm afraid I'm just a little . . . confused, is all."

Ian dropped the candlestick and held out his hand. "My name is Ian. Ian Fossor. I'm the Gravedigger's son."

The stranger went to shake Ian's hand. Ian shuddered. The long fingers gripped around his own were like icicles.

"Nice to meet you, Ian. My name is Jacob. Jacob Tanner."

Fiona gasped. She held a hand over her mouth, eyes wide in disbelief.

Jacob Tanner.

Ian struggled to remain calm, gawking at the man whose funeral he'd spent the whole day preparing for. He'd dug the grave himself. Helped Bertrum settle the tombstone into the ground. Yet here Jacob Tanner was, standing in the foyer, alive as ever.

Jacob smiled. "I . . . I'm glad I found you then, young Fossor. Nice to see a friendly face after all of this."

Ian continued to stare. *How?* All the color had drained from Fiona's face.

Jacob noticed and released Ian's hand. "My dear, are . . . are you all right? You look troubled."

Fiona took a step back.

"Ian," she said, "you . . . you didn't Speak the Words, right?"

"No," Ian said, staring at Jacob, who looked at each of them, perplexed.

He doesn't know, Ian realized. *He has no idea he's dead. He thinks he's just woken up from a dream. How is this possible? How can he not know?*

Ian tried his best to act calm. "Jacob, listen to me. There's something I need to tell you. That place you crawled out of tonight, it was your—" He struggled with the last word. How could he tell him that he'd just crawled out of his own grave?

For a moment, none of them moved. Fiona was still transfixed at the sight of Jacob looming over her.

Ian's mind was a whirlwind. How had Jacob risen? Corpses didn't wake unless they Called. Fiona would have heard it. And then Ian would have had to Speak.

Bang! Bang!

The corpse's gaze shifted to the door. "It seems you have a lot of visitors this evening, young Fossor."

Ian swallowed hard.

Beware what the Moon brings.

Bang! Bang!

His hand trembled as he reached for the doorknob.

Strength now, Ian. A Digger does not cower. A Digger fears no darkness.

He threw the door open, and a familiar voice greeted him through the fog. A voice Ian had thought he'd never hear again as long as he lived.

"Ian! Just the Digger I was looking for. You owe me an explanation or two, I should think."

Thatcher's skeletal feet *tap-tap-tapped* on the hardwood floor as he marched into the house with long, confident strides.

"Ahhh!" Jacob let out a terrified scream, stumbling back through the library doorway. His lanky frame flopped back over a table, sending him crashing down with a loud *thud.*

He stared at Thatcher as he sat up, scooting back even farther as the skeleton took a seat at the bottom of the staircase.

Ian was dumbfounded. Returning Thatcher to rest was one of the most difficult things he'd ever done. Now, the troublesome corpse was back, walking above ground as if everything were completely normal.

"Thatcher . . ." The name caught in Ian's throat. It wasn't possible. It defied the laws of nature. The laws of

Gravedigging! Unless someone had dug down and Spoken the Words, there was simply no way. "Thatcher, how—"

"What is *that*?" Jacob called from his hiding place behind the couch.

"It's all right, Jacob," Ian said. "His name is Thatcher Moore."

"How can that . . . *thing* have a name?"

"Hey!" Thatcher snapped, "what happened to manners, eh? You're not exactly a vision either, friend."

Ian held up his hands. "Please! Calm down, both of you."

"What is this . . . this *creature* doing in the house?"

"He's not a *creature*." Ian sighed. "He's a corpse. So are *you*."

Jacob gasped. "I am no such thing!" he huffed.

"It's true," Fiona whispered.

Jacob looked down, examining himself. "But that can't . . . that can't be," he muttered.

"That place where you woke up . . . that dark place you had to climb out of . . . that was your grave, Jacob."

The lanky corpse gasped, his giant Adam's apple bobbing up and down. He fumbled at his clothes, lifting his hands to touch his own face, his filmy eyes widening.

"That's why you walked through all those stones tonight," Ian told him. "You woke up in your cemetery plot. But *I* didn't wake you. Something else did."

"I don't like this, Ian," Thatcher said. "Something's not right."

"I should think not!" Jacob agreed.

"And we're not the only two corpses wandering round out there. The others are stirring, too. Could be the whole cemetery. Passed more than a fair share on my way to your door tonight."

Ian's mind was racing. Something was lifting the barrier between worlds. Something sinister was at work. He paced around the room, struggling to make sense of it all.

"How many?" Fiona asked.

Thatcher shook his head. "Hard to say. Lost count around a hundred."

Ian nearly tripped over his own cloak, catching himself before he tumbled into Jacob. *A hundred?*

"More," Thatcher said. "Far more. Stinks of Weavery, if you ask me."

The word hit Ian like a punch to the gut.

Weavery.

Beware what the Moon brings.

This is what Olivia had warned him about. That moon. The green fog. It was carrying something through the air, tainting the ground, waking the thousands of corpses resting beneath the soil. Destroying the very place the Fossors held sacred.

Taking the Dead and thrusting them into the world of the Living, whether they wanted it or not.

He remembered his grandmother's words. She said the rift was thinning. That the balance between worlds would fail, that the two would become one.

She hated the Gravediggers. Ian could see why. But *this*? Resurrecting the entire cemetery? She wasn't just targeting the Fossor family. No, she was attacking everything it held dear—the very lives over which the Gravediggers were tasked with keeping a close watch.

"Thatcher," Ian said, trying to calm himself, "you didn't see her, did you? My grandmother? Did she speak to you?"

The skeleton nodded, the bones in his neck popping. "I

heard her voice," he said. "Just one word: 'Wake.' Then I was up and about."

After herding the group into the dining room, Ian squirmed uneasily in his chair. Thatcher stared at him through those black eye sockets. Jacob looked more worried than ever, nervously glancing at the window every few moments. Only Fiona remained calm, focused.

Ian wished there was someone else who could take charge.

Fiona cleared her throat. "First thing's first. We have to go out there."

"We do?" Jacob asked nervously.

"I don't like it either, Jacob," Ian said, "but Fiona's right. We need to see what my grandmother has done. There must be a way to fix this."

Thatcher nodded. "Reasonable, but dangerous."

"Well, we have to," Fiona said. "It's no use hiding in here all night. The Weavers wanted a fight." She slammed her fist down onto the table. "We'll give them a fight."

Jacob anxiously pulled at his collar. "Can't you just put them back? The Dead, I mean?"

"I can't," Ian croaked. "Not by myself." He felt his cheeks redden. "I'm not strong enough, Jacob. Not on my own."

"But you are," Fiona said. "You can Speak just as well as any Digger. I've seen you."

"It won't be enough," Ian said.

"I'm proof of that," Thatcher said. "Whatever a Digger can conjure with those Words of theirs, the old woman's spell seems to cut right through it." He made a cutting motion with his hand. "Like a knife through butter."

"Well we have to try," Fiona said, her voice rising. "We

can't let them do this to the graveyard." She gestured to the window. "All those poor souls outside . . ."

Jacob turned to Ian, "What do you say, young Fossor? What shall we do?"

"Whatever you need, I'm with you," Thatcher said. "I have a debt to repay. Probably more than I can ever pay back in this life. But wherever this thing takes us, I'm there." He placed a skeletal hand atop Ian's. "You showed me the Great Beyond, Ian. You have no idea how wonderful it is. My parents are there. My friends! Now they're all old . . . older than I'll ever be, but it's still them. You showed me that Death isn't the end. It doesn't have to be."

Ian stared at Thatcher, pulse pounding as he listened to his words.

Fiona took Ian's other hand. "Being a Digger is the last thing you want. We both know that. But tonight . . . just for tonight, you have to be. Bertrum's out there, somewhere. He needs us. And we need *you*. None of us can Speak, Ian. Only you have that power."

Ian measured their words, suddenly finding that he was no longer afraid. With Bertrum missing and his father gone, he was the only one left who stood a chance against the Weavers. The only hope those poor corpses roaming the cemetery had of returning to peace. The only hope of making sure his friends were safe.

"That graveyard is my home," Thatcher said, "but it's not just mine. It's not just for the Dead. It's your home, too."

It took a long time before Ian found the strength to stand, his wound burning like wildfire. Thatcher was right. It *was* his home. He couldn't let it fall into disrepair. He couldn't let his grandmother tear apart the land of his House. After so long, he was realized the only hope they had was for him to become the thing he feared most: a Digger of House Fossor.

"All right," he said, finally. "I'll try."

As Ian went to retrieve his cloak from the study, he saw his father's letter sitting on the side table. Picking it up, his eyes settled on a single line:

Remember, Ian: The Yard is in your care, now.

When he fixed the cloak over his shoulders, he felt like a knight donning his armor. He caught a glimpse of himself in the mirror, sighing at the cloth hanging loose around his drooping shoulders. He fixed the wool cap over his ears, shuddering as his thoughts drifted to what awaited him outside. *Not exactly the bravest knight in the realm, then.*

Fiona was waiting for him in the foyer. "I know you're scared," she said. "I am, too." She studied him dressed in the Digger clothing. "This doesn't have to be who you are," she told him. "Not forever."

"I want to believe that," Ian said. "Really, I do."

"After all this is over, you're talking to your father," she said, "You're coming with me to the Guilds, even if I have to drag you by the ear."

"I know," he said, forcing a smile.

"Are you ready?"

He wasn't ready at all. But he couldn't back out now. Jacob and Thatcher were waiting, watching his every move. They hadn't asked to be woken or to be thrust out into the world of Living without warning, without care or love. He couldn't let them down.

"Ready," he said, hoping they believed him.

Fiona threw the door open.

Ian squinted into the impenetrable green fog before taking the first step to set things right.

Thirteen

The sickly moon hung low as the misfit party made its way to the manor gate. Thatcher took the lead, his bony frame marching, proud and fearless toward the cemetery grounds. Jacob brought up the rear, wringing his hands as he hummed softly under his breath. Fiona slipped her hand into Ian's, tapping her finger gently against his palm. It was the only comfort he felt as they approach the graves.

He felt like he was marching toward his own doom.

"'The Dead are not the Living,'" he chanted to himself. "'They shall not walk above ground, nor breathe the air of mortal men.'"

The rusted iron squealed as the Thatcher swung the gate open. "The others should be just beyond here," he said. "The ones by the forest were the first to rise."

Ian swallowed.

The Dead are not the Living.

They shall not walk above ground, nor breathe the air of mortal men.

The Dead are not the Living.

Please, please let that be true.

Corpses wandered aimlessly through their burial grounds. Ian could only watch, horrified, as they shuffled through the cemetery in numbers beyond count. Some were old, nothing more than bones. Others were not quite skeletons, but not too far off, either, flesh hanging from their faces like strips of tattered cloth, shambling in their grotesquely-rotted burial finery like a attendants at a nightmarish ball. Some wandered alone, others banded together in mismatched groups, their moans echoing through the air in a gut-wrenching chorus of pain.

Jacob pointed to a woman, young and beautiful, her milky white skin glowing in the strange moonlight. "You know her, young Fossor?"

Ian swallowed as she walked past them. The woman paused for a moment. Their eyes met. She looked away and continued on, stumbling her way through the headstones.

"No," he answered.

And it was the truth. Ian realized that, without the name on the stone, he was blind. He looked out at the sea of corpses, strangers, all of them. Names floated through his head without faces to match.

Jacob shuddered. "This is all so very . . . very . . ." The lanky corpse shook his head, "*Eerie.*"

Before Ian could take another step, another woman drifted out from behind a tombstone. She clutched at Ian's arm, her pale fingers colder than icicles as they dug into his skin. "Please, Digger . . ." she whispered, voice strained as if she were choking, "Tell me . . . where *am* I?"

Ian looked into her eyes, which were wide and full of fear. "You're . . . you're in the graveyard," he said.

She looked down at her dress, then touched a hand to her face, shuddering. "This . . . this wasn't supposed to happen," she said, squeezing tighter. "This body is so *cold*! Not as I remember it. Not at *all*. Why am I *here*?"

Ian ripped his arm out of her grasp. His mind raced to find words of comfort.

Because the Weaver cast a spell, he thought. *Because she wants to bring House Fossor to ruin. Because she wants to lay waste to everything we stand for.*

He couldn't say that.

"It will be over soon," he assured her, not entirely believing the words, himself. "I'll make sure of that."

She slowly backed away, her pale face glowing as she disappeared into the sea of corpses.

"Digger!" one called.

"There he is!" a second screamed.

Ian felt as if he were drowning, his breath coming short, chest heavy as the Dead surrounded him, moaning and growling like a pack of feral hounds.

"What *is* this?" one demanded, shaking Ian by the collar of his cloak. His eyes were orbs of pure white, skin gray and wrinkled as ancient parchment.

"Why are we *back*?" another asked.

"The air, Digger! It burns my lungs!"

"These legs o' mine are useless! Rotten flesh can barely carry me weight!"

Ian stepped back, heart racing, as spindly hands reached for him from all sides.

"The Void," they cried. "It spat us out!"

"I need to see my family!"

"My children!" someone screamed.

"My wife!" another wailed. "She needs to know I'm back!"

Ian tried to bat the hands away, but soon they were all over him. The corpses surrounded him like moths to a flame. He was afraid. They were so upset, so unpredictable. Fiona tried to shoo some away, but they paid her no mind. All eyes were on Ian—the lone Gravedigger.

A Digger endures, he told himself.

A dead man pulled him in close, his ghastly face awash in dread. Ian peered deep into his filmy eyes, and suddenly he felt the fear drain from his body. He understood.

They weren't angry. They were *confused*.

Ian looked out at the pack of corpses, flailing and shouting. Torment shone in their eyes. They were just lashing out from fear.

"Ian, we need to get them back in the ground!" Thatcher called, trying to shoulder his way through the crowd.

Ian knew the skeleton was right. He just didn't know *how* to make that so.

His grandmother's words rang in his ears: *That graveyard of yours can use a bit of life.*

His heart raced as he climbed up on top of the nearest headstone, looking out over the sea of the Dead. Lost and scared, each and every one of them. Some stood by their own graves, crying out as they clawed at the names inscribed in the stones. The more hysterical ones began kicking over their own markers, knocking granite and slate to the ground, slowly turning the cemetery to a pile of rubble. Others ran off, dragging their wretched, broken limbs along the ground as fast as they could. Where they were going was a mystery, but Ian didn't suppose *they* knew, either.

He'd always thought of the graveyard as a silent city—a city of sleepers. Of bones. Yet, as he watched the thousands of corpses lurching through the fields and meadows, through the mausoleums and ossuaries, he wasn't sure *what* it was anymore.

So far, the Weaver's plan seemed to be working.

"Come!" he heard one of them cry. "With me! To the village! Let's go home, lads!"

Ian jumped down from the headstone, holding out his hands to try and stop the rush of corpses making their way toward the gates. "No!" he cried.

But it was no use. Ian tried to push them back, but they kept coming. The rest of his band joined him, forming a line to hold the crushing wave of the Dead at bay.

Still, they came.

Bertrum's voice echoed in Ian's mind: *The Dead are dead, and nothing can change that. Mortal life is a gift given only once. It cannot be lived eternally.*

They couldn't go back to the village. He wished they could see that. It wasn't their place anymore. If they tried going back to their old lives, it would set the world of Living awry. The villages and cities outside the graveyard would fall into chaos if corpses began flooding in. The Dead couldn't roam the world of the Living. The Code had to be upheld.

"And the bones of the Dead must return to the earth," he heard himself say. He gripped the obsidian shovel.

I *must return them.*

One of the corpses knocked into Ian, and he fell to the ground, tasting the dirt in his mouth. He tried to reach up and grab a hold of one of the passing Dead, but his fingers slipped through empty air.

A roar echoed across the Yard. Ian flinched. He knew that shout.

Bertrum.

Fiona reached out a hand, helping Ian up off the ground as the group of corpses shambled past them and into the fog.

"That came from the Children's Yard!" she cried.

As the pair pressed deeper into the cemetery, they dodged hordes of the undead, zigging and zagging through the crush. Ian realized he'd never seen so many people in one place, living or dead. It was years' worth of bodies. Decades'. *Centuries'.*

The Dead are not the Living. They shall not walk above ground nor breathe the air of mortal men.

"Ian!" the old corpse shouted. "Thank the stars yer all right! Gimme a hand here, will ye?"

Bertrum was waving to them down from the entrance to the Children's Yard.

The undead children were wreaking havoc. Everywhere, little skeletons were running and jumping, moving so fast Ian couldn't keep track of them all. Some cried out joyfully as they raced around their tombs, leaping off stones and weaving around frost-covered bushes. Ian watched one climb onto the rusted rocking horse leaning against a headstone. He rocked his bony frame, ribs and spine rattling as the ancient toy creaked and groaned to life. Some of the other childish ghouls climbed up onto the taller tombstones, clapping and cheering him on.

"Quite a scene to stumble into," Bertrum growled. "Found these blasted kids on my nightly patrol. Been tryin' to settle 'em ever since."

Ian ducked as a ball whizzed by his head. A tiny skeleton giggled and chased after it, followed by three more.

"I know that one," Thatcher said. "Oswell Barnes. Right little troublemaker."

"The little ones are the worst," Bertrum said. "Overexcited tiny terrors. Can't even grab *one*! They're too wily. Slip outta yer grip like snakes." He pulled Ian in close. "How is it out there?"

"Not good. They're all awake."

Bertrum gave a low, gargling growl. "It's that blasted grandmother o' yers. Don't know what she's aimin' to get from all this mess, but I can tell ye, it ain't good. No way the two of us are goin' to be able to put all these dirt-breathers to rest, and she knows it."

"We're here to help," Fiona said.

"Aye. And I thank ye for it, lass. Honest, I do. But even with the extra hands, so . . . there's just too many of 'em. We need to close the main gates. Keep 'em confined to the grounds. They can't get loose, or we'll never gather all of 'em back. I'd have done it myself, but these little 'uns are impossible to wrangle."

"I'm on it!" She grabbed Thatcher by the wrist. "You're with me. Let's go."

Ian held out a hand, but he was too late, only brushing the side of her skirt as she ran by.

"Be careful!" he called after them.

"Don't worry about us," Thatcher shouted over his shoulder in that singsong rattle. "I'll handle them. Just figure out how to send us back, and we'll call it even!"

Ian watched as the pair disappeared into the fog.

Bertrum rested a meaty hand on his shoulder. "I've sent word to yer father. No tellin' where he is at the moment, but until he arrives, we've got to make do, eh? Chin up, lad. I've trained ye as best I could. But there's no rule for this. I know ye think me to be a stickler for the rules"—he smiled and gave Ian a wink—"but even an old grump like me knows when it's time to break 'em. Life's not all about followin' the same path, after all. Sometimes it's best to stray a bit. That's how we learn *new* rules."

"New rules," Ian repeated.

"Aye, and rule number one: undead children oughtn't climb so high." He pointed up at the gate. A little girl was perched on top of the wrought iron, wavering and wobbling as she clambered along, finally reaching the ledge of the wall surrounding the Children's Yard.

"Hey!" Ian called to her. "Get down from there!"

The little corpse stuck out her tongue. "I don't want to, and you're not the boss of me, Digger!" She gave a sly grin as she turned back to the statues, dancing around them like an acrobat.

Ian watched as she moved closer to the edge. Her foot slid off as she twirled. She yelped and grabbed a hold of a statue, dangling in the air.

"Ungrateful little brats," Bertrum muttered.

"I'll handle it," Ian said.

The girl was giggling as she swung from the statue's wings. Ian bit his cheek as he watched her inch toward the edge of the wall. She wasn't as durable as Thatcher. If she dropped, she'd shatter like glass.

"One more chance," he warned her. "Come on down."

She stuck out her tongue again before pulling herself up and hugging the statue. It teetered from its place on the wall. Laughing, she pushed and pulled at it until it came free.

"Careful!" Ian called out.

Bertrum shook his head. "Don't think she'll listen, lad."

The sound of children's screeches filled the air as he began his climb up the wall. Dew dripped from the cracks in the rock, making it hard for him to get a good grip. He looked down, hoping the little dead girl wouldn't put up much of a fight. Ian hated heights. Luckily, he never had to deal with them. It was much safer to dig below the ground. Being high above it was something new. He pulled himself up slowly, fingers numb as he found his grip inside the cracks of the stone. His stomach lurched the higher he climbed. "Don't look down," he told himself, gritting his teeth. His back ached by the time he finally reached the top, letting out a sigh of relief when he hoisted himself up and over the ledge.

"Come and catch me! Come and catch me!" the girl taunted, hiding behind one of the statues.

Ian steadied himself as he maneuvered toward her.

She was close.

He lunged forward, hoping to snag her before she could scurry away. She darted behind one of the cherubs. Ian grunted. "Please come with me," he begged. "You're not in trouble, I promise. I just need you to come down."

"You can't make me!" She laughed.

"Fine," he said. "Stay up here if you want. All I'm asking is that you—"

Before he could get the words out, a brilliant beam of light flashed in the distance. It was followed by a piercing clap of thunder, shaking the foundation of the wall. It was as though the sky, itself, had broken open. The little girl gasped. Mesmerized, she slowly shimmied over to Ian, grabbing onto his wrist. He was so entranced by the light, it took him a moment to even notice.

"I'm Anne," she whispered.

He smiled. "I'm Ian. Nice to meet you."

She pointed with her free hand. "Look what it's doing to the lake!"

The beam grew brighter, hovering above the black water. Bolts shot from its sides, striking the surface of the lake with loud *cracks*, sending brilliant veins of purple light pulsating just beneath the surface.

"It's so pretty!"

Ian squinted, trying to make out the path of the beam; it was centered over the lake, stretching from the moon all the way down to his mother's tomb, bursting from the spire like a giant torch. Anne was right. It *was* pretty. It may have been the most beautiful thing he'd ever seen.

Or the most terrifying.

"Come on," he said gently. "I think we should get down now."

Anne nodded.

Ian bent down, gesturing for her to climb onto his back. She wrapped her arms around his neck, holding on tight as he made his descent. When they reached the bottom, Ian plopped her down onto the grass like a little doll.

Bertrum was waiting, shielding his good eye, watching the flashing light.

"I have to go there," Ian said matter-of-factly.

"Don't know if that's a good idea, lad."

"She knows what's going on here," he said. "If my mother is awake, she'll know."

"Might be that's true."

"It *is* true. If anyone knows, it's her. It *has* to be. She's one of them. She can stop this. She's faced Weavers before. If my grandmother is free, she can send her back. Use the spell one more time."

"She may not be awake."

Ian watched the green light shoot from the lake.

"What else could that be?"

"You don't want to see her."

There was something in Bertrum's tone that that took Ian by surprise, a certain sadness in his voice.

"I may not want to, but I have to."

"Ye don't have to put that weight on yer shoulders."

"It *has* to be me, Bertrum. You know that."

The blacksmith let out a heavy sigh. "I don't like this, boy. If it were up to me, I'd send ye back to the house and lock ye in yer room. But ye got that look in yer eyes. Been seein' it a lot these last days. Ye never had it before." He leaned in. "Makes ye look older. More *serious*-like." He grinned a wide, lopsided grin. "I like it, though. It's a good fit for ye."

They stood in front of the boathouse. The gray wood was chipping and splitting, half-rotten and latticed with cobwebs.

A heavy chain held together by a big, rusted lock sealed the entrance.

Bertrum took a step toward it, grunting as he reached up and gave the chain a good tug. It fell, coiling on the ground like an iron snake. "Looks like someone got here before us." He gave the door a push. It creaked open slowly. "Best if ye wait out here while I take a look," he said. "Can't be too careful." He disappeared inside.

Ian waited by the door, listening to the old corpse *clang* and *bang* around.

He turned back to watch the light over the tomb, wondering if he really did want to see his mother. A part of him longed for her—longed to see her face, to match it with the memory of her voice. It had been haunting him his whole life. He'd dreamed about what she'd looked like for as long as he could remember. Beautiful, he'd imagined. More than words could express.

He entered the boathouse, ducking beneath hanging ropes and sail canvas, nearly tripping over cracked jugs of paint, piles of rotting lumber, and spools of fishing line. The dank, musty smell of mold and was overpowering. The windows were covered in a thick layer of soot, allowing very little light to pour in as Ian felt his way through heaps of ancient tools and piles of canvas. Bertrum was at the back of the room, struggling to yank something out from under a tarp.

"Here she is, boy. My canoe. Grab hold and give her a good pull."

Bertrum counted back from three and, using all their strength, the pair was able to pry the vessel loose from under its cover.

"Rowboat's missing," Bertrum muttered. He ran a finger along the length of the canoe. "That grandmother o' yers has started a riot out there. Let's get this boat in the water afore she cooks up somethin' even worse."

Ian's legs wobbled as he stepped into the canoe. It bobbed, threatening to overturn. Bertrum steadied the craft as he handed Ian an oar.

"Now it may seem hard at first, but ye get used to it pretty quick." He made the paddling motions with his arms. "Just go nice and slow. Let the boat do the work. Current will carry ye faster than yer arms will. Don't need to wear yerself out."

Ian sat down, getting a feel for the motion of the water. As the waves rolled beneath him and rocked him up and down, he suddenly longed for dry land.

"Row straight there. And no matter what ye do, don't touch the water."

Ian looked over the side, captivated by the pulsing, purple lights snaking around him.

"Don't know what kind o' foul things are in there now." Bertrum paused, looking out at the island. "Ye sure ye don't want me to come along?"

Ian took a deep breath. "No," he finally said. "I have to do this alone."

Bertrum gave a curt nod. "So be it."

Ian plunged the oar into the water.

"Wait!" As Bertrum limped back into the boathouse, Ian waited, clutching onto the oar as he listened to the old corpse bang around the shed. He emerged carrying a heavy object in his hands.

A sledgehammer.

Ian gasped as the blacksmith dumped it into the bow. The small vessel listed from the weight.

"Just in case," Bertrum said.

The old corpse looked Ian dead in the eye. Did he know about the nightmares? Ian had never told him about those dreams.

"Yer father made her that casket from stone. Who's to say she didn't wake? Might be she did. And if that's the case, might be ye want to free her. Only *you* can decide that. But if ye do, I just want ye to know this, lad. Some things are better left in the past. Memories can't be remade. 'S the whole point, really. If they could, they wouldn't be memories at *all*."

With that, Bertrum gave the canoe a great push, shoving Ian out onto the open water.

Fourteen

A biting wind blew across the lake. Ian pulled his cloak tighter around his shoulders. The light burning over his mother's tomb cut through the fog like the beacon of a lighthouse. He rowed faster, filled with a newfound determination. It felt as though he were sailing toward an unknown horizon, a cliff at the edge of the world itself.

On and on, he rowed.

And, for the first time in a long while, he felt completely alone.

He wasn't.

The shadows had returned. They twisted and wound around him, whispering and hissing. He'd never seen them out in the open before. They'd always hidden behind the headstones, or hovered over the mausoleum roofs.

Now they whisked close to his face, spiraling like gigantic bats. He reached up and tried to grab one, but his hand met only air. They were shadows, after all.

The island was drawing closer, looming up from the black water. Ian rowed harder, trying to ignore the shadows' taunts. His wound was throbbing again. The burning sensation flowed from his elbow to the tips of his fingers, searing like boiling tea bubbling through his veins.

A shadow floated just in front of his nose. *AFRAID*, it hissed.

Another dropped down from above, swirling around the first.

HE'S AFRAID.

Then it broke into two. The new wisp circled the canoe like a tattered, black kite. *AFRAID*, it whispered. *AFRAID! AFRAID!*

AFRAID! Another one echoed.

THE DIGGER PUP IS FULL OF FEAR.

LOOK AT HIM.

HE SHAKES.

HE QUAKES.

HE SHIVERS.

Just ignore them, Ian told himself. *Fight through it. They're not real. Only shadows. Only in your mind.*

He kept his eyes trained on the tomb, rowing even harder, struggling toward the green light.

NOT STRONG, they hissed.

NOT LIKE HIS FOREBEARERS.

THIS ONE IS SMALL.

THIS ONE IS WEAK.

HE'S BROKEN THE CODE.

BETRAYED HIS ANCESTORS.
HALF-WEAVER.
FALSE DIGGER.
OATHBREAKER.
"Enough!"

Ian lifted the oar out of the water, wielding it like a battle-ax as he swung it through the air.

"I am no oathbreaker!" he screamed. *"Or a false Digger!"* Another swing. *"And I'm not weak!"*

"I'm Ian!" he cried. *"Of House Fossor!"*

He brought the oar down with a mighty crash, using the last of his strength.

Swoosh! The shadows dissolved as the oar sliced through them, disappearing in a chorus of shrieks.

As he drew close to the island, he spotted the stolen rowboat. It looked as though it had run aground, beached in the stony shallows of the small cove. Ian paddled as quietly as he could, moving slowly until the canoe came up alongside the little boat. He kept alert, scanning the rocky outcroppings for the boat thief.

Nothing.

He rowed the canoe up onto the sand, careful not to touch the water as he stepped out. He could hear the lighting *sizzle* and *pop* as he stalked along the beach.

Across the sand were origami boats. Ten years' worth. They bobbed gently in the shallows, water-logged and half-rotted. Their flowers were long gone. Ian searched for traces of them along the shore, but saw just sand.

He'd only seen the tomb from his bedroom window and the edge of the lake. It had always seemed so tiny, no bigger than a thumbnail. But as he ventured farther into the island, he found himself confronted by a colossal marble structure bathed in the pale glow of the light cast from its spires.

As Ian neared the entrance, he thought that it looked like the front gate of a castle. It should be protected by a moat and guarded by armor-plated knights.

Just a few more steps, he told himself. He edged up to the door, heart racing. His fingers tingled. He could barely feel his legs, and his toes had gone completely numb.

There was a fuzzy tickle in his brain and a tremendous sense of déjà vu swept over him. He'd been here before. He'd spent countless nights crossing the lake to enter this tomb in his dreams. His mother was just a few feet away, right inside that door. All he had to do was walk a few steps and she'd be there.

He gripped the sledgehammer, readying himself for whatever waited on the other side.

Torches burned from the sconces of the tomb walls, casting the interior in a soft, orange glow. Ian's heart raced as he took those first few steps inside, watching the lightning crack behind the stained glass windows. His footfalls echoed in the cavernous room. His mother's coffin sat at the center of the chamber, just as he recalled from his dreams, a gigantic stone square atop a pedestal, torches burning on either side.

His feet crunched on something as he drew nearer. He looked down and gasped. The floor of the tomb was littered with rose petals—white and blue—tens of thousands of them, covering the floor. Everywhere he looked, he saw flowers—his flowers. Some were still in bunches, resting along the pedestal. Others sat on top of the coffin itself. They were tied in bouquets and wreaths hanging from the walls, sitting on the floor in vases. He recognized a few of the arrangements. Ian held back his tears as he took in the blooms, more bright and beautiful than they ever grew in his garden. Every year, he'd watched as the paper boats disappeared across the lake, thinking they floated to simply land on the opposite shore, or fell apart during the crossing. Instead, they'd reached his mother. Each and every one he'd ever picked, ever touched.

As he reached the coffin's side, he hoisted the sledgehammer off of his shoulder. His pulse pounded in his ears as he ran his hand over the cool stone, tracing the name inscribed on the lid.

Elizabeth Fossor. She sleeps now in starlight.

Ian felt the salty tear rolling down his cheek and onto his lips.

His mother's name was Elizabeth.

He'd never even known her *name*.

Ian wished he could go back. He wished he could have done something to stop the Weavers. He'd only been a small baby wrapped in a blanket, too tiny and weak to matter. If he'd been bigger, maybe he could have done something. *Anything.*

It was time to face his fears. Time to banish the nightmares.

Ian took a deep breath as he lifted the sledgehammer over his head. He closed his eyes and gritted his teeth as he prepared himself to take that first mighty swing . . .

A hand caught his wrist. "No!"

Olivia pulled his arm down, letting the sledgehammer *clang* against the marble floor. She looked so much smaller in the tomb, her dark hair frizzy, drooping down from the hood of her soiled cloak. Nora and Clara were with her, both looking equally ragged.

"How . . ." Ian began, unsure if he was seeing things. "How did you get here?"

"We stole a boat!" Clara said.

Olivia jabbed the little Weaver with her elbow. "We didn't *steal* it. We only borrowed it."

Ian looked at his cousin, so worn and weary. Olivia seemed to have shrunk since he'd last seen her last. She didn't seem like the same girl he'd met in the forest, outside that wooden cage.

She seemed . . . frightened.

"She didn't wake," Olivia said, pointing to the stone coffin.

Ian looked at his mother's name inscribed on the slab. Deep down, he knew Olivia was right. If his mother had woken, Ian felt that he would sense it. He so badly wished that she had. There was so much he wanted to say, so much he wanted to know. He closed his eyes and pictured her rising from the granite tomb, feeling a hot tear run down his cheek.

"So many nights I dreamed of coming here," he said to Olivia. "So many nights I wished she would come back."

"I'm sorry, Ian."

He looked into Olivia's eyes and was surprised to find that she meant it.

"Grandmother tried to expel her from the Great Beyond," Olivia said. "But it didn't work. She couldn't find her. Grandmother doesn't know we came here." She nervously dug the toe of her boot into the rose petals on the floor. "We needed a place to hide. I didn't know where else to go, after she told us . . ." Olivia's face twisted up, and tears welled in her eyes.

"After she told you what?" Ian asked.

"*Everything*!" she blurted out, voice muffled by her sobs. "About the spell she's been working. About *you*. That night we took you . . . I didn't know what I was doing. Grandmother ordered me to, so I did. She scolded me day after day, telling me that I wasn't acting like a true Weaver. She . . . she forced me to help her, to work the Dark Weaves." Olivia swept an arm over the tomb. "She said she'd been watching me, said she could see into my soul. She said I needed to change, to become a true Weaver. I didn't know she was doing it to cause all *this*."

"The spell," Ian said. "What is it?"

"Here!" Clara chirped up. She lifted a leather-bound book from inside her robe, and held it out to him.

He ran his hand over the spine, unable to read the markings.

"Open it," Olivia said.

Ian flipped through the yellowed, brittle pages until he saw an illustration of the tied-up Digger being sacrificed.

"Grandmother's never been able to leave that forest," Olivia said. "There was a spell that kept her there. A spell your mother cast, long ago. But ever since Grandmother got ahold of you, the spell's lifted. I took these two and ran. We needed to get out of there. Grandmother . . . she was going to punish me. Punish us."

"Why? What did you do?"

"She knew I was coming to the edge of the woods. That I was watching you, and that I was curious of the world outside. She . . . she said that Weavers have done the same thing in the past—and that they were punished. That they got what they deserved." Olivia wiped the tears from her cheeks. "Ever since she found out about what I was doing, Grandmother's changed. Something in her, something dark and evil seemed to wake. I couldn't stay there anymore."

"Speak for yourself," Nora said. "I didn't want to leave."

Olivia shot her sister a cool look. "Nora took some . . . convincing."

"We had words," Nora said.

"Words?" Olivia lifted a handful of her hair, showing Ian the uneven, singed-off ends. "We had a bit more than words. You tried to take my head off with your Threads!"

Nora folded her arms. "You started it."

"You were right to leave," Ian told them. He turned his attention back to Olivia's book. "Something in here will help?" Ian asked, running his hand over the strange words.

"It should be the next one," Olivia said, gently turning the page.

An illustrated moon glowed up at Ian, and beside it, a swirling vortex was inked in the sky.

"This is what you were trying to warn me about?"

Olivia nodded. "Grandmother's emptying the Void. The Great Beyond, too. I wouldn't have believed it, if I hadn't seen it. Your blood . . . she said it was special. She said it was a *key*. I tried to talk her out of it, tried to reason with her while you were chained, but she struck me and said that if I didn't help, I'd end up just like . . ." Her eyes drifted to Elizabeth's stone coffin.

"Like my mother," Ian finished.

"She'll do anything, Ian. Anything to hurt you and everyone else."

"Emptying the Void?" He thought back to the old woman's words. The green fog, the giant moon . . . *That's* why the

Dead were rising from their graves. The home of restless souls had been shut. Without the Void or the Beyond, there'd be no place for them to go but back into their bodies, thrust once again into the world of the Living.

Nora read from the book: "*Only blood can shift the balance: one part Weaver, one part Digger. This, mixed with the bones of the First Spoken, shall tear the Void asunder and smash the Gates of the Beyond, plunging the world of the Living into the Forever Dark.*"

Forever Dark. The words sent a chill through Ian.

Nora leaned forward, tapping her tiny finger on the page. "That means *you*," she said.

"One part Weaver, one part Digger," Ian repeated.

"The one who's blood is equal parts," Olivia said.

"And the First Spoken was your skeleton friend," Nora added.

Ian closed the book and stared at her. "Why are you helping me?"

Her lips quivered. "Because we're *family*."

The word hung in the air like a thick fog.

"Like I said, Grandmother told us everything . . . about what happened to your mother. About the fight. About our parents. She kept it from us for all this time. I didn't know. I never *knew*." Olivia shuddered, tears streaming down her cheeks as she threw her arms around Ian's shoulders. "I feel sick, Ian. *Ashamed*. All my life . . . the Diggers . . . We were told so many stories . . . so many awful, *dreadful* stories. But when you came into the forest, when you spoke to me, I started to realize . . . it was lies, all of it."

"Grandmother was wrong," Nora agreed.

"Diggers are *nice*!" Clara beamed. "See?" She lifted up

her robe, revealing her knobby knees. "My scrape's all gone!" She pointed to the skin where the pricker had stuck. The wound was healed over.

"She told us that Diggers round up victims for their graveyards," Olivia said. "That they needed to fill their graves with the bones of children. But even when I first met you, I realized that wasn't true." She pointed to Clara's knee. "The Diggers from grandmother's stories wouldn't have done *that*."

"We watched you yesterday," Nora said, "putting that man in the ground. We saw the respect you gave him and his family. You didn't kill him, or eat his bones. I . . ." She struggled with the words, wincing. "I suppose we were wrong."

"Grandmother *frightened* us," Clara squeaked.

Olivia pulled them in closer. "I couldn't keep Nora and Clara around her. They were terrified. The look in Grandmother's eyes . . . it was . . . *horrible*. I couldn't stay in those woods and let her harm them. We had to leave, and I needed to see this place. I needed to make sure it wasn't at all like Grandmother said it was."

Ian realized that he and Fiona were right about Olivia. She'd only done what her grandmother told her to. Seeing her shivering and afraid, clutching her two little sisters, his heart felt heavy, like a chunk of lead slowly sinking in his chest. He didn't want them to live in fear.

They didn't deserve that. No more than Fiona did, or Thatcher, or the countless corpses wandering the Yard. He couldn't sit back and watch everyone around him fall into despair.

"How do we stop it?" Ian asked. "Do you know how to break this spell? Can it be reversed?"

Olivia shook her head. "I don't know. Not yet, anyway. There are things at work, Ian. Terrible things. I saw . . . I saw so many vile . . ." She choked on the words.

Ian placed a hand on her shoulder. "What?"

"The Underrealm," she whispered. Nora and Clara both shuddered.

Ian felt his whole body grow cold, as if he'd suddenly plunged into the Void. His father had told him about the Undderrealm just once, long ago. No one could *see* the Underrealm. He didn't think so, at least. It was a horrible place. The home of demons, of eternal night. A breeding ground for wickedness and nightmares, the deep, dark lair of evil souls unfit for the Great Beyond. The Diggers had no dealings there.

"She summoned the beings there," Olivia said. "Those nasty, evil *creatures*. They . . . they rose from the ground, out of that cauldron she used when she cut your . . ." Olivia hugged her arms across her chest and closed her eyes. "I . . . I couldn't bear to watch."

Ian couldn't believe what he was hearing. Even with black magic, the Underrealm was a dangerous, nearly impossible place to reach. If his grandmother had found a way to go there . . .

"We have to stop her," he said, slinging the sledgehammer over his shoulder.

"How?"

Ian racked his brain for an answer, but found he had none. It seemed like the entire world was falling apart. If the Void was emptying, the balance would be destroyed. All those restless souls with no place to go . . . the Gates of the Great Beyond had broken. The gates of the Underrealm, too.

Spirits both good and evil would descend upon the world of the Living.

"I don't know," he admitted. "But if there's a way, we'll find it. *Together.*"

"If we're going to do something, we'd better hurry," Nora said. "Grandmother's not one for wasting time. Not anymore."

The three Weavers moved to the entrance of the tomb. Ian hesitated, turning back to his mother's coffin.

He gazed at her statue resting atop the marble, up to her delicate, peaceful face. He rested his hand on top of hers, wishing that he could touch her warm skin, not a cold, stone carving. Still, even so, he felt close to her. Closer than he'd ever been in his life.

"Mother," he said, "I don't know if you can hear me. I don't know if you can see me from where you are. But I want you to know that I came for you. I . . . I wanted to see you. I love you. If you should wake, Call Fiona. She'll hear you. And if you need me to, I'll free you from this tomb. Even if it takes everything I have." He knelt down, resting the side of his face against the cool marble. "I wish you were here, Mom. I need you. People are depending on me, but I don't know if I'm strong enough. If you can hear me, please . . . tell me how."

He waited in silence, surrounded by magic torchlight and bright flowers.

"Ian," Olivia said softly, "we need to go."

He picked himself up, gently placing one of the flowers on top of his mother's stone hands.

"Someday, I'll see you," he whispered, stroking her marble cheek. "I'll make things right. I promise."

"The plan," Fiona huffed. "What's the *plan?*"

The group huddled among the headstones clustered near the manor gates, sharing worried glances and wild theories. Bertrum kept a wary eye on the three young Weavers, though Ian had explained everything and already told the old grouch to behave. It had taken a while, but Bertrum had finally agreed to let them stay, as long as they stayed where he could see them.

"We *should* be hunkering down," Thatcher said. "Go inside the manor . . . Fortify ourselves. But does anyone listen to me? No. Of *course* not. Why would you? No, let's all just stay here, out in the open, like a gaggle of geese, ripe for the plucking."

"Mind your tongue, lad," Bertrum said, puffing on his pipe while he sharpened his blades with a stone. "Give us a moment to think, eh? All yer blabberins' givin' me a right headache."

No one spoke. They sat, looking warily out into the fog. Waiting.

Ian watched Olivia. She was shaking, knees pulled up to her chest.

"What's wrong?" he asked.

"I can feel Grandmother's Weave. It's leaving the forest. It's . . . it's coming to the graveyard."

Bertrum cast a wild eye to the distant trees. "What are we expectin', lass?"

"I don't know. The spell she was working on, I'd never heard anything like it before. I couldn't understand the words. It was like some other language. Something old. Ancient."

"Well *that's* reassuring," Fiona said.

Thatcher scoffed. "Yeah, I don't think she'll be stopping by for a *friendly* visit. She's cookin' something up, alright. Only it's not honeycakes, that's for certain."

"If she *does* come, I'll try my best to stop her," Olivia said.

"Me, too," Nora said. "Grandmother showed me the Dark Weaves." She cast an apologetic look at her sisters. "She said I had a talent for them. It may not be much, but we can put up a fight if we have to."

Bertrum glanced up from his sharpening stone, looking at the tiny Weaver in surprise. "Good to know," he said. "We got us one warrior in a small package, at least."

Ian stood and stepped into the circle, arms clasped behind his back.

"Well?" Bertrum asked.

"The first thing we'll need to do is gather the Dead," he said. "This curse woke them, but there's no telling what will happen next. Grandmother could have other plans for them."

"But how?" Fiona asked. "There's too many of them."

"The lass has a point," Bertrum said.

"We could group them together," Nora offered. "Corral them into a single spot."

Thatcher bristled. "They're not *cows*," he snapped. "They're *people*."

"I don't think she meant any disrespect," Jacob muttered. "And she *does* have a point. Young Fossor can't chase each one of them down single-handedly."

"Won't work with just one o' you, lad," Bertrum said. "One Digger, *hundreds* o' Dead."

"Thousands," Jacob corrected.

"Well there has to be *some* way," Fiona said, stamping her foot.

"Aye," Bertrum muttered. "And by the sound of it, it won't be nothin' good."

Ian turned to Nora. "You're the strongest Weaver we have. Anything you can do to help gather them?"

Nora frowned. "Even if I tried, I'm afraid it wouldn't work. The Weave Grandmother cast is strong. I won't be able to do much unless she's weakened."

Ian pulled his cloak tight around his shoulders. He'd secretly hoped his father would have returned to save the day, or that his mother would have woken to tell him what to do. But as Ian paced in the fog, he realized that no one was coming to save them. He was their only hope.

"There is one way," he said, finally. As soon as the words left his mouth, he fell silent, casting a nervous glance toward the graveyard.

"Well?" Thatcher prodded.

"*Hush*," Olivia said. "Give him a chance to think."

Ian cleared his throat. "Before anything can be done about the Weaver, our first priority has to be the Dead. They *must* be handled, and handled with care. Now I know I'm the only Digger . . . but there are more in this graveyard." He pointed to the Fossor Family Crypt, its warped spires rising from the fog like a demon's horns.

Fiona shot him a worried look. "Ian . . . you're . . . you're not thinking of . . ."

"I am."

"A Digger's never woken another Digger," Bertrum said, his gravelly voice barely above a whisper "Ain't never been done. Even in the most dire of times, it's—"

"*This* is a dire time," Ian urged. "Trust me. I understand what I'm proposing may be dangerous, but if we have any hope of setting things right, my ancestors *must* be woken. I know it's against the Code. But we're desperate. I . . . I can't fix this by myself. The Void and the Great Beyond need to be restored."

Bertrum frowned. "Resurrecting that many at once—"

"Will be hard, I know." Ian sighed. "It scares me, too. Honest, it does. But there's no one else." Ian turned and pointed to the forest. "And it will be the last thing *she'd* expect. She thinks we're frightened and weak. Let's see how she feels when there's an *army* of Fossors at our backs."

"Well," Bertrum said, sheathing his ax, "I'll not stop ye. Things'll be dangerous no matter what we decide, I reckon."

"I wish it didn't have to come to this, but . . ." Ian looked at Fiona. "I'll need your help. To resurrect so many at once, I'll have to Speak the Words through a Voicecatcher."

"I'll do it," she replied.

"I know you will. We can do this." He turned to Bertrum.

The blacksmith stood to attention, limbs snapping into place.

"While we're down there, I'll leave the defense to you. Keep Thatcher and Jacob close. They're your charges, now."

The old corpse threw up a meaty hand in salute.

"Need to fetch the rest of my weapons from the manor," he said. "We'll start fortifying the doors and windows so none of the Dead get in. I'll meet ye back here once yer done."

Finally, Ian turned to the girls. "Olivia, Clara, Nora. I'll need you with me. I don't know what we'll run into down there. I may need you to cast a Weave, something to protect us. Can you do that? We'll need to be brave. *All* of us."

Olivia wiped a stray tear from her cheek. "We'll do our best."

Nora gave him a long, searching look. "Everything in my power, Digger. It's yours."

"We're with you!" Clara chirped.

A cold chill swept through Ian's bones as the small band tiptoed into the Fossor Crypt.

Fiona lit the torches, slowly illuminating the room. In the center was an enormous opening. As Ian peered in, he saw a huge circular cut in the stone floor. The upper level of the crypt sloped down, forming a walkway that spiraled down as far as he could see.

"We have to go down *there*?" Clara asked.

"I don't like this," Nora said. "This place is invested with magic. *Old* magic. I'm not familiar with it."

The air grew cooler and more damp as they descended. Ian breathed in deeply. It was the familiar comforting mineral smell as an uncovered grave. Fiona stopped every few feet to light another torch, slowly summoning the passage to life.

Above each torch was a painting of one of the Diggers and, under each picture, another rule of the Digger's Code. Ian gazed up at a picture of Ishmael Fossor the Sailor, the Digger who made the long journey across the seas. He was standing on the deck of a great galleon, hand resting on the ship's wheel, eyes fixed on the horizon. Underneath him was the fourth rule: *The Dead are dead, and nothing can change that.*

Once they descended farther down, the engravings ended and unadorned torches lit the way. Ian was no longer sure just how far down they'd traveled. With every step, he'd grown more nervous. He wasn't sure he was ready to meet his ancestors. It was a strange idea, and yet he felt as if they'd been around him his whole life. They *had*, in a way. Their portraits covered the walls of the manor. Their eyes had always looked down on him from on high, constant reminders of his inevitable fate.

But the thought of seeing them in the flesh made him feel uneasy. They'd be paintings and stories and history come to life. *People.* He felt a weight on his chest—the weight of history and tradition.

His breath came rushed and shallow at the thought.

When they reached the bottom of the spiraling walkway, they were in a long, stone tunnel. Ian lifted a lantern sitting beside the wall and lit it with the last torch. He held it up high so the rest of the group could see the path forward. Droplets of water plopped down on his head, splashing into pools of moss and mushrooms sprouting from the cracks in the earth.

The tunnel stretched for what seemed like miles. He tried to picture the cemetery above, wondering just how far they'd traveled. They must've been under the Children's Yard by now. No. Much farther. Maybe the Flower Gardens. They'd been walking so long, perhaps they were near the edge of the forest.

After a while, they stopped before another iron gate. Ian raised the lantern to read the words mounted there:

HERE LIE THE DIGGERS OF THE HOUSE OF FOSSOR. LONG MAY THEY REST IN PEACE.

Ian swallowed.

Well, he thought, *their long rest is about to get a bit shorter.*

He handed each of the others a torch as they entered the crypt, praying that they'd find the help they needed.

The crypt was the most magnificent thing Ian had ever seen. The ceilings stretched up at least fifty feet, painted black with white, silver, and golden stars. He grew dizzy looking at them, a swirling series of constellations glowing in the darkness. For a moment, he forgot he was a half-mile beneath the earth. Throughout the room, obsidian pillars rose, so large he wondered how they were even transported down to the chamber. Yet even the majesty of the painted ceilings and stone pillars paled in comparison to what he saw resting in the middle of the room.

Coffins everywhere. Some sat in rows along the floor, some on raised platforms. Others rested in carved shelves inside the walls. Each one was crafted from gleaming black obsidian, almost wet-looking in the torchlight.

Ian edged closer to the nearest one and saw that it was more of a sarcophagus, carved to look like the Fossor resting inside, his ancestor's calm stone eyes staring up at the stars above.

One day, in the distant future, his own face would be carved into one of these coffins, and it would be *his* body lying inside.

Ian felt like he was looking into his own grave.

The largest of the coffins was in the center of the room, beneath an enormous statue of Ingmar Fossor. Ian cringed just looking at him, a mountain of a man, imposing in his armor, one arm resting on the hilt of a deadly-looking sword. Ian considered what Ingmar would say to him in that moment, a small boy cowering in fear. He needed to steel himself, if he were going to go through with the plan.

"All right," he finally said. "Everyone, gather around." He motioned for them to form a circle in the center of the crypt. "We'll need to join hands," he told them. "The bond needs to be strong, and it will take all of us working together to hold it."

Ian stood between Olivia and Fiona. The Weaver hesitated a moment before taking her cousin's hand.

"It'll be all right," he told her, noticing the doubt in her eyes.

"I'll need to reach out to all of the Fossor spirits at the same time," Fiona whispered. "I don't know if we'll be able to do this, Ian. It's going to be very difficult. It's like . . ."

"Like trying to see in the dark," he said. "I know. You can do this. Keep your consciousness open. As I Speak the Words, let them flow through you."

The circle tightened. Ian's palms were soaking wet as he held on to Fiona. He watched as the Voicecatcher's eyes rolled up into her skull as she tapped into the essence of the Void.

Ian took a deep breath before launching into the Words. "Fathers, I have traveled deep, and I have reached you. Hear me now, ancestors. I seek your help and your guidance, and have journeyed down from the land of the Living. With these words, I give you breath. With these hands, I give you life. Never before have I sought you. Never before have I begged for your aide. Yet now that time has come. Rise and speak now, Fossors of old, for your descendant is in need. Let my words guide you. Emerge from your slumber and walk among the Living once more."

Ian's world went dark as he flung himself into the Void, only this time, it looked different. Lights flickered in the swirling black, spiraling like lightning bolts on the waves. He felt like a leaf floating in the eye of a hurricane. He reached out to the light, hoping to grab onto something to steady himself. But before he'd even gotten his bearings, the torchlight of the crypt returned. He was splayed out on the cold, stone floor.

A penetrating silence had fallen over the room. It was as if all sound had suddenly been sucked out. Fiona's eyes returned to normal. The young Weavers were shaking.

"What happened?" Olivia asked. "Did you see them?"

Fiona's eyes went wide. "I saw them."

Ian perked up. "And did they hear?"

"They heard."

He waited nervously. Watching. Listening.

Clara fidgeted. "Are you sure it worked?"

Ian gazed out around the Crypt, looking for signs of life. He found none.

"Something should have happened by now," Fiona said. She turned to Ian. "Right?"

He held up a hand. "Listen," he whispered. "They're awake."

A low rumble echoed through the Crypt. It was quiet at first, but soon grew deafening. The ground shook. Fiona and Ian tumbled against each other. Olivia steadied herself against one of the pillars, her face turning a deathly white, while Nora and Clara clutched onto her legs, terrified.

The sarcophagi wobbled and shook as the obsidian lids crashed down to the floor. One by one, the Gravediggers of old emerged from their graves.

Ian watched, transfixed, as they slowly sat up in their coffins, shaking the centuries-old dust from their black cloaks. The first few stepped out into the crypt, stretching out the limbs they were using for the first time in ages.

Many of them were tall, like his father. Some were gaunt, others muscular like oxen, and still others were tubby, heavy in the midsection and squat. He spotted Iago Fossor, with his giant gut and flabby chin. And there was Imbert, tall and skinny as a stork. The Gravediggers came in all shapes and sizes, he realized. Yet there was one thing they all shared: their hair, all snow-white.

Ian was amazed at how perfectly preserved they all looked, as though they'd only been hibernating. He'd expected some of them to look like Thatcher—little more than bones. Or Jacob, at least. He saw Ishmael still wearing his captain's hat. The tails of his black coat dragged on the floor as he plodded across the chamber on a wooden leg. Strings of white hair dangled from beneath his cap, framing his wind-worn face.

Isaiah the Scribe stood beside Ishmael. He was much shorter than the rest of the clan, slightly hunched, with rounded shoulders. He was draped in a black robe, his spindly, paper-white hands clutching a quill and roll of parchment. His inquisitive eyes shifted around the room like a nervous hawk, rapidly taking in his surroundings. Ian took comfort in how fragile and frail he appeared, far less imposing than the other Fossors.

Ivan the Builder came next. He looked like more of a bear than a man. With the burly arms bursting through his torn, black vest, Ian could easily picture him wielding a hammer and saw. It was said that no mortal man could build structures faster and more beautifully than Ivan. Then Isidore approached. Known as the Painter, he was the one responsible for most of the portraits. His cloak had presumably once been black, but as he stepped into the torchlight, Ian noticed that it had been flecked with paint, turning it into a brilliant, multicolored smock. Even his white hair was caked in the stuff, the white mixing with every shade of the rainbow.

The crypt was suddenly alive with the Diggers of House Fossor. Hundreds of them, some whose names Ian remembered, others who appeared as total strangers. They formed a circle, towering over him like trees. From every direction eyes stared down at him. Ishver's eyes. Ibrahim's eyes. Ivan's and Igor's. Ilion's and Isidore's. The reanimated Fossors quickly filled the room that had seemed so massive just moments before.

Fiona leaned in and whispered Ian's ear, "Is this all of them?"

He scanned the room. The Diggers stood there, silently waiting. Only their eyes moved. Ian struggled to read their expressionless faces.

He was about to speak when the assembly of Diggers slowly parted—one by one, the Fossors stepped aside, the shuffling of their cloaks resounding through the tomb like a gust of wind. Each one suddenly knelt, the sound of their knees *thudding* on the stone floor sending vibrations underfoot like an earthquake.

It wasn't until the last row moved aside that Ian saw who they were making way for. Ingmar Fossor's hand reached up from his sarcophagus. Ian jumped as the gauntlet shot up into the air, clenching into a tight fist. The ancient Gravedigger climbed out and began his clanging march down the steps.

He was bigger than the stories made him out to be. *Much* bigger. Ian always thought his father was the tallest man he'd ever seen. The tallest man who ever *lived,* maybe. But Ingmar stood well over eight feet. Towering wasn't even the word. *Terrifying,* more like. His face looked exactly like it had in his portrait: cold, gray eyes; gaunt cheekbones; strong jaw; long, thick hair tumbling down to his shoulders like a lion's mane; a curled mustache draped over a pair of thin lips, which were straight and unmoving. He was clad in a suit of black armor with silver chainmail that rattled as he walked. He didn't look like a Gravedigger—Ian couldn't picture him shoveling dirt. He was a warrior, through and through. A long sword hung from his belt, the blade glinting in the torchlight, etched in the same runes that decorated the Diggers' shovels.

Ian knelt as Ingmar stopped before them, pressing his hand to his forehead in the Digger's greeting. He motioned for the others to do the same. Then the great knight folded his arms across his chest and stared down at the miniature Digger and his terrified companions.

"Rise," he said. His voice was the deepest Ian had ever heard. The force of it shook the ground like thunder.

Ian shot up to his feet.

"Ian," the ancient Gravedigger boomed.

Ian nodded, swallowing nervously.

"Long have we watched you from Beyond. A good lad, and true." Ingmar paused, gesturing with a sweeping motion around the crypt. "But tell me . . . who has summoned us? We heard the Words of Resurrection."

Ian glanced nervously at the other Diggers as they leaned

in, waiting for his answer. His heartbeat pounded in his ears, louder than war drums.

"It was me," he said.

Ingmar's brow furrowed.

"*You?*" Iago snapped.

Isaiah jumped. "You've Spoken? But . . . but you're so young! *Much* too young . . ."

"His gift shouldn't be strong enough," Isidro said. "Not yet."

"I should say!" Ivan roared.

"It's true," said Fiona, jumping to Ian's side and squeezing his hand. "I helped."

Ingmar turned a cold eye on the Voicecatcher. Both children froze, unsure what the Father of Diggers would do next.

Without warning, he shot out his arm and snatched the hood off of Ian's head.

Another round of gasps echoed through the crypt as the Diggers glimpsed Ian's pure white hair.

"It . . . it can't be," Isaiah whispered.

"He's just a child!"

"A Novice!"

"How could this have happened?!"

"So soon!"

"It can't *be*," Isaiah repeated.

"Enough!" Ingmar thundered. He knelt before Ian, placing a gauntleted hand on his many-times-grandson's shoulder. "We've felt a disturbance," he said. "The Dead have been restless of late. The Netherworld teems with despair, the Void steeped in turmoil . . . the Great Beyond plagued in confusion. The souls of the Dead cry out as one. Tell me, what evil has befallen our Yard?"

"A curse," Ian answered.

Isaiah the Scribe teetered forward, nervously tapping his quill against a rolled-up scroll.

"A curse?" he asked excitedly. "A curse of what nature? Perhaps I've heard of it. . . . I've studied several . . . No two are ever the same . . . Always a solution. Always!"

"Here we go." Isidro sighed. "Calm your nerves, Isaiah."

"Let him speak!" Ingmar thundered.

"A curse is a curse is a curse," Iago mused, his enormous belly jiggling as he spoke. "And all curses can be lifted." He snorted. "If it *is* a curse, that is."

"What is the nature of this one?"

Ian hesitated, taking time to choose his words carefully. "The Dead have risen. All of them." He pointed up toward the domed roof of the crypt. "Listen!"

Silence fell as the Diggers lifted their heads up to the ceiling, listening to the faint footfalls rumbling above.

"Hmm," Isaiah muttered, tapping his quill on his chin. "The Dead rising from their graves . . . a powerful magic . . ."

"Weavercraft," Iago spat. Imbert and Isidro nodded in agreement.

"I know the coven," Isaiah said.

"Aye," Ivan the Builder growled. "That dreaded family in the forest."

"A powerful family," Isaiah mused.

"They should have been dealt with long ago," Iago said.

"It wasn't our fault," Nora said, stepping in front of her sisters with a defiant glare.

Ivan and Iago stared at the girls.

"You've brought them here, into these hallowed halls?" Iago shrieked. "*Weavers* entering the Fossor Crypt . . . Where is your brain, boy?"

"This isn't their doing!" Ian said.

"Oh, but it *is*," Iago said. "A good many things would have been different if the Weavers had been banished swiftly. But *someone* decided to make that blasted pact." He shot a look at Ibrahim.

Ian didn't like Iago's tone. He could see why Thatcher didn't care for him. Or Bertrum, either. Iago the Disagreeable—he was certainly living up to his name.

Ian felt ashamed. He was half-Weaver, after all. If his blood hadn't been used in the spell . . .

"Yes, yes," Ingmar said. "I've heard of these Weavers from many of you. Curious that none of *you* ever attempted to do anything about that problem, save for our Isaac. Hear me, Iago: Bravery is more than talk. Talk is nothing more than hot air. Now is the time to *act*."

Ian breathed a sigh of relief. At least someone was on their side.

"Tell me," Isaiah said, unfurling one of his many scrolls. "Do you know the details of this curse, young Ian?"

Ian thought back to his captivity in the woods. His arm still burned where the dagger had pierced his arm.

"It's all in here!" Olivia said, holding up the book.

The Father of Diggers stared down at her with those intense gray eyes as Isaiah snatched the tome from her hands.

"Oh, my!" the Scribe muttered, nose buried deep in the musty pages.

Iago lumbered forward. "Ian Fossor? I still can't believe the whelp's actually *Spoken*." He grabbed ahold of Ian's wrist, slowly lifting his arm. "These arms are still skinny. Legs like a chicken. Can you hold a shovel, boy?"

A few of the Diggers laughed.

Ian felt his cheeks burning. He looked up at his ancestor, unsure what to say. With everything he'd been through, he didn't feel like he needed to prove himself. Why did they have to be so cruel? What did *they* know? They'd been asleep for hundreds of years. Sure, they were family, but it didn't give them the right to judge him so quickly. He could feel the anger boiling up inside, and he was ready to burst.

Ian ripped his arm from Iago's grasp. "I've wielded the obsidian shovel of my father, Isaac Fossor. I've used it to Dig, and to Speak. My arms are stronger than you might think."

Another Digger stepped out from the group into the light. Ian recognized him immediately— Ishver, his grandfather.

"Ian," he said, voice filled with warmth. "Come closer, my boy. Let us have a look at you."

Ian took a few apprehensive steps toward the old man. Ishver smiled and patted him gently on the head, his gloved hand sweeping through the white-flecked hair.

"He's Spoken. There's no mistaking it." He beamed. "I always knew our little Ian would surprise us. I wasn't sure when, and I wasn't sure how, but I always knew it would happen."

"Aye," Iago spat. "And I don't think the surprises will end there. The boy's *blood* is tainted. His mother's side is to blame." He pointed a fat, sausage-link finger right at Ian's chest. "And if you ask me, *he's* the cause of all this mess. Diggers and Weavers aren't meant to marry. A union like that is bound to produce a failure. Anyone who knows *anything* knows this."

"Hold your tongue!" Ingmar snapped.

Ishver frowned. "A child is never to blame for his parents, Iago. Am *I* to blame, for letting my son marry the girl he truly loved? Is *Isaac* to blame for that old crone's actions? Is *Ian* to blame for being born? No. I gave my life fighting for this boy. Isaac lost his wife fighting for this boy. Ian lost his mother. The old Weaver is cruel, I'll grant you that. And powerful beyond words. But this is not Ian's doing."

Iago slowly slunk back into the crowd.

Ishver bristled. "How old where you when you first Spoke, hmm? Eighteen? Or was it twenty? How old were *any* of you when you learned to Speak? Far older than this young Digger, I can tell you. His gift is strong in him. Little, yes. Scrawny, a bit. But he's still a Digger, through and through. A *Fossor*. And we should listen to what he has to say."

Ian froze as every eye in the crypt focused in on him. "I-I was with her," he stammered. "Th-the Weaver . . ."

He told them everything: about Speaking to Thatcher for the first time, about chasing him into the woods, about meeting his Weaver cousins he never knew existed, about their autumn spell. He told them what it was like to be trapped in the cage, and about his grandmother's shack. How she'd pierced his arm with the dagger and collected his blood in a chalice. The smoke and the smell and the look in her eyes as she cast the spell. About Bertrum coming to save them and the green fog and the beam over his mother's tomb. He told them of the Dead rising from their graves like a decaying tidal wave and of the chaos of the Void as he floated through the stormy abyss.

By the time he finished, Ian was exhausted. He stood there, knees trembling as the Diggers gaped, captivated by his story.

"Curious," Isaiah said finally, and to no one in particular.

"Now you see why we need your help," Ian pleaded.

Ingmar folded his arms. "A Digger's blood is powerful. In the hands of a Weaver, there's no telling how terrible it can be."

"She means to destroy us," Ian said. "I heard her say so myself."

"And she may have," Ingmar answered, smiling mischievously, "if you hadn't woken *us*." He turned to address the rest of the Diggers. "All right, you lot. It seems we're going to have a long night ahead of us. We've got a Weaver to stop."

"The Dead must be dealt with first," Ian said.

The father of all Diggers nodded gravely. "Yes. The Dead will find rest, Ian. Don't you worry about that. I've longed to Speak these past thousand years. It will be good to hear my own Voice again. The Void must be repaired if those souls are to sleep once again. Lead the way, young Fossor."

Fifteen

The Diggers spread out across the graveyard. Their black cloaks made them look like dark clouds as they swept through the headstones, intent on wrangling the wandering packs of the Dead.

Ian watched his ancestors from the front steps of the manor, impressed with how they managed to round up thousands of corpses with so little effort, gentle shepherds directing their wayward flock.

Yet even as the Diggers of old moved about, gathering the Dead, the green fog drifted over the graveyard, rank with the sick, slimy feel of Weavery. With the Void and the Great Beyond in disorder, there would be no rest for the souls. Not until the balance was achieved once again.

Ian saw Imbert leading Jacob away. The young Digger

was sad to see the recently-deceased corpse go. He'd developed a soft spot for poor Jacob. But it would be better for him to be laid back to rest. He'd be safer in his coffin, six feet under the ground. And he really wouldn't have been much help fighting the Weaver, anyhow. At least Ian could relax a little knowing that at least *one* of his friends was now out of harm's way.

Bertrum stepped out of the manor door and growled, his eyes fixed on the woods. Ian noticed his hand wavering near the ax on his belt.

"It'll be all right, Bertrum. We have help."

The blacksmith's eyes stayed fixed on the trees.

"Don't be so sure, lad. A whole army can crumble before a single Weaver, if she's strong enough."

Ian cringed. Those weren't the rousing words he was hoping to hear. As he looked out at the forest in the distance, a loud crack of thunder echoed through the sky. Bertrum grabbed onto Ian's shoulder as a dark vortex began to swirl overhead—a black hole gaping next to the green moon. The air grew bitingly cold as the black mass grew and grew, until the moon, itself, disappeared.

"Grandmother!" Olivia cried. "She's finishing the Weave!"

Ian shielded himself as frigid gust of wind followed, blowing so hard, he feared the trees would be pulled up by their roots. The hunting hood flew from his head.

"Bertrum!" he called over the deafening *whoosh*.

The old blacksmith grimaced as one of his ears blew off in the wind, tumbling across the grass and out of sight into the fog. "Blasted Weaver!" he cried, touching his hand to the hole on the side of his head. "Ye'll have to speak up, lad!"

One by one, the stars flickered out.

"It's the Void," Ingmar called, eyes narrowing. "She's brought it into this world. Never have I seen such trickery."

"What does it mean?" Ian asked.

Ingmar shook his head. "With the Void here, this realm is vulnerable. It can be warped, used. Destroyed, even. The Weaver can do with it as she pleases."

"We can't let that happen!" Ian cried over the roar of the wind.

Ingmar drew his sword. Ian jumped back as the obsidian gleamed in the green light.

"No," the Father of Diggers said. "We cannot." The ancient Digger leaned in close, his lips pressed up against the blade of the sword. He whispered softly to it. Ian moved closer, curious to hear his ancestor's words, but wind was so strong, Ingmar's voice was drowned out. As he spoke to the blade, the engraving began to glow. Bright, archaic runes, just like the ones on Ian's father's shovel. They flickered and blazed like the embers of a great fire, orange and yellow, cutting through the fog.

One by one, the other Diggers appeared through the fog, gathering around Ingmar. Ian looked on in awe as they each lifted their shovels, holding them high above their heads. The sky blazed as the shovel's runes ignited around the ring like a trail of wildfire.

They hummed in unison, their low, rumbling drone slowly cutting through the shrieking wind. Ian felt a warm, soothing sensation flow through his body as he listened, and while the vortex still swirled overhead, the winds died down. The only sound left was the gentle Diggers' song.

"Ian," Ingmar said, "come, raise your shovel and join us."

The other Diggers all turned their attention to him as

they held their glowing shovels high in the air. Ian's gaze traveled around the circle, moving from one pair of ice-gray eyes to the next. "Me? But I don't have my own."

"Here, lad," Bertrum said softly, limping over with Isaac's shovel.

Ian looked down at it, wrapping his fingers around the handle. His arms were shaking. The shovel was just as heavy as before, and even heavier than the sledgehammer in his mother's tomb.

Bertrum kneeled down, resting a hand on Ian's shoulder. "Listen to me, lad. They need ye, now. Just as ye need them. They're working an old magic, here. The Digger's Storm."

Ian looked into Bertrum's good eye, then down at the obsidian.

"An ancient power," Bertrum said. "Never covered it in yer lessons, son. Never got that far. It was done once, long ago when all the Gravedigging Houses fought together."

"I can't," Ian said, awkwardly hefting the shovel. "I'm not like them . . . not truly."

The corpse smiled. "I know, boy. But they're yer family. Yer *blood*. Sacrifice, Ian. It's about *sacrifice*."

"We need a living Fossor to complete the circle," Ingmar called. "Come, Ian. You must add your strength."

Ian looked over at his ancestors, then up at their glowing shovels, flashing like a hundred stars.

"Go," Bertrum said. "I'll take Fiona back to the manor. Make 'em proud, eh? Make *me* proud."

Ian nodded, trying to quiet his nerves as he marched over to take his place with the rest of the Fossors.

He saw the gravestones standing solemnly in the fields beyond the manor gates. Those thousands of restless souls,

236

terrified and lost, trapped in a world where they didn't belong. *I'll do this for them*, he told himself. *All of them. If this curse is to end, I'll be the one to end it. Even if it scares me to death. Even if it means giving up on my dreams.*

"Raise it high, now," Ingmar instructed. He hoisted his sword above his head. "Do as I do."

Ian followed the command, sweat pouring down his face as he lifted the shovel high into the air. His muscles ached and burned, and his knees buckled as he struggled to keep the obsidian high.

Ian listened, then joined his voice to theirs. As he hummed, the warm sensation came back. His arms stopped trembling. The butterflies were gone. Suddenly, heat burst from his fingertips. When he looked up, his shovel was glowing, just like the rest. He watched, awed, as the engravings flickered and danced across the black stone, glowing like rubies in the moonlight.

"Recite after me!" Ingmar thundered. "*Where darkness lingers, let light shine. The Balance must be struck! Let thy light pour forth, and cast the darkness into night. The Balance must be struck!*"

Ian joined in the chant, the Diggers' voices melding as one.

"Aim, now," Ingmar cried. "With me!" He pointed his sword toward the vortex, and with a great thrust, he sent the beam of light screaming toward the sky's wound. The other Fossors followed, and the giant beam careened into the Void's darkness. It sizzled and cracked through the swirling blackness, flashing against the nothingness. Slowly, the vortex grew smaller.

"It's working!" Ishver cried.

Ian's hands began to burn as he clutched the handle of his shovel. For a moment, he thought he smelled his own flesh burning. The pain was becoming unbearable, as if it was draining his soul.

"I can't hold on!" he cried, but no one could hear him over the roaring and crackling of the light.

As the Diggers continued their work, the Void began to pulse deep, menacing red, casting its bloody glow over the graveyard.

Ian held on as tightly as he could, cheeks burning as a biting wind blew down from the opening in the sky. He struggled against the howling wind, trying to keep his balance as it threatened to blow him away.

The days of the Digger are over!

His grandmother's voice boomed inside his skull, pounding against his eardrums like the clarion blast of a trumpet. He nearly dropped the shovel. His head pounded and muscles wrenched as though he'd been struck by lightning.

Ian closed his eyes and saw the old Weaver's face, as clear as day.

"The Void will be shut," she hissed. *"And the Great Beyond is next. There will be no rest, Ian. No peace. Every soul thrown to the pits in the Underrealm, and the Diggers will naught but watch!"*

Ian opened his eyes and realized the handle of his father's shovel was glowing bright red, like metal in Betrum's forge, burning through his gloves and singeing his skin. Before he dropped it, the obsidian blade of the shovel shattered in a brilliant flash of green.

The Diggers of House Fossor were thrown to the ground as the Void thundered and roared, swelling even larger in the sky, spinning and swirling.

Ian tumbled to the grass. Sprawled out on his back, head pounding, he watched the obsidian shards of his shovel shower down around him like black snow. He reached out a hand and touched a fragment as it drifted down, feeling the stone turn to ash on his fingertip. His spirit sank as he watched the remains of his heirloom sizzle and burn, completely destroyed. His father's shovel . . . the sacred tool Isaac had crafted with his own hands, burnt to ash. Ian knew how much his father loved that tool, how much he depended on it, almost as if it were an extension of himself.

And I'm the one who destroyed it.

He closed his eyes, fighting the urge to cry.

"I wasn't strong enough, Dad. I wasn't strong enough!"

"Ian?"

The voice cut through the darkness, soft and familiar.

Ian opened his eyes and saw his father standing over him.

"You're . . . you're back," he whispered, unsure if he was dreaming. Isaac was a half a world away, far from the troubles of the graveyard. He couldn't be here now.

Perhaps I'm dying, Ian thought. *Perhaps he's just a dream.*

Isaac knelt beside his son. "I'm back," he said, resting a hand on his Ian's arm. "I came as soon as I received Bertrum's letter." He looked to the ash pile, then to the splintered handle of the shovel.

Ian sat up, his head still pounding from the blast. "Dad, I'm sorry, your shovel, the Yard, I—"

Before he could finish, his father grabbed him and held him in a warm embrace. Ian felt Isaac's chin resting atop his head. He could feel his father sobbing as he pressed Ian's face to his chest, holding him tighter.

"You've nothing to be sorry about," Isaac said, taking

Ian's head in his hands. "A Digger's shovel is precious, but not more than his *son*."

He knelt down in front of Ian. "I'm the one who's sorry. For leaving. For not telling you the truth. For . . . for keeping so much locked inside all these years. Forgive me."

Ian looked into Isaac's smoke-gray eyes, finding that they were filled with pain. He hugged his father again, burying his head in Isaac's broad shoulder.

"It's all right," he said, through his sobs. "I understand, Dad. I understand."

They embraced for a long time. Ian didn't want it to end, but Isaac finally stood.

He ran a hand through Ian's hair. "You've been busy."

Ian's heart pounded. There was so much he wanted to say. So much he wanted to explain.

Isaac smiled and offered him a hand to help him to his feet.

"Isaac!" Bertrum stomped forward and pulled Isaac into a great bear hug. "Ye were sorely missed," he said, then nodded to Ian. "The lad's done well. Ye should be proud."

Isaac returned the blacksmith's embrace. "I am," he said. "More than you know."

The other Diggers gathered around them, dusting themselves off. Isaac watched them, then turned to Ian. "You've led them this far," he said. "Lead them now."

Ian looked up at his father, finding himself lost for words. *Me?*

All this time, he'd prayed for Isaac's return. For his father to come and save them all.

"Dad, I can't. I'm . . . I'm not like you."

Isaac laid a hand on Ian's shoulder. "No, you're not. You're stronger than I ever was. Braver than I could ever hope to be. You're *better*." He gestured to the other Gravediggers. "We're all with you."

"I don't know where to go," Ian said. "I'm not a warrior like Ingmar."

"The manor gates," Isaac said. "Lead them there. It's a good place to make a stand. I've seen the way they look at you. Their eyes shine with pride. They'll follow you, Ian."

Ian nodded, turning to his ancestors. When he spoke, he found his voice more firm and powerful than it had ever been. "With me, fathers. To the manor gates!"

Isaac pulled Ian in close as they marched to the manor, gesturing to the tomb across the lake. "I'm sorry I never told you about your mother," he said. "All this time I thought I was protecting you, but I can see now that keeping her such a secret did more harm than good. That was unfair of me. You have no memories of her. I'll regret that forever. But I'll tell you all about her. Once this curse is lifted . . . once things get back to the way they were. Bertrum told me about the conversation you had." Isaac sighed. "You deserved to hear it from me, first."

"It's all right, Dad. I know how hard it was for you. You just needed time."

Isaac clenched a powerful fist. "I should never have let your grandmother escape to the forest. I thought the spell your mother cast on her would protect us. She didn't think your grandmother would ever be able to break it." He pointed toward the trees. "But it seems even that wasn't enough.

"I've let this go on far too long. She means to hurt us, Ian. She means to bring our House to ruin, to destroy everything we stand for, everything we hold dear in this world." Ian looked up at him, watching as his gray eyes burned in the moonlight. "But tonight, it ends. We can't let her harm our family any longer."

Ian felt a deep sense of relief wash over him as he listened to his father's voice. Maybe they did stand a chance. His father would know what to do. He always did. For as long as Ian had been alive, there'd never been a problem that Isaac Fossor couldn't fix.

"We can do this, Ian. Together, we can stop her."

As the group marched toward the manor, a cry ripped through the silence.

"Someone, help!" Olivia screamed.

Ian raced ahead and found Fiona convulsing in the young Weaver's arms, her eyes rolled up into her head, skin pale as milk. Olivia gently dropped her onto the grass, gasping as the Voicecatcher flopped around like a fish out of water.

Ian kneeled down next to her, trying to keep her steady as he pawed through his satchel trying to find something to help her.

"What's happening?" he cried.

Olivia took hold of Fiona's face. She gently pulled beneath the Voicecatcher's eyes, looking deep inside. "She's having a vision."

"What kind of vision would do *this*?"

"She's communing with Grandmother," Nora said, gently running her fingers down Fiona's cheek. "Grandmother's in Fiona's mind, infecting it like a fever." Nora cringed. "I don't want to know what she's seeing right now."

Fiona's body wrenched, arms and legs bending in ways Ian didn't think the body could bend.

"Shhh," Olivia cooed, stroking her hair. "It will be okay. You have to fight it, Fiona. Listen to my voice. Follow it. Follow the sound."

Fiona's eyelids flickered as Olivia spoke. Ian bit his nails.

"Back away," Nora said, rolling up her sleeves. She traced patterns through the air, the tips of her fingers pulsing with light. "Grandmother taught me these. Weaves that can stop someone from entering your dreams." Her fingers fluttered around Fiona's head. "I've never used these before. Hold on."

Muttering something under her breath, Nora traced a pattern just above Fiona's forehead. The web of light grew bright, igniting like flame, gold and nearly blinding. Nora stood, took a deep breath, and shouting a word in a language Ian couldn't understand, she swiped her hand down in a slapping motion. The web of light sank down, pressing into Fiona's forehead.

Fiona screamed as the Threads made contact with her skin.

Ian reeled. They seemed to be burning her.

"It's not working!" Olivia cried. "Nora, get rid of it!"

The little Weaver whipped her hands through the air, drawing both hands toward her body as if pulling an invisible rope. Slowly, the web of light began to fade before finally disappearing from Fiona's skin.

Nora shook her head. "I don't know what else to do."

Ian felt the panic rise in his chest as he watched his best friend writhe in pain. "How long will it last?"

"There's no telling," Olivia replied. "Once Grandmother gets inside your head, it's hard to get her out." She jumped up and grabbed onto Fiona's face with both hands. "Listen to me!" she shouted. "Leave her alone. Get out! Come and face *me* if you want to hurt someone, you hear? LEAVE HER ALONE!"

Ian's mind raced as he sifted through medicine after medicine. There had to be something he could do.

He rummaged frantically through the satchel until his hands grasped the wide clay jar nestled in the bottom. He lifted it out and gave it a shake, listening to the powder sift inside.

"This might do it," he said.

"What is that?" Olivia asked.

"It's called Watchman's Dust, a powder made from ground black salt crystal. Magic may not have an effect, but maybe this will."

You always wanted to be a Healer. So Heal.

"Take two pinches and put them in each nostril," Ian said. "Not too much, or her heart may stop."

"You think it will get Grandmother out of her head?"

"I don't know," Ian answered. "But I do know that it's very potent. Healers use it to bring people out of comas. Usually when people go into shock, they lose consciousness. Watchman's Dust acts as a stimulant. It should snap her out of it, I hope."

He upended the satchel and looked from vial to vial until he found them: nurnroot and foxfrost. He gathered his mortar and pestle, dumping the contents of the vials into the stone bowl and grinding them until the leaves and roots were a thin, flaky powder. He steadied his hands, trying not to tremble as he poured the mixture into an empty vial, adding water from a leather bladder until the mixture swirled inside.

"More medicine?"

"Nurnroot and foxfrost," Ian said. "It should keep her body temperature down. The Watchman's Dust will give her a great deal of energy, and that could be fatal. This will balance things out."

He grabbed the last object he needed: a glass tube with a plunger affixed to one end. He carefully poured the medicine into it, then looked up at Olivia.

"I'll need you to open her mouth."

Olivia did so, prying until Fiona's lips parted and her mouth hung open. Ian leaned forward and placed the glass tube inside, pressing the plunger with his thumb. The medicine shot out in a steady stream. Olivia tilted Fiona's head back, allowing the medicine to go down.

"Please work," Ian whispered.

He leaned forward and blew hard into Fiona's nose. The two pinches of salt shot into her nostrils.

Suddenly, Fiona's body jerked. Her eyes popped open as she sprang upright, pupils small as pinheads. She let out a loud groan. Ian breathed a sigh of relief, gently cradling the back of her head before setting her back down on the ground.

"Easy," he said. "You're all right, Fiona. You're back."

"Is she going to be okay?" Clara asked nervously.

"Let her be," Olivia said. "Best to give her some space." She looked up at Ian. "You have a gift," she said. "You were able to save her when magic couldn't."

Fiona closed her eyes and seemed to fall back into a trance. Olivia shot Ian a worried glance.

"It's okay," he told her, pressing his finger to Fiona's wrist, feeling her pulse. It was fast, he felt. Too fast.

As Ian moved his hand from her arm, Fiona clutched her throat and sat up, gasping for air. "No!" she screamed.

Olivia threw her arms around her and rocked them gently back and forth.

"It's all right," she said. "She's gone now. It's over."

Tears slid down Fiona's cheek as she struggled to catch her breath.

"Child," Isaiah said, taking a few sheepish steps toward her. "What did you see?"

Fiona looked up at him. Ian cringed when he saw her eyes. Those emerald eyes that had always been so full of fire were now filled with fear.

"Death," she whispered, before collapsing back onto the grass and staring up at the sky. "She showed me the world, Ian. How it will end. How the Underrealm will rise and swallow us whole."

Ian knelt down next to her.

"She won't hurt us," he said. "I won't let that happen. Ever." He handed her a small jar of green liquid. "Take this," he said. "It smells like moldy frogs' legs, but it'll calm your nerves."

Another tear slid down Fiona's cheek.

Ian brushed it away with his sleeve. "It will look better in the morning," he whispered. "Everything looks better in the morning. Remember?"

Dark clouds blotted out in the sky as everyone gathered at the gates of the Fossor Manor.

Bertrum growled as he looked to the woods.

"Things may get bad, lad. And if they do, I need ye to stay behind me. We'll make our stand here. If Dehlia gets this far, I need ye on the other side of this wall, ye hear me?"

Ian looked back at the house. "I want to be out here with the rest of you. I *need* to be here."

"I think it's best to do what Bertrum says," Isaac said. "Take the girls and keep them safe."

"If it's all right with you, Uncle, we're going to stay," Nora said.

Isaac looked down at the tiny Weaver, studying her with a curious gaze.

"We can fight," Nora added. "And you'll need Weavers to defend against her spells."

"I'd keep 'em close," Bertrum agreed. He gestured to Nora. "Especially that little sprite."

Isaac pondered his words for a moment before nodding. "Very well," he said to the girls, "but I want to keep you as safe as I can. We Diggers will attack first, should it come to battle."

"We'll do our best to cover you," Olivia said.

Bolts of lightning flashed and cracked over the woods.

Clara tugged on Ian's sleeve. "She's coming. *Grandmother's* coming."

Ian watched as the lightning bolts danced over the trees.

"Be brave," he said to her, trying his best to keep calm.

As soon as he said the words, he saw her.

Off in the distance, a figure in white emerged from the woods. Barely a speck on the horizon, Dehlia grew larger as she approached, walking slowly—calmly. Ian tried to keep his breathing even as headstones shattered and mausoleums toppled in her wake, ignited by the bolts cast down from the sky.

The Weaver halted only a few yards from the gate. A final burst of lightning rippled through the sky, burning out over the horizon like a blood-soaked comet.

"Now," Bertrum grunted over his shoulder. "Close to me, lad." He motioned to the girls with his ax. "Get ready, all o' ye. It's time."

The air grew colder as the old Weaver stood there, pale as death in the moonlight.

Isaac took a few steps forward. "That's close enough."

Ian watched as Bertrum marched up next to his father. The rest of the Diggers formed a loose column at their backs. Olivia, Nora, Clara, and Fiona kept watch from the sides of the group. They began to work their Weaves, sparks sizzling at their fingertips.

Dehlia smiled.

"We had an agreement," Bertrum said. "Each family's to keep to their own side o' the wood."

"Agreement?" the old woman snapped. "I recall no agreement. I recall a spell, cast to keep me trapped. And I've grown tired of sitting idly by."

"Why?" Bertrum asked.

The Weaver threw her head back and cackled, though it didn't quite sound like laughter. The noise made Ian shudder. She pointed to Olivia. "I have my reasons. Her, for one. Just like her aunt." Her long, crooked finger then landed in Ian's direction. "And him. Young Ian. Oh, how my Olivia so wanted to follow him." Her eyes hardened. "You'll be the first, young Digger."

Isaac shook his head. "There'll be no more blood spilled here."

The Weaver eyed him as though he were a fly in her stew. "Blood calls for blood. I've waited long enough, Isaac Fossor. I've bided my time. I've been bound to those woods for longer than I could stomach. Years. *Ten* years I've languished, and while you've lived on, I've done nothing—*nothing*—but sit, and think, and wait . . . and watch."

"I've lived on?" Isaac said. Ian could hear the rage building beneath his father's voice. "I've *lived on*? You think it's as simple as that? No, Dehlia. I've done anything but. You took everything from me that night—"

"I didn't take *everything*. Your son lives . . . or are you so enamored with your Digging that you hadn't noticed?" She smiled. "Your son for my daughter. Even trade."

"You'll not touch a hair on his head," Isaac said, his voice dangerously low. "Think of what you've already lost. Your daughters. *All* of them. Isn't that enough? What is there to gain?"

"Revenge," Dehlia spat. "Revenge for their lives. Revenge for all you took from me when you lured Elizabeth out of those woods. Ten years ago, to the night. Did you know that, Digger? Ten years since I lost everything I held dear. She was happy before she left. She could've had anything. Anything she desired. Our family was strong. And now . . . now, my own granddaughters seek to leave me. They've been tainted by your ways, the fools!"

"Elizabeth wanted to leave. It was her choice. And your family *was* strong once, but not anymore. You made sure of that. Your grandchildren have found safety here. They've found peace. Something your daughter always wanted."

"My daughters died because of *you*. Because of your family. This isn't just for them. All those years ago, you Fossors pushed us out. Banished us from our land, swept us deep into those woods. We were here, once. In the fields and meadows. Out in the sun, beneath blue skies. Voicecatchers, working side by side. Not the things you forced us to become. Not trapped in seclusion like animals."

"Your ancestors made a pact with evil!" Isaac thundered. "They desecrated the bones of this Yard to work the Dark Weaves. They chose their path. They chose to worship the dark of the Void, the black depths of the Underrealm. You had a choice. You could have stopped. Any one of you could have *stopped*. *That's* why Elizabeth left. She saw there was more joy in good than in evil. More happiness in light than dark. Now your granddaughters have learned the same. And if you think I'm going to let you come here and hurt the people I love, then you're even more blind than I thought."

The Weaver shook her head. "No, Isaac. I'm neither blind, nor weak. I've simply learned from my mistakes. And I won't make the same ones again." She paused. "I wanted to thank your son, too. Without him, I wouldn't have found the strength I needed."

Ian winced as the wound on his arm began to burn.

"But it will all be over soon. Maybe I'll take you first, Isaac. First the father," she said, motioning to Ian. "Then the son. Then . . . everyone else, I suppose. I really have no use for them."

Bertrum threw his crutch aside and raised an ax. "One more step, Weaver," he growled. "Take it. I dare ye to."

The Weaver pursed her lips. "Oh, come now, Bertrum. Don't threaten me."

She took a step forward.

Before her other foot touched the ground, Bertrum let his ax fly.

Ian gasped as the blade sailed through the air faster than

he could blink. He steeled himself, preparing to see the Weaver cut down.

She raised a hand, and it froze in midair, hovering just inches from her face.

With another flick, the ax disappeared in a black puff of smoke. A moment later, a bat emerged from the acrid haze, screeching toward Bertrum's face. He tried to swat it away, but it was too late. Ian watched in horror as the winged creature sank its claws into the blacksmith's neck. Bertrum fell to the ground.

Isaac sprinted to his side.

"I've grown weary of you, blacksmith. Sometimes, I wonder why I didn't do this all those years ago. The thought of keeping you around entertained me, I suppose." Dehlia's lips curled in a twisted grin. "But my amusement has grown stale. I no longer care for the taste."

Ian watched as Olivia's whole body began to shake. "This isn't right," she said, fuming. "They can't stop her. No matter what they do, it won't be enough." She took a deep breath. "I can't let her do this. I've sat back and watched her my whole life. I'm sick of it." Ian tried to grab her, but it was too late.

"Olivia, no!"

"I have to, Ian. You keep safe."

She ran past the rows of Diggers, stopping just short of where Bertrum lay.

"Grandmother!" she called.

The Weaver turned. "So," she said, "you've run into their arms, and the world's all right, eh? It's been done before. They won't keep you safe, you know. They can't. Your aunt thought it was a good idea. Things ended badly for her. And for your mother, as well."

"Aunt Elizabeth was right to do it," Olivia said, her voice hard like stone. "I see that now. All my life, you've taught me to hate these people. But there's nothing to hate. It was all a lie. *Your* lie."

"I suppose you feel brave, don't you?"

"I don't know what I feel," Olivia said. "But I know one thing, Grandmother. I'm strong. We all are. You made sure of that."

Dehlia laughed. "Don't pretend, child. You're afraid. I can see it. I can *smell* it. You reek of it."

"That may be," Olivia shot back. "But how I feel doesn't matter. This has to stop!"

"And you're the one to stop me, hmm?"

Olivia nodded.

"Us, too!"

Nora and Clara joined their sister, wild Threads of light flowing around their bodies like spiraling rope.

"This has been coming for a long, long time, children. And if you think that you're strong enough to so much as *bruise* me, you really haven't learned anything at all."

"We've learned enough, Grandmother," Olivia said.

Nora raised a hand, illuminated with purple light. "All those books. All those spells. I've memorized each and every one of them. I can Weave the Threads just as well as you can." She smirked. "Maybe better."

"Stupid girl. There are things in this world you don't understand. Things that can't be found in any *book*. You think I'd really be so stupid as to teach you everything?"

Ian steadied himself on Fiona's arm. He wished he knew some kind of spell or trick, something to stop them before they destroyed themselves. He didn't doubt his cousins' bravery. He worried about his grandmother's strength.

Ian watched the Weavers position themselves, the webs around their bodies growing in size and brightness until he was nearly blinded. The Fossors had all stepped back, giving the girls space.

His grandmother moved her hands through the air, her long, slender fingers working as though she were a spider spinning her silk. A red light began gathering at her fingertips, growing larger the faster she moved her fingers, pulsating and flicking like flames.

"*NO!*" a voice thundered from the darkness.

Thatcher came bounding out from behind a headstone, his skeletal frame sprinting at the Weaver.

"Leave them be!" He stopped between them. "If you want to hurt someone, hurt me."

"Even the *dead* boy is feeling brave!" The Weaver laughed. "You're all full of such surprises." She narrowed her eyes, then raised her arms. The red light grew so bright that Ian had to shield his eyes. "Be gone!"

The light shot from her fingertips in a extraordinary flash. Thatcher cried out and tried to jump away, but it was too late. The blast shattered him; ribs and vertebrae rained down upon the manor grounds.

Thatcher's skull rolled across the grass. Ian watched, horrified, as it came to rest at his feet. The empty eye sockets looked up at him. "Well," Thatcher's head remarked, "I tried."

Ian picked up the skull and held it up in front of his face. Even in pieces, Thatcher still looked like he was smiling.

"This is a bit embarrassing," the head quipped, "don't you think?"

"Thatcher . . . why?" Ian asked.

"Just doing my part. You stuck your neck out for me. Figured I'd return the favor. Looks like I mucked it up a bit. Should've planned more. But I was never much for plans, really."

Ian sighed as he crouched to rest Thatcher's skull down alongside the stone wall. "You did your best, Thatcher. More than anyone could ever ask. You're . . . you're a good friend."

"Better late than never," the skull replied. "Debts have to be paid."

The Weaver edged closer to Olivia. Thick, black tendrils emerged from the palms of her hands, curling through her fingers like smoke.

Olivia took a step back as they wormed their way toward her. She bent down on one knee and clasped her hands together as if she were praying. Ian saw her close her eyes and whisper to herself. As her lips moved, a bright light formed a perfect orb around her body.

At the same time, Nora and Clara joined their Threads together until a massive cord of light rose into the air, flying at Dehlia like a gigantic whip.

Dehlia's web grew around her like a shield. Clara and Nora's whip crashed against it and vanished.

Dehlia cursed under her breath. She shot her hands out once more. The smoke serpents multiplied, writhing toward Olivia in tangled groups, shrieking with a sound like nails scratching against slate.

The light around Olivia grew brighter, a searing white. The first serpent struck it and burst into mist. But they kept coming, one after another, their shrieks echoing across the graveyard. Finally, one broke through the light's defenses and wound its way around Olivia. She cried out as it twisted around her waist. Two more lurched out and wrapped themselves around her arms, tying them up behind her back.

Nora worked golden Threads through the air, forming them into the shape of eagles. The magic birds soared into Olivia's protective shield, clawing at the serpents. Yet more and more appeared, strangling the massive birds, taking them by their wings and dragging them down, screeching.

Olivia fell to the ground as the smoky tendrils enveloped her, until she was completely buried under their weight.

Ingmar sprang forward, sword drawn, his ancient battle cry thundering through the night. Still, the old Weaver was too fast. With the flick of a wrist, Ingmar's sword disappeared in a glittery *poof*. He skidded to a halt and looked down at his empty hands, eyes widening in confusion.

Black smoke rose from the ground, gathering around his ankles and taking the form of a hand. The long, skinny fingers clenched around his boot and gave a powerful yank, sending the Gravedigger sire plummeting down. Ingmar reached into his boot and withdrew a dagger. Gritting his teeth, he slashed at the shadowy hand. It released its grasp before disappearing back into the ground.

The Gravedigger picked himself up and brushed the dirt from his armor.

"You'll need worse than that to stop me, Weaver."

The old woman laughed demonically as she raised her hands up to the night sky. She pointed at the moon, her eyes suddenly turning a horrifying shade of red.

More tendrils shot from her palms. Ian cried out as they shrieked toward his father. Ingmar moved to block their path.

"Here!" Isaac shouted, throwing his ancestor a shovel.

Ingmar caught it and planted his feet, wielding the shovel in front of himself like a spear. With a mighty swing, he knocked the tendrils away. They exploded in a smoky mist.

The Weaver grinned. "I should have destroyed that cursed shovel long ago, when I had the chance."

"There'll be no more chances," Ingmar replied. "House Fossor will stand."

"We'll see," she hissed. "There are some things you can't slash and dig your way out of."

The lightning returned in a fiery blaze, scorching the earth around Ingmar's boots. The ground shook, then slowly began to splinter and crack, until it split open. Ian watched, horrified, as tombstones sank into the ground. All around them, as the earth crumbled away, trees and rocks fell into the ever-expanding pit. A gigantic crater had opened before Fossor Manor, gaping like the maw of some terrible beast.

Then a red light sprang from the charred dirt near Ingmar's feet. It flowed up around the Digger, forming into a dome of sizzling energy. He swung at it with his shovel, but the obsidian cracked against it before bouncing back.

Olivia's face went deathly-white as she gazed into the pit. "The path to the Underrealm," she whispered. "You've opened it. Freed it upon this realm. Grandmother . . . how could you?"

"Unspeakable, Weaver!" Ingmar thundered from within the confines of his light prison. "To bring such darkness to this world. You've cursed us all! Do you not see?"

The rest of Diggers backed away from the pit as screeching, long-limbed demons began clawing over its edges—misshapen, gruesome things, like living shadows stitched together.

Ian and Fiona took shelter behind the manor gates. Ian tried to make out the creatures' faces, but only their eyes and jagged fangs shone in the evening gloom. They weren't like the shadows he'd seen all those late nights before in the graveyard. They were monstrous and wretched, beings of the Underrealm, made up of complete darkness, bred to destroy.

As they heaved themselves from the ground, the shadow creatures multiplied, lurching their way forward like a nightmarish army. Ian got a queasy, sick feeling as he watched them drawing nearer.

Isaac stood defiant before the shadow hordes. The other Diggers took their places beside him, forming a long, unwavering line. Ian wanted to join them, but Nora and Clara were clutching at his cloak, trembling. He couldn't leave them behind.

"This is where it ends!" Isaac called, his voice hard as stone.

"No," the Weaver said. "This is where it begins."

The creatures of the Underrealm surged forward in a rush of smoke and shadow.

"What's happening out there?" Thatcher called out.

Ian went numb. He felt the cold sting of fear in the pit of his stomach, that horrible sensation that had become all too familiar. His nightmares had become real, after all. The shadow creatures were almost at the manor gates. He covered his ears as they screeched, high-pitched and terrifying.

The shadows crashed against the line of Diggers, breaking over them like churning waves against rock. The Diggers fought against them, kicking and punching through the ever-thickening black cloud.

Nora and Clara shot magnificent beams of light from their palms, Threads that formed into a rain of golden arrows that screamed down from the sky and plunged into the demon hordes. Many of the creatures dropped, pierced by the young Weavers' barrage, yet they still advanced.

Dehlia laughed, calling more creatures from the abyss.

There were simply too many, Ian realized. Even with every Digger from House Fossor standing firm, they would never be able to push back the Underrealmlings. "A Digger fears no darkness," Ian whispered to himself.

Yet, even as he spoke the words, he realized that that's all they were: *words*. Silly words. And as he repeated them, they seemed to lose all meaning, twisting into a jumble of sounds. He didn't even know why he continued saying them. As he felt the darkness creep in, he finally understood that no words would save him now.

And the darkness was stronger than ever.

Sixteen

"Now," Dehlia said, almost to herself, "where is he?"

The Weaver made her way through the charred battleground, packs of shadow demons following in her wake. She approached the manor slowly, sidestepping the Diggers on the ground, pinned by her Threads. Iago tried to shout at her, but as soon as he opened his mouth, a shadow hand flew out from the darkness and covered it. Imbert tried to kick out at her, but smoky talons held him firmly in place. Ingmar could only look on, helpless and trapped from inside the sizzling dome.

Clara and Nora lay strewn on either side of Olivia, all three trapped under the writhing smoke serpents.

Ian was still frozen behind the gate.

"Ah," Dehlia said, "there you are. I thought you might

have run off. *Brave* boy." Her smile twisted into something sinister. "*Stupid* boy."

A beam of light shot out from her hands. Ian lifted an arm to shield himself, knowing it would be of little use. Her beam enveloped his body. That was a relief, at least. He'd been sure her plan was to make him explode into a million pieces like Thatcher. But he felt only warmth, like butter melting on a piece of toast.

Slowly, his body lifted off the ground.

"To me, now," she said.

Ian rose higher, his body drifting out of the gate and into the cemetery-proper. He tried to grab the bars as he passed them, but his fingers slipped off like the metal was coated in grease. He slowly drifted along, feeling like a prisoner being carried toward the executioner's ax.

Packs of demons gathered below, howling and hissing wildly as Ian floated just out of their reach.

"Ian!"

A hand shot up out of a tangle of smoke. It passed through the light rays and grabbed hold of his ankle. Ian felt his body stop in midair. The old Weaver tugged at him like she was working a lasso, but she couldn't draw him any closer.

Ian looked down and saw his father's face emerge from writhing shadows.

"Listen to me, Ian," Isaac choked, "You're the only one left."

"I can't do this alone!"

"I know," Isaac coughed. "You won't have to." He held out his hand. "Take it."

Ian struggled against Dehlia's pull, reaching out to clutch his father's hand.

"Your mother," Isaac said. "Think of her. The song. The one she sang to you. Do you remember it?"

"Dad . . ."

Isaac's hand slipped away.

"The song!" he cried. "Remember the song!"

Ian's watched as his father disappeared back into the dark smoke. He closed his eyes, trying to picture his mother's face. And as he did, fear gripped his heart like a vice. *I'll see her soon*, he realized. *This is the end.* Once he reached his grandmother, he'd be dead. Soon, he'd see the Great Beyond for himself . . . if there still was a Great Beyond left to go to.

Ian began to hum his mother's lullaby. He'd always heard it in his head, but he'd never actually voiced it before. Now, the melody poured from his lips. As he sang, a warm rush of energy floated through his chest. His mother's voice flowed through him strong and full, alight with love.

"That song," he heard his grandmother hiss. "What is that *song*?"

Before Ian could reply, his entire world vanished in a blinding flash of white.

He found himself in the middle of a glade dappled in pale, hazy sunlight. The grass beneath his feet was soft and bouncy, and when he looked down, he saw that it wasn't green, but silver, with light reflecting off the blades as they swayed in the breeze. Dotted throughout the clearing were white trees—too white—completely smooth and shiny like ivory. Strange, beautiful flowers blossomed from their branches, bright pinks and purples, and wooden charms laced in garlands of pine and painted gourds. Even the smell of the air was strangely different, inviting and comforting, like a beloved relative's perfume.

"Ian . . ."

The voice lilted through the clearing like a song. That same voice he'd heard every night in his dreams. The voice he swore he'd never forget.

A woman emerged from behind one of the trees. Ian stared as she approached, taking in her face, the face he could never remember and had only seen that brief night in the tomb, carved in stone. Her skin was dark, like Olivia's, not the milk-white he'd conjured in his dreams. Her nose was slightly bent, and beneath it was a mouth with thin, almost blue, lips. Her cheekbones were very hollow, almost as deep set as her mismatched eyes, one blue, one green. Charms of pine cones, feathers, and pieces of carved stone adorned her black, oily hair.

She wasn't the perfect beauty of his dreams, Ian realized. She was *more*. Of all ways he'd imagined her over the years, nothing compared to the beauty that stood before him, a wild beauty, imperfect and perfect all at once.

"Mom," he said, barely able to get out the word.

"I've waited for you for so long." She wrapped her arms around him. Ian felt his knees go weak. He thought he might cry. And laugh. For the first time in his life, he felt complete. For just that moment, everything seemed to be right.

"I can't tell you how happy I am to see you here," she said. "You've followed my song. I've been watching you."

Ian looked up at her. "You have?"

"I sang it for a reason, Ian. I knew I wasn't long for the world. I sang it so you'd find me."

She smiled. "Let me show you." She led him through the clearing, gently running her fingers along marble-white branches as she swept between the trees before stopping at a small pond, ringed in flowers. The water was still, like silvery ooze—not even a ripple danced across its surface. Ian thought he could walk on top of it, if he tried.

His mother bent down at the pond's edge and pointed, beckoning him nearer. "Look closely. See what I've seen."

Ian took a step toward the edge. He thought he would see his own reflection. Instead, he saw himself as a small boy, running through the graveyard with Fiona. They laughed and tumbled and rolled in the fields and meadows, leaping over the headstones and chasing each other through the flower beds.

"See?" his mother said. "You've always been with me. And I've always been with you."

She bent down and ran her hand over the surface of the water. It rippled only once, and the images faded and changed.

Now Ian was slightly older. He was standing at the lakeside with his father and Bertrum, pushing the paper boats out toward his mother's tomb.

"I've loved those flowers," she said. "That was a very sweet thing to do."

"I saw them in your tomb," Ian said. "None of them died."

Elizabeth Fossor nodded. "As long you carry me with you, they never will."

Again, the image faded. Ian watched himself picking plants from his herb garden, then placing them in the mortar and pestle to make his salves.

"You have a great talent. And a kind heart. A Healer's qualities."

"I wish I could have been there, that night," Ian said. "I wish I could go back in time, look after you when you were sick."

His mother pointed to the silvery pond. "I live in the past. That's my burden, Ian. But you don't have to. The future is wide and endless. You'll get plenty of chances to set things right."

With the wave of her hand, the water rippled and the image faded once more. Ian looked down and saw he and Fiona sneaking through the graveyard and digging up Thatcher.

"Now this wasn't a surprise," she laughed. "You were always so curious. You get that from me, you know. I never learned to be 'proper.' Not the way your father meant. I have too much of the woods in me. You always had a touch of mischief. Even as a baby, I knew you had it in you."

"I do?"

"A mother can sense those things. It was the way you looked. Your eyes. They were always on the move, so big and filled with wonder." She laughed softly, "I'd try to show you the secrets of Weaving, you know. I'd trace patterns of gold Threads above your crib, and you'd laugh and laugh, trying to reach out and touch them." She grinned. "Your father never wanted me to show you such things, but what he doesn't know can't hurt him. You're my son, too. Just as much a Weaver as a Digger."

"I can't Weave, though," Ian said, confused.

"That's why you're here, now. Your grandmother will never stop, Ian. Not until everything that's good in your world is charred and black and broken. I won't let her do that to you." His mother gestured to the glade surrounding them. "Before I died, I fashioned this place. It lies between the Void and the Great Beyond, separate and safe. I needed somewhere my spirit could live on, somewhere my mother could never find me."

Ian looked back at the water and saw himself as a baby. He was laughing as he crawled around the garden. His mother was sitting beside him, smiling as she stroked his pudgy cheeks. All the while, baby Ian giggled and tumbled through the grass. When he sat back up, his mother placed flowers buds in his hair. Little Ian reached up and grabbed one, holding it in front of his face with a curious frown. His mother picked him up and twirled him around, singing to him in that sweet, soft voice. She draped a necklace over his head, a thick hemp cord with dangling frogs' legs and rabbits' feet. Ian could hear the words, now:

> *Sing, and touch the blackened sea*
> *The Void it gives the gift to thee*
> *Inside the dark the powers be*
> *And from the dark the light is freed*
> *Sing, and touch the blackened sea*
> *To craft whatever your fancies be*
> *Breathe to life the Threads of gold*
> *Breathe to life the Threads of old*
> *Shape them into things untold*
> *Weave the webs of solid light*
> *Weave the webs and give them life*
> *Weave the webs to set you free*
> *Weave the webs and all will see!*

It was too much for Ian to handle. He averted his gaze, moving away from the edge of the pond.

"Doesn't it make you sad?" he asked. "Seeing those things all the time?"

"Not at all," his mother said. "Those were the happiest moments of my life. Even if I can't relive them. But I understand. We can't look back on our pasts and not feel a certain sadness. It's impossible not to, even if they're nothing but good memories. It's sad to realize that they've come and gone. Sad to realize everything you've left behind. Things that could have happened, but never did."

"I wish we could just go back and stay there forever," Ian said. "Can we? Is there a way? You made this place. Surely—"

"I wish there were. You have no idea, Ian. No idea how many times I nearly Called. I wanted to reach you so badly. So many times, I've stopped myself from passing between worlds. It would be too hard, you realize. For your father. For you and Fiona. Even for Bertrum. I just couldn't." Her face darkened. "There's so much I wish I could have taught you. Had you learned the secrets of Weavery, perhaps my mother wouldn't have done what she did. She's angry for so many reasons, Ian. Angry that I left, angry that I had you."

She pressed the wound on Ian's arm. "I watched her do this to you," she said, and then pointed to her own arm. Ian leaned close, noticing a crescent-shaped burn scar, white against her dark skin.

"A Weaver first learns to work the Threads in one of two ways," she said. "The first is intense focus and meditation. It takes a long time."

"And the second way?"

"Pain."

Ian ran a finger over her raised scar. "She did this to you?"

"I was around your age, still unable to Weave a single

Thread. So my mother branded me. She told me to focus on the pain and nothing else. That the pain would lead me to the Void. And it did."

Ian's heart sank as he pictured his mother as a child, helpless and tortured into working magic. He felt his own arm begin to burn.

"I don't understand," he said, gesturing to his scar. "She wanted me to be able to Weave?"

"No," his mother said. "But she *did* hurt you. You can still use that pain, Ian. You can use it against her. The dagger was infused with Weavery. It's in you. All you need to do is focus."

Ian took in his mother's words, finding them difficult to comprehend. The thought of embracing his other side, the Weaver side . . .

You have to try, he told himself. *People are depending on you.*

"Weavers and Diggers both touch the Void," his mother said. "If you can weave the Threads along with Digger magic, you have a chance of restoring the Void and the Beyond once and for all."

Ian rubbed the wound on his arm. It felt like far too much to learn in so little time. He felt so much pain as it was. He didn't think he could handle any more. The thought of focusing on it, using it as a weapon . . .

The sky darkened. A harsh wind picked up and whisked through the glade, through the silver grass, tearing flowers from their stems, whipping petals across the pond.

His mother's face darkened.

"She's found us."

A flash ripped through the air, exploding just over the trees, sending mother and son tumbling. Ian watched as his grandmother appeared before them, climbing out of a portal that hung in the sky like a tear in a sheet. She stepped down onto the silver grass as the black maw of the Void opened in the sky.

"Did you think I wouldn't find you?" Dehlia spat. "I can move between worlds better than you can, child. Make no mistake. The Void is empty. The Underrealm teems with the restless. Did you not think I could travel to this hidden cove?"

"Don't listen to her," his mother said.

"Step away from him, Elizabeth," the old Weaver spat. "You can't protect him, no matter how far he runs."

"Just shut her out," his mother whispered. "She has no power here."

The Weaver cocked her head. "No power? I have more than you can dream, dear."

"I'm not questioning your abilities, mother. But this is a place of peace."

"Peace? You speak to me of *peace*? Whatever peace there was shattered the moment you left me. The moment you married that Digger. The moment you brought *him* into this world." She pointed at Ian with a long, gnarled finger. He shrunk back.

"Mother . . ."

"*Don't*, Elizabeth."

The Weaver took a step forward, sparks flickering at her fingertips. "Everything changed the day you left. You ruined us. You ruined *everything*. And now . . ." Dehlia gritted her teeth. "Now my own granddaughters have fled." She let out a maniacal laugh. "Traipsing off to the graveyard to be with the

Fossors, just like you, Elizabeth. All my family, gone! And *you* . . . you were the first. You planted the seeds inside their dim, little minds. I know you did! You left, Elizabeth, and our family suffered."

"Because you refused to change!" Elizabeth said. Ian watched the wild flare in her eyes. Familiar lights of Thread magic began swirling between her fingers. "You never *listened* to me. Never once considered how I felt. Since the time I could walk, you filled my head with that darkness. Did you ever for one moment consider that I didn't want to follow you?" She walked toward the old woman, robes billowing in the wind. "Weavers were good, once. They Wove the Threads of Light. I tried to explain it to you . . . but you refused to listen. You sought only the Dark, as your own parents did. You didn't *give* me any choices. Everyone must find his or her own way in this world. I found mine."

"You forsook everything, broke the oath. You killed your own family! Your sisters! Those Fossors banished our kin to the woods. But you, stupid girl, you ran right into that filthy Digger's arms." Ian watched the spittle fly from the old Weaver's lips as her screams grew louder. "Betrayer!"

"*Betrayer?* It wasn't betrayal. It was escape."

"You had natural-born abilities," Dehlia said. "Wasted. All *wasted*! For *what?*"

"For my *family*! The family that *I* chose."

"They're no family of mine," the old Weaver snapped.

"What would you have had me do? Stay with you, cooped up deep in those woods, reading from those horrible books? Helping you cover this world in darkness?"

"It would have been better for you. You could have done great things. You could have *been* great."

"No, Mother. I *did* do something great. You just couldn't see it. I brought light into this world, and he's standing here in front of you. Something pure. Something *good*. A family. A son." Golden Threads wrapped around her arms. "And your black magic stole the life from me!"

As his mother spoke, Ian saw something in the old Weaver's eyes that he'd never seen before. They were filled with fear. It was strange, seeing such a powerful, terrifying figure shrivel and shrink. Ian wasn't sure what she'd do. Anything was possible.

There had to be something to stop the madness. Some way to make it end. He couldn't watch his mother get hurt again. But he had no shovel this time. No satchel. No friends or medicines or Healing manuals. Just himself.

The wound on his arm burned with a searing he'd never felt the like of before. He rolled up his sleeve, watching as the black puncture mark began to glow. He winced, wanting so badly to cry out, but he needed to stand his ground. He did as his mother said and focused on the pain.

Feel it, he told himself. *The pain, and nothing else.*

He took a deep breath. Beneath his skin, a pale green glow moved along his arm, down to his wrist, into his palm, flowing up his fingers.

Suddenly, a flood of memories—memories not his own— burst into his mind like a tidal wave, washing all sense of reason away. Ian couldn't keep the tears from flowing down his cheeks as wave after wave of pain and misery flowed through him, filling his soul with unbearable heaviness, like heaps of sharpened lead. He tried to scream, but couldn't. His knees buckled, and he sank down, clutching his stomach, retching as every muscle in his body seemed to harden to stone. All at once, he could feel their pain. His father's. His mother's. Anguish, torment, regret . . . all of it tore through his mind. He couldn't stand it. But the more he struggled, the hotter the wound seared.

Ian gave himself over to the pain, seeing through the eyes of his mother, his father, and most of all, to his surprise, his grandmother. The old Weaver's memories overwhelmed him, obliterating any sense of light or warmth, filling Ian's brain until he feared his head might burst.

When he could stand it no longer, he lifted his arms, and the pain left him, oozing out into the ethereal tangle of Threads. He stumbled back, feeling as if he were seeing with total clarity for the first time in his life.

His mother's song echoed in his head.

Weave the webs of solid light

Weave the webs and give them life

Ian paused, looking at his fingertips, glowing bright green, like the cursed moon his Grandmother summoned over the graveyard.

How can I use this?

He concentrated on the pulsing warmth, feeling it flow through his muscles and veins. Slowly, he flexed his fingers. A long, flowing thread of green light curved above him, arched like a rainbow after a strong rain.

The pain, he realized, looking at his grandmother. *Her pain.*

Dehlia took a step back, threading her own Weaves around her until she was sheathed in an armor of red light.

Ian nervously approached his grandmother. His fingertips burned, still not used to the feel of the Threads. "You never wanted any of this to happen, did you?" His voice shook, barely above a whisper.

Then he saw it. She flinched.

"*What?*" she snapped.

"It's all right," he said. He held up his hands. "I know that things have gotten out of control. Isn't that right?" Without realizing what he'd done, a large spiral of green Threads surrounded him, twisted and thick as vines.

"Ian!" his mother screamed, lunging herself between them. "No! You don't know the power of the Weaves!"

Dehlia took a step forward, Threads sparking dangerously from all around her. "You challenge me? Have you gone *mad*, boy?"

Ian ignored her. His own Threads continued to spiral and swirl, weaving around each other in impossibly complex shapes. He couldn't help it. He couldn't control their strength and shape. All he could do was try to talk . . . try to reason. "You're hurt, Grandmother. I can see that, plain as day."

His Threads expanded, encasing the glade in a thick dome. Dehlia hissed, and a spear of light flew from her hands, sailing toward Ian. Before it could strike, his own Threads gathered in a swirling mass, overwhelming his Grandmother's.

Dehlia stared, agape. Her killing Weave had failed. As Ian's Threads multiplied, her own began to fizzle and fade. "What . . . what is this?"

The Weaver looked to Ian, then to his mother, her face twisted in pain.

Ian walked toward her. "When my mother left, it hurt you. You couldn't understand why anyone would want to leave, right?"

"I . . ."

"Except you did. You *did* understand, and *that's* why it

273

hurt so badly. You talk about your family being banished to the woods, all those years ago. The oath they took to never leave the wood. *Your* mother kept *you* in those woods. She taught you everything—everything you needed to work black magic. But it wasn't really what you wanted."

The Weaver shuddered. Red flashes of light crackled around her, burning the ground at her feet.

"ENOUGH!"

Wind tore through the meadow as the Void swirled and roared above. The trees were ripped from their roots and flung through the air like twigs. Ian felt like he was wrestling with a hurricane, barely able to stand as he shouted over the howling.

"You never wanted it! But it was forced on you. You took your hatred and tucked it away deep inside. You used it. It made you stronger. But it ate away at you, too, year after year. And before long, you forgot that what you were really feeling was pain. It became normal. It was a *part* of you. You taught it to Olivia and Nora and Clara."

His mother gasped. "Ian . . ."

"When you had children of your own, the hate was still there. You passed it on to them. Tried to make them just like you. But when one of them decided to live a different life, you couldn't bear it. You couldn't stand that she left, that she found a way to live in happiness!"

"She left us," the Weaver whispered.

"You wish you had the courage to do the same thing. You saw your daughter do what you'd always *dreamed* of doing, but you gave up on that dream a long time ago. You see Olivia doing it, now. And Nora and Clara. They're starting to see the good in the world."

The sky started getting lighter. The winds slowly died down, leaving behind only a gentle breeze. Even the water on the pond had gone calm. The Weaver's lips were trembling.

Ian's Threads grew even longer, swirling around the glade in a blinding shimmer. "You saw the family your daughter had started, and it drove you mad that it made her happy. So you did the only thing you knew how to do. You tried to hurt her. You tried to destroy all the joy and happiness she'd found, because you knew you'd never have it for yourself."

He watched as the fire faded from his grandmother's eyes. His mother looked at the old Weaver. "Is that true?"

Dehlia tried to speak, but something caught in her throat. She stood there in stiff, stunned silence.

"I know how it feels," Ian said to her.

"How?" the Weaver finally managed to say, the words sounding thin and hollow. "How could you *know?*"

"Because I was being led into a life I never wanted, too." He felt a sting of panic as the words came tumbling out—for so long they'd only lived as thoughts in his head. Now he felt an overwhelming sense of guilt, but at the same time, it felt good. There was no going back now. He felt free.

"I know what it's like, being somebody you don't want to be. All my life, I've been training to Dig. Training to Speak with the Dead. And all that time, I've known deep down that it's not who I am. It never was. But I'm a Fossor, so there's no escaping it for me. I know what it feels like to watch other people live out their dreams while you're stuck on a path you never chose. It's lonely. Some lucky people can choose who they want to become. It doesn't feel great being one of the unlucky ones."

His green Threads pulsated, forming a tight web above his grandmother. Slowly, the web descended.

"Oh, Ian . . ." The Weaver fell to her knees. She was shaking. "I never meant for it to come to this."

"I know," Ian said.

"I just wanted my family back!" she wailed.

"We're here," Ian's mother said.

Dehlia shook her head. "It's too late. I'll never be able to go back to the Other Side, to the world of the Living. Not after what I've done. There's nothing left for me there."

"You don't have to go back," his mother said. "Not if you don't want to."

The Weaver stared at her daughter for a long time. Ian watched as her eyes took in the glade, the trees, the grass, the pond.

"I was never good to you, Elizabeth. *Never*. Everything your son said was true."

Ian studied the swirling Void gaping open in the sky. "It's not too late," he said, pointing.

"How?" she asked. "How can that be true?"

"We can shut the Void," he said. "Break it. Banish it!"

"*Ian* . . ." his mother said, worry in her voice.

He felt the warmth of the Threads as they swirled around his body, between his legs, up around his shoulders. "We can do it," he urged. "I know we can." He turned to his grandmother. "Think of the good it will bring. No more restless souls. No more pain in the afterlife. With the Void gone, there won't be darkness for the Dead. *Ever*. They'll all be able to reach the Beyond. All of this can be for *everyone*."

Dehlia gazed up at the Void churning above.

"You know what it feels like to hurt," Ian told her. "Imagine what it would feel like to *help*."

A warm glow surrounded his grandmother as she

considered Ian's idea. "With all three of our Weaves, it's possible. He's a wise boy, Elizabeth. Wise beyond his years."

Elizabeth smiled. "Yes."

"You would have me stay? Are you sure?"

"I am," Ian's mother said. "Things can change. No matter how bad they get, they can always change."

The old Weaver's expression softened. She let out a deep sigh, relaxing her shoulders and, for the first time, Ian could see that beneath it all, she was an old woman who'd finally found peace after a long, long life.

"Start over," she said. "I'd like that very much."

Ian watched his grandmother move her hands through the air, weaving her way deep into the Void.

His mother weaved her own Threads, joining with Ian's as the three of them focused their power on the vortex hovering above the glade. Dehlia reached into the swirling light and pulled it apart, making the bright opening large enough for him to step through.

"This will send you back to your own world," she told him. "You'll feel pressure, like a piece of dough flattened by a rolling pin, but keep moving through. Once you're inside, speak the words I told you. Do you remember them?"

Once the portal was opened, Ian joined his mother by the pond. He settled down next to her, watching the images dance across the silvery water. It was him as a baby, being rocked to sleep in his cradle as his father read him stories from Isaiah's book.

His mother brushed his cheek.

"Was that true, what you said about not wanting to be a Gravedigger?"

Ian took a moment before answering. "Yes," he said. "I wasn't sure about it for a long time. But I am now."

"You have a gift for Healing," she said again. "Not only bodies, but minds, too. Use it." She wistfully ran her finger over the water. "When you get back home, talk to your father. He needs to know."

"He won't like it."

"No," she said, "he won't. But you're his son. He'll listen to you. It won't be easy, but he'll understand."

"The portal is closing!" Dehlia called.

Ian and his mother stood, and she hugged him once more.

"You've turned out even better than I hoped, Ian. I can't tell you how proud you make me. *Every day.* And I'll be with you the whole way, watching, so don't ever feel alone."

"I won't, Mom."

She drew him close again. "I love you, Ian. More than you'll ever know. It will be a long time before we meet again. Live the best life you can."

He fought back tears as he stepped into the portal, shutting his eyes and plugging his nose before jumping into its blinding light. The glade faded away as he slipped between worlds, and the Void pulled him in for a last embrace.

Epilogue

"There. That oughta do it."

Bertrum moved the rake along the freshly-tilled soil, giving the final row one last pat with the tool before setting it down. Ian followed behind with a trowel and sack of seedlings, creating neat, ordered rows.

"Garden's twice as big, I reckon'," Bertrum said, lighting his pipe as he surveyed their work. The autumn spell had been lifted, and everything was lush and green again, the air filled with the sweet aroma of late summer. Ian wiped the beads of sweat from his brow, happy to be out in the warmth of the sun.

He looked over the herb garden with pride, walking gingerly between budding rows of mint and sage, star moss and frost juniper. Soon, the garden would be in full bloom, larger than ever. With the amount he'd planted, Ian doubted he'd have trouble refilling the jars and vials in his satchel. Medicinal plants of all kinds would soon grow and blossom, reaching up to the sunlight, bursting from their rows in a surging chorus of green.

Bertrum flexed his fingers, gazing at the stitching around the battered knuckles.

"Ye did a fine job sewin' me back up, lad. I took a real wallopin'."

"I'm sure it won't be the last time." Ian laughed.

The old grouch grinned crookedly. "No, I suppose not."

"Ian!" a voice called.

He saw his father waving to him on the horizon, far across the meadows and fields.

"Ah, is it that time already?" Bertrum asked. "Best run along now, lad. You don't want to be late." He leaned in. "Nervous?"

"A little bit," Ian admitted.

Bertrum grinned. "Ye'll do fine, boy. Just fine. I've taught ye well, if I say so meself."

Ian ran through the graveyard, leaping over the weathered stones and markers. In the distance, he could see the ancient Fossors working, rebuilding the broken tombs and mausoleums under Ivan's guidance.

As he neared the manor, he spotted Isaiah making his way down the cobblestone path, scribbling furiously in a book.

"What have you got there?"

The Scribe furrowed his brow as he jotted down some last thought.

"My book," he answered, without lifting his eyes from

the page. *A Compendium of Fossors Past.* Your father was kind enough to let me peruse the library. It's been a long, long time since I've made any new entries. I was hoping one of you newer Fossors would take up the mantle and continue my work. It's a good thing I'm here. The last entry was Igor. That was nearly four hundred years ago! I've had a lot of catching up to do, my boy. Lots of catching up." He tapped his quill against the side of his head. "It's a good thing old Isaiah is still sharp as a needle. My memory is still strong as ever; though I'm afraid I can't say the same for these fingers. They're aching something terrible with all this scrawling."

"May I see what you've written?"

"Of course." Isaiah leaned in close as he handed the book over to his many times-great-grandson. "I'd flip to the back, if I were you," he said, with a wink.

Ian skimmed through the new pages, glancing at each name etched in flowing letters. Igor. Ilion. Iago. Isidro. Ishver. Isaac. He turned to the last page and nearly dropped the book.

Isaiah grinned as he watched Ian's eyes go wide. "You didn't think I'd leave out the most important Fossor since old Ingmar, did you?"

Ian's hands shook as he read the entry:

Ian Fossor, Son of Isaac and Elizabeth. Ian holds a special place in Digger lore, for he is the first of our kind born of a Weaver. On one terrible eve in the first year of his birth, his grandfather, Ishver Fossor, fell in battle with the Weavers of the Black Wood. His mother, Elizabeth Fossor, died of an unknown sickness soon after. Ian survived to be the first Digger to Speak in the eleventh year of Life.

Surely, a feat that only those with the strongest Voice can achieve. It was Ian Fossor who healed the Void, and in doing so, ushered in a new era of peace and tranquility for the souls of the Dead.

Ian's couldn't believe he was reading about himself in the book he'd been listening to his father recite since he'd been born. He turned the page, but the other side was blank. "There's no ending," he said.

"Well, naturally," Isaiah replied. "Because *you* haven't ended yet, have you? Maybe you can fill in the rest when the time is right. You have a long life ahead of you, my boy. The possibilities are endless." He smiled and patted Ian on the shoulder. "We must write our own stories, Ian. How they *end* is up to us."

Olivia, Nora, and Clara were waiting for Ian back at the manor.

"You better hurry," Olivia said. "It'll be here soon."

Ian nodded and ran inside, bounding up the stairs to his room. Inside, he searched through the piles of books and laundry until he found his satchel.

"Hey," a voice snapped from atop the dresser. "What's all this? You're going without me?"

Ian looked up and saw Thatcher's skull watching him.

"You want to come with me? I thought you hated your schooling."

Thatcher's jaw clicked. "Yeah. I did. I *used* to, at least. But it's been a while since I've been. Figured if I tagged along with you, it'd be all right. There's a lot of fun to be had when the two of us are together. Lots of mischief to be made. What do you say?"

Ian stared at his bag as he mulled it over.

"Just for today," he finally replied.

He grabbed the skull and gently fit it into his bag.

"Little cramped in here," Thatcher mumbled. "But it'll do."

Downstairs, Isaac was waiting in the foyer. Ingmar was with him, polishing his huge, obsidian blade.

Isaac knelt down in front of them.

"Here," he said, wetting his hand and flattening Ian's cowlick. "Better." There was a glint in his eye as he looked fondly at his son. "You're taking a big step today. I'm proud of you."

"You are?"

Isaac laughed. "Of course I am."

"But who . . . who'll look after this place?"

Before the words left his mouth, Olivia walked into the foyer. Ian gasped when he saw the black cloak draped over her shoulders.

"You . . . how . . ." The words came out in a jumble. His cousin was draped in Digger's garb.

"I hope you don't mind," she said, lifting up her arm. "I had to take it in a bit. Bertrum said I could make my own, but I figured since you're going to the Guilds, I could just use yours."

"Of course," Ian said, his head still swimming.

Isaac noticed the look of confusion on his face. "My son is going to follow his dreams, but my niece is still discovering hers. We'll manage, Ian. We've never had to deal with anything like this before, but there's a first time for everything. Still, there will always be work to do around the Yard. Death does not sleep. People will still need burying, and the ones they leave behind will still need consoling. A Digger's work is never done." He pulled Ian in close. "You had the courage to face your fears. The courage to find your mother. Now it's time to find the courage to live your life. A life of *your* choosing. It's not up to me to decide for you. You've shown me that. The time has come for a change."

Ian clutched onto his satchel, beaming up at Isaac. "Thanks, Dad. I love you."

And he meant it.

Ingmar clasped Ian on the shoulder. "It's a noble calling, to be a Healer," he said. "Perhaps it *is* time that House Fossor helped the Living. They need us now. More than the Dead. I wish you luck, child." He held out his gauntleted hand. Ian took it, feeling the cold, icy skin. Ingmar peered deep into his eyes and, for a moment, Ian saw a twinkle pass through them like a shooting star.

As if reading his mind, Ingmar leaned forward. "I *do* smile, you know. From time to time. And I think this occasion is as good as any to do so."

Ian turned to Olivia. "You sure about this?"

"I'm sure," she said. "After I came here, I . . . I fell in love with this place. It's so open. So *peaceful*. The meadows, the way the sunlight hits the grass . . . It's good to be out of that forest. And when I talked to your dad about it, he offered to teach me your ways. Bertrum says I'm a natural."

Isaac grinned. "She's already learned how to properly sharpen the shovels and how to plot a gravesite as well as that old grump can. I think she'll will make a fine Digger." Isaac laughed as he gently mussed her hair. "She's not a Fossor, but she's family. I couldn't ask for a better replacement."

"I would agree," Ingmar said.

"I'll soon learn to Speak," Olivia said. "I'll start being useful around here. I owe you, after all." She brushed Ian's hand. "Don't worry. This place will be safe with me. I promise. Wait here one second . . . I have something to show you!" She scurried off into the next room, returning with a large object wrapped in burlap. She placed it on the ground, yanking off the covering, and Ian nearly gasped. There was the obsidian shovel, gleaming and good as new.

"I fixed it," Olivia said. "My mending spells aren't as strong as they might be, but I think it turned out just fine."

Ian smiled, still surprised by the sight of the Weaver in his cloak. He reached down and brushed his fingers along the engraved shaft. Olivia was beaming as she picked it up, wielding it lovingly in her arm. "I'll take good care of it," she said. "And just think . . . soon I'll make one of my own."

"I know you will," Ian said. He hugged her tight. "I'm glad you're here, Olivia."

"Now," Ingmar said, gesturing to the door, "let's get you out there, my boy. They should be here, soon."

Ian found Nora and Clara waiting for him outside.

The three walked down the gravel path, past the gate, and toward the main road to town.

"So, this thing's big, right?" Clara asked. "*How* big?"

"Bigger than anything you've seen, probably," Ian replied.

Clara tugged on his sleeve. "And it's pulled by horses? That's a strange thing for . . . what's it called again?"

"A *carriage*," Nora said. "It's called a carriage."

"How many people fit in it?"

"Lots," Ian said.

"Other children? Like us?"

"That's right," he said, laughing. "Others like us."

"I hope they're nice," Clara said.

"They will be," Nora assured her. "At least they'd *better* be."

Ian laughed, dreading the thought of someone getting on his little cousin's bad side.

"Will the Capital be scary?" Clara asked.

Ian gave her hand a reassuring squeeze. "New places are always a little scary, I suppose. But it'll be fun. The king lives there. You can see his palace, if you want."

Clara smiled. "I'd like that."

They fell silent as the *clip-clop* of hoofs sounded in the distance.

Clara clutched tight to Ian's hand as they watched the bend in the road. The rumble grew louder as it approached. Finally, the carriage appeared from behind the trees, moving down the long, narrow road beside the cemetery. It was the largest one Ian had ever seen, at least ten horse-lengths, with eighteen enormous wooden wheels and six cabins. The driver pulled up on the reins and slowed to a stop in front of them.

Ian looked through the rows of windows. Inside, he saw faces—children's faces. Some were looking at him. Others gazed down at their laps. Some laughed with others in excited conversation. It was strange seeing so many people his own age. *Living* people.

The door creaked as the driver swung it open. Ian paused at the steps leading up, locking eyes with him. The driver smiled, ushering them forward with a tip of his feathered cap. Ian took a deep breath before climbing onboard.

He nervously scanned the sea of faces as he walked down the narrow aisle, unsure of where to go.

"Ian!"

A hand shot up in the back. Ian was glad to see Fiona's fiery red hair.

"Here," she said, tapping the empty space beside her. "I saved you a seat."

She gave him a big hug as he settled himself beside her.

"You ready?" she asked.

"Ready," he said.

The door swung closed, the horses neighing as the carriage lurched forward. Ian looked out the window, watching as the cemetery rolled by, the gravestones growing smaller and smaller as they sped off into the morning light.

Acknowledgments

No book is written alone. I'd like to thank the following people for bringing this story to life:

My amazing editor, Alison Weiss, whose tireless work made this book what it is today. Thank you for your boundless guidance and wisdom. Honestly, I don't know if you ever get a chance to sleep.

My agent, Brent Taylor, who never gave up on Ian. Truthfully, Brent should be listed as co-author, as he contributed to this story in countless ways. Brent, I am eternally grateful for your insight and support, and for "Thanatopsis." The Yard would be far less exciting without you.

Graham Carter, who brought Ian's world to life in the

most magical of ways. I couldn't image this book without your wonderful artwork. Cheers.

To my parents, who fostered my deep love of reading at an early age. Thanks for letting me climb up on all those bookshelves in the living room. I met some great people up there.

Emma, for being the coolest sister on the planet.

To the folks at TMS for their continued encouragement and support. In case any of you were wondering, this is what I was doing on all those lunch breaks.

Special thanks to Uwe Stender and the rest of the team at Triada US Literary Agency, and to Whitney Gardner, without whom Ian would never have discovered his love of plants.

Kate Camizzi, who has seen this entire process unfold from Day One. I can never thank you enough for guiding me through the good days and bad.

My thanks for all the staff at Miller Memorial Central Library in Hamden, Connecticut, for providing this writer with all the books on botany, gardening, and natural medicine he could get his hands on.

To my readers and fellow 2017 debut authors: thank you all for the input and support. I wouldn't have made it this far without you all in my corner.

To Megan, who inspires me every day, and encourages me to follow my dreams. I'm glad you decided to keep me. I love you.